AGATHA AWARD-WINNING AUTHOR

$1 25

KATHERINE HALL PAGE

AUTHOR OF *THE BODY IN THE BOOKCASE*

THE BODY IN THE BIG APPLE

A FAITH FAIRCHILD MYSTERY

Enjoy more delightfully perplexing
FAITH FAIRCHILD mysteries by

KATHERINE HALL PAGE

AGATHA AWARD-WINNING AUTHOR
KATHERINE HALL PAGE
author of *The Body in the Fjord*

THE
BODY
IN THE
BOOKCASE

"A HIGHLY
ENTERTAINING
SERIES"
Booklist

also
THE BODY IN THE FJORD
THE BODY IN THE BOG
THE BODY IN THE BASEMENT
THE BODY IN THE CAST
THE BODY IN THE VESTIBULE
THE BODY IN THE BOUILLON
THE BODY IN THE KELP
THE BODY IN THE BELFRY

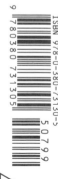

EAN

THE BODY IN THE BIG APPLE

"New Yorkers and suburbanites alike should enjoy this fast-paced mystery; and gastronomes will relish the aptly apple-flavored recipes."
—*Publishers Weekly*

And praise for Agatha Award-winner KATHERINE HALL PAGE's previous Faith Fairchild mysteries:

"Scrumptious suspense."
—*Boston Herald*

"This highly entertaining series effectively mixes modern-day moral dilemmas with charm, warmth, and humor."
—*Booklist*

"Her literary concoction is satisfying and surprisingly delicious."
—*Los Angeles Times*

"Page has kept her Faith Fairchild series fresh by making each novel distinctly different."
—*Ft. Lauderdale Sun-Sentinel*

"Murder most delicious!"
—*Tulsa World*

Faith Fairchild Mysteries by
Katherine Hall Page
from Avon Books

KATHERINE HALL PAGE

The BODY in the BIG APPLE

AVON BOOKS
An Imprint of HarperCollinsPublishers

AVON BOOKS
An Imprint of HarperCollins*Publishers*
10 East 53rd Street
New York, New York 10022-5299

First Avon Books paperback printing: February 2001
First William Morrow hardcover printing: November 1999

Avon Trademark Reg. U.S. Pat. Off. and in Other Countries, Marca Registrada, Hecho en U.S.A.
HarperColllins® is a registered trademark of HarperCollins Publishers Inc.

Printed in the U.S.A.

10 9 8 7 6 5 4

To my mother,
Alice M. Page,
with love and joy

ACKNOWLEDGMENTS

I would like to thank Dr. Robert DeMartino once again for his invaluable medical advice and our years of friendship.

Many thanks also to Faith Hamlin, my agent, and Zachary Schisgal—an editor who edits.

And I am especially grateful to Patricia Hero of Arlington, Virginia, who suggested the title years ago at a bookstore signing!

The present contains nothing more than the past, and what is found in the effect was already in the cause.

—HENRI BERGSON

The BODY in the
BIG APPLE

Prologue

Memories are our waking dreams.

Certain scenes recalled fill our minds with the immediacy of the present, though the event is long past. We hear words and are convinced we are remembering what was actually said. We see a room in exact detail. The particular drapes at a window—the fall of the fabric, the texture of the cloth. The flowers in a vase, their fragrance tenacious. The taste of a perfectly ripe pear, its juice sticky and sweet. Not the vague recollection of someone, but his very presence. Warm skin—in need of a shave, the feel of the slight bristle against the caress of a cheek.

Yet other memories can be revived only obliquely. These tend to move persistently out of reach, slipping further and further away as we struggle to remember them. Tantalizing. How old was I? Which house was it? Who was that person? They retreat until it is only the face and the place in the photograph we are holding in our hands and not real memories at all.

Ephemeral, fleeting—perhaps dreams have the ad-

vantage over memories. Certainly bad dreams do. Even our worst nightmares diminish over time. But the waking terror of a vivid recollection is with us for life. It comes unbidden, not merely an uninvited guest, but an unwanted one. We're in the shower, driving, reading, talking, and suddenly these scenes push everything to one side, and, hostages, we can only watch helplessly, forced back into the past. The voices are too loud to ignore. The words repeat over and over again.

This tale is that kind of memory.

—Faith Sibley Fairchild, 1999

One

"Is there a back way out of this apartment?" the young woman asked anxiously. The caterer turned in surprise. It was a line she had heard only in the movies. "There's a service door past the maid's room," she answered, indicating the direction with a wave of her hand, still clutching the pastry tube she was using to pipe florets of dilled mayonnaise onto timbales of smoked salmon mousse.

The woman's next line, although equally surprising, was not from a script.

"Is that you, Faith? Faith Sibley?"

It was.

Faith put the tube down and focused on the person in front of her. Startlingly large deep blue eyes, chin-length burnished red-gold hair, skin like veritable alabaster. It was a measure of the kind of concentration that Faith brought to her work not to have recognized Emma Morris, now Emma Stanstead, immediately. They'd spent most of their school years together, in school and out.

3

"Emma!" Faith flung her arms around her friend, mindful of Emma's black Ralph Lauren evening suit and the dark mink over one arm. "Emma! It's been ages." Emma hugged her back. No air kisses, just a good, hard hug. Air kisses—on both cheeks if it was a *really, really* close friend or celeb—the greeting of the eighties.

"But what are you doing in the kitchen?" Emma asked.

Faith would have thought her white jacket, checked trousers, and toque supplied the answer, yet Emma, while not stupid, had tended to approach life at a slower, more gentle pace than that of her fellow classmates.

"I'm a caterer now, with my own company, Have Faith. Surprisingly, I've gotten only a few calls from people looking for an 'escort' service—or God. Most of the calls are to do parties like this, and things have been going amazingly well." Faith stopped. She was gushing; plus, she was getting absolutely no response at all from her audience. Emma was listening with the air of a woman who is sure the ringing phone is going to be her doctor with news of a fatal diagnosis. Faith surreptitiously rapped her knuckles on the table for the continued prosperity of her fledgling business—and for her friend's well-being.

Her impression was confirmed by Emma's reply. "That sounds like fun. The food was lovely. Some little shrimp things?" Emma's voice trailed off and she looked in the direction of the exit. The earlier note of fear in her voice was back—full force.

"Are you okay? What's wrong?" Faith asked, putting her hand on Emma's arm and pulling her away from the kitchen bustle and over toward the windows.

4

Outside, the stars were obliterated by the lights of New York City, several million watts, brighter than usual at this holiday time of year. It was bitterly cold and those below on the sidewalk walked quickly, heads bent.

Emma seemed momentarily transfixed by the view—or some other view in her mind's eye. She looked very much the same as she had when they were in high school together six years earlier—extremely beautiful and not much older. So far as Faith could tell, the only changes were that she was a bit more slender, had cut her hair—and was terrified.

She released her grasp and faced her friend, repeating the question more forcefully. *"Emma,* do you need some help? What's wrong?"

"Wrong? What could be wrong?" Emma said. Faith's query had dropped a penny in the slot, and Emma began to move. She shrugged on her fur and pulled gloves from a pocket, dropping a Christmas card she'd been holding in the process. Faith bent down to retrieve it for her, but Emma swooped—all but knocking Faith over—grabbed the card, and was out the door in an instant. Since she was Emma and had been raised properly, "Thank you so much. Lovely to see you" floated back.

Faith stood staring after her, puzzled. Emma's perfume lingered, at odds with the fragrance wafting from the tray of bite-size wild mushroom quiches one of Faith's assistants was transferring to a serving dish.

"Put some of the crab cakes with those and they'll be ready to go," Faith instructed, focus back. Emma receded.

Except Emma was back, and once more Faith was startled.

"Could you meet me tomorrow? At the Met. Inside the front entrance at noon?" she whispered in Faith's ear.

"Tomorrow?" Faith found she had lowered her voice in response to Emma's tone. Then noting the desperate look on Emma's face, she said, "I'll be there." Emma nodded and vanished. This time, apparently, for good.

Focus now totally shot to hell, Faith tried to think what could be going on with Emma. They'd lost touch when Emma transferred to boarding school for her senior year, and then they'd ended up at colleges far apart, seeing each other sporadically when home. Faith had been invited to Emma's wedding when she'd married Michael Stanstead, a lawyer—two, or was it three years ago?—but Faith had been in Europe at the time.

Granted, it was a stressful time of year—as was life in the Big Apple at any season, particularly in the circles Emma traveled in—money had married money, and Stanstead was involved in politics, too. But the fear on Emma's face hadn't been that of someone worried about finishing her Christmas shopping or getting her cards out. It wasn't a "What am I going to wear to the United Nations Association benefit next week?" look or "Did I send our contribution to Covenant House?"

It was fright, as in "I'm scared."

"You can go, Howard. The two of us can finish up. As usual, you were magnificent." Faith blessed her lucky stars often; in this case, for delivering Howard, the perfect bartender/waiter. He was attractive, but not so arresting as to divert attention from the food. Bright and funny, maybe the best thing about Howard was that he didn't want to be an actor. Or a writer. Or a composer. Or anything else except what he was.

It was after nine. Tonight, Faith could afford to take her time. She didn't have another job, or she would have been long gone. This one had been described initially as "cocktails for a few business friends with a few nibbles." "A few" had become a crowd. The "nibbles" heartier. Howard reported that—as often happened—this *was* dinner for many of the guests—the "juniors," he called them. Faith was glad she'd prepared plenty of food—filling food. She'd known from the host's choices that sashimi and white wine were out. These guys still ate red meat— and they were mostly guys with a few trophy wives or girlfriends scattered about the room like tinsel on a tree. She was cynical enough to know that the host would have asked some guests to bring arm candy and some not.

"A good party?" Josie, her full-time assistant, was looking for some strokes.

"A very good party—and I should know." Faith smiled.

She'd been to enough of them over the years. Born twenty-three—almost twenty-four—years ago to the Reverend Lawrence Sibley and his wife, Jane, née Lennox, a real estate attorney, Faith had grown up in Manhattan with her sister, Hope, one year younger. Children's parties and the delights of Rumpelmayer's had given way to increasingly less innocent pleasures, culminating in New York's club scene and parties, endless parties. Wasn't that what the eighties were all about?

Unlike Hope, whose career aspirations had been

well defined by age ten, when she'd asked for a subscription to the *Wall Street Journal* for Christmas, Faith hadn't had a clue about her future for many years. It had been pleasant to consider the world her oyster and contemplate any number of possibilities for a while. Then one morning early in the fall after she'd graduated from college, she'd awakened—late—and realized she was very, very bored. The unexamined life was not worth living, she knew from her father's sermons—and Plato—so she'd lain back and thought. She could get married. There were several possibilities in that department, but she wasn't in love—and she wasn't *that* bored. She could get a job. Her mother had taken to leaving the *Times* on the kitchen table, open at the Help Wanted section. It made sense, but what kind of job? She could go back to school. Most of her friends seemed to find it necessary to add more initials to their names, yet Faith did not feel called in that direction.

It had not escaped her notice that lately she'd been paying more attention at parties and restaurants to the food—the way it was served and the way the table was set—than to her companions. And all with a highly critical eye. She'd always loved to cook and had taken as many courses as she could get away with in her college's famed culinary arts department while still earning a B.A. in English. She'd sat up in bed, the previous night's dinner still before her eyes. I could do that, she'd thought, and much better.

She'd traded her social life for an apprenticeship with one of the city's top catering firms and courses at the New School in how to run your own small business. Her family had watched with bemusement and some skepticism. Then, when Faith had announced she was dipping into the modest trust fund left by her grandfather to launch Have Faith, she'd encountered some resistance.

"Have you considered the rate of failure for such ventures?" her mother had asked, pulling a computer printout from her Prada purse at lunch at Le Bernardin. The restaurant—new, hot, and specializing in seafood—was Faith's current favorite. She'd known her mother's spur-of-the-moment invitation had been as calculated as her own acceptance. She'd reached into her own purse—Longchamps—and pulled out the numbers she had crunched. Her mother had been surprised—and impressed. By the time the coffee had arrived—strong and black—Jane Sibley had seemed close if not to approval, then to acquiescence. But still she'd wavered. Faith could legally use the money as she wished, yet she had wanted her parents' blessing. Then she'd hurled her last spear.

"It's because having a daughter who's a cook doesn't give you the same reflected glory that having one who's cornering the market does, right?"

"Good heavens, no. The other way around these days. And what a mean thing to say, dear. I won't repeat it to your father."

"Then what is it? You want me to get married? You want grandchildren?"

"Oh, you silly, I'm worried you're going to lose all your money, of course."

"Well, I'm not. Trust me," Faith had heard echoes of earlier talking-tos from mother—conversations about things like curfews.

Her mother had reached over to pat her hand. "I do." And that was that.

Faith's aunt, Charity Sibley, had been enthusiastic

about the idea from the beginning. Stretching far back into the highest branches of the tree, the Sibleys had named the first three females in a family, Faith, Hope, and Charity. Faith was convinced that the reason she had merely one sibling was her mother's aversion to the name Charity and her awareness that it was a tradition Lawrence wouldn't have even fleetingly thought to break.

Charity Sibley was a natural ally for Faith, having started her own extremely successful ad agency when she was only a few years older than Faith was now.

"Such a hot field," she'd said, congratulating her niece. "After Black Monday in '87, everyone moaned and groaned about all the money they'd lost—serving spritzers instead of a glass of wine. All those boring purées and coulis—cheap, but not very filling. Happily, things are back to normal now and entertaining is entertaining. You can do my Christmas party. Lots of fun food and music. I don't want any sad faces." She'd been alluding not to junk bonds, but to her decision to sell her business and her apartment at the San Remo, overlooking Central Park on the West Side. She'd already purchased a rambling old house with acres of land in Mendham, New Jersey—a decision that had shocked and saddened her many New York friends. "Jersey!" one had exclaimed on Chat's answering machine. "Why not Forest Lawn!" Chat had stuck to her decision, smilingly confident that anyone who really wanted to see her—and her pool, tennis court, whirlpool, sauna, and other amenities—would manage to find a way to cross the Hudson River.

"I always get lost in New Jersey" had been Faith's sole comment.

"I'll give you a map," Chat had replied.

That settled, there was no question that favorite aunt and favorite niece would continue to see as much of each other as before.

Have Faith had edged into the highly competitive New York catering market in early fall and quickly established itself by word of mouth, lip-smacking mouths. Before, in many circles, snaring Faith Sibley as a guest had been considered a coup. Faith was not yet swamped by business, but the future looked promising. On the strength of the tide, she'd moved into her own place—a studio on West Fifty-sixth Street, but a studio with a doorman in a prewar building with an enormous, beautifully landscaped inner courtyard. Not that home, a spacious apartment on the East Side, was bad. Jane Sibley had married Lawrence, the son and grandson of men of the cloth, with the proviso that he find a calling on her own turf in Manhattan. God knew, there were as many lost souls on the island as anywhere else. She had hoped to maintain a modicum of privacy this way—privacy unavailable in the village-type parsonage of Lawrence's youthful dreams. Watching her struggle to keep the blinds drawn, as well as their father's only occasionally reasonable hours, had convinced both Faith and Hope to avoid men without button-down collars and Windsor knots.

Nesting into her studio, Faith didn't miss the larger baths and reliable heat across town. She was on her own at last. She had also recently signed a lease for a new, expanded location for the business. Grown-up papers to sign. Grown-up fees to a lawyer.

Yes, it had definitely been the right decision and she had never been so happy, she reflected. There had been plenty of glitches and near catastrophes, but tonight's catering job had been a piece of gâteau. They were almost finished packing up. This had been one of the better kitchens to work in, recently remodeled and, from the sparkling appearance of the appliances, plus the absence of anything save champagne, orange juice, caviar, and DoveBars in the refrigerator/freezer, one seldom used.

Josie had gone down to the van with the first load. Faith gave a last look around to make sure they weren't leaving anything. The table was bare again, except for today's paper. Idly, she pulled it over. She hadn't had time to read it yet. Hadn't, in fact, read the paper for days. There was no escaping today's lead. The headline was unusually sensational—and large—for the *Times*. As well it might be.

Underground Radical Leader Nathan Fox Dead
Apparent Homicide, Say Police

She sat down and began to read the article, wondering at the same time why she felt so shocked, so stunned. According to the paper, he'd gone underground in 1970. She'd only been three years old. He'd had a tremendous effect on another generation, but not much on hers. Still, she felt shaken. She looked up as Josie came back.

"Did you hear about Nathan Fox?"

"Where have you been? It's been the only thing on the news all day. Never mind. I know where you've been." Josie laughed. "It is pretty amazing. All these years they haven't been able to find him, and now he turns up dead in an apartment on the Lower East Side."

Faith read out loud, " 'Police say there were no signs of forced entry at the apartment off Grand Street that Fox rented under the name Norman Fuchs two years ago. They speculate his assailant or assailants might have been known to him, but burglary has not been ruled out as a motive. A source, requesting anonymity, close to the investigation revealed that the book-filled apartment had been completely ransacked.' " She paused. "They must have thought he had something valuable. I wonder what they were looking for?"

"Not the money from Chase Manhattan Bank. He was a much better talker than doer. Remember? He and two others were going to rob the bank and distribute the money to the truly needy or whatever, but as soon as they passed the note to the teller, they were caught. Didn't get so much as a roll of pennies. I didn't hear how he got away exactly."

Faith, who had been scanning the newsprint, answered, "The article says there was a fourth accomplice waiting in a car. Fox managed to get away from the bank's security guards before the police arrived. He knocked one of them out, which added assault and battery to his charge."

"He was armed, but he didn't shoot. They should have given him credit for that."

"How do you know so much about all this?" Faith asked. Heretofore, any conversations about politics with Josie had consisted in wondering what Mayor-Elect David Dinkins would serve at his inaugural at Gracie Mansion compared to his flamboyant predecessor, Ed Koch. Josie was even more dedicated to food than Faith. She'd grown up in Virginia, raised by a grandmother who was apparently famous over several counties for her fried chicken. Josie had come to New York several years ago and started working at any food-related job she could get, taking as many courses—and covering as many cuisines—as she could squeeze in. She was all set to open Josie's as soon as she had the money—and the perfect location. Dream, nothing, she'd told Faith. Josie's was fact. Future fact, but fact.

"I told you. There's been nothing else on the news all day. Every time I turned on the radio, there was some piece of the story—or some guy talking in one of those serious 'This is nothing but a test' voices about how it's the end of an era."

Faith knew what Josie meant about the voice, which was intended to be reassuring, yet managed instead to imply the button had just been pushed and everyone was doomed.

She had turned to a profile of Fox on an inside page and was studying his photograph, taken shortly before he disappeared.

"Not bad-looking," she commented. "No, make that definitely acceptable, and this looks like a lousy picture." He had the regulation long, flowing locks of the sixties and wire-rimmed granny glasses, but behind the frames, his eyes were bright and intelligent. He had a full, sensual mouth curved in a slightly mocking smile. She could almost see him shrugging. Like, What's the big deal? She wondered where the picture had been taken, what the context had been. Suddenly she felt sorry for the man. All those years on the run. Granted, he had tried to rob a bank, a big bank, but he hadn't killed anybody, and now he'd been killed. An "apparent homicide." Why did they always say that? He'd been shot and the weapon was missing. There was nothing apparent about it at all. Murder. He'd been murdered. In broad daylight. The medical examiner estimated the time of death as 4:00 P.M. She gave a slight shudder. She liked the Lower East Side, and the blintzes at the Grand Dairy restaurant were the best in the city. Grand Street would mean something else for a while now. Something other than long-ago pushcarts and present-day discounts—and the blintzes.

" 'The end of the sixties at the end of the eighties'— that's what the commentators having been saying all day. His death is supposed to be some kind of significant event, like it was planned as a big period for the decade. John Lennon in 1980; Nate Fox in '89. I don't think junkies are into this kind of political, philosophical shit—and you know that's what it's going to turn out to be. Junkies looking for something to hock."

Faith laughed and agreed. Nobody she knew could puncture a balloon like Josie. "Every obit this year has had 'Swan Song for the Eighties'—first it was Lucy, then Olivier, then Irving Berlin. I thought when Diana Vreeland died in August, that would be it. But they trotted it out again for Bette Davis."

Josie was putting on her coat, but Faith was still lost in the article. She'd have to pick up a paper on her way home. How had he stayed hidden all these years? Obviously, he must have had a network of friends, people sympathetic to his ideas. Family? But the FBI would have been keeping a close eye on any relatives. She skipped to the end, where they always listed survivors. "No survivors." Nobody? It was an amazing thought. No siblings, parents dead. Never married, or if so, divorced. She began to construct his life rapidly. Where had he grown up? Born in Newark, New Jersey, the article said. Newark before the '68 riots.

Newark, home of Jewish intellectuals and an up-wardly mobile middle class. Weequahic High School. Philip Roth country.

There were many facets to Faith Sibley's personal-ity, some in direct contradiction to others. She was both open-minded and given to snap judgments; label-conscious and down-to-earth; somewhat self-centered and overly generous. The one dominant trait for which there was no antiphony was her curiosity. There had never been a time when she hadn't wanted to know everything about everybody. Curiosity and an exceed-ingly active imagination. She was the original "Why?" child, and Jane had almost been driven mad by her daughter's questions. Faith's father, Lawrence, had greeted her inquisitiveness with joy. An infant episte-mologist. He'd answered at great length, in excruciat-ing detail. Faith had soon learned to engage in interior monologues, and she was doing this now. What if Fox's death was tied to the movement and not a ran-dom act of urban violence? Why not the FBI itself? A bust gone wrong? But if you'd known Fox was Fox, he'd have been worth more alive than dead. There was a large reward for his capture.

"Come on, boss, I want to go home and take a long soak in a hot tub with lots of bubbles."

Faith stood up and carefully placed the paper back exactly as she'd found it. It hadn't appeared that any-one in this household had read it, either. It was proba-bly the maid's paper; the *Times* and *Wall Street Journal* would be left at the front door each morning by the doorman and read on the way to work—or with white gloves to keep the nasty, smudgy type from one's man-icured hands by wife or mistress left in bed. Nathan Fox's death wouldn't affect the market. Therefore, it would have been of only passing interest, good for a crack or two about radicals, hippies, phases outgrown or merely transformed. One of Faith's recent dates had entertained her for an hour with his elaborate theory that Yuppies, whose "death" was celebrated in the '87 crash, were the flip side of the coin from hippies. "Same sense of entitlement, self-interest, self-righteousness, same segment of the population. Grazing and arugula versus macrobiotics and grass. Coke versus acid. Different taste in clothes, yet same awareness and disdain for deviations. What, no beads? What, no Rolex? See what I mean?" Faith had, and it made sense. There weren't any hippies anymore, only "aging hippies," and that was a pejorative. Nate Fox was fifty-six, an aging radical. She tried to imagine how he must have looked at the time of his death. Significantly different, or he wouldn't have been able to hide in plain sight. Maybe the FBI had lost interest in him. There were bigger fish in the sea. Maybe they'd stopped looking.

"Ah, I'd hoped you might still be here." It was the host, rubbing his hands together after pushing through the kitchen door, followed by two other men, almost indistinguishable from himself. They looked to be in their early thirties in well-cut dark suits with well-cut dark hair, and their clean-shaven faces were slightly flushed—but not too flushed—as evidence of a good time. One of them was smoking a cigar.

"Wonderful job, Faith. It all went off rather splendidly, don't you think?"

While not above giving herself a pat on the back, Faith wasn't sure how to reply. A "Yes" was terribly self-congratulatory; a "No" unthinkable.

17

"People seemed to have a good time."

"Yes, they did, and I thank you. We have something coming up in February for some out-of-town clients. I'll call you with the date next week." He took a bottle of champagne from the refrigerator, confirming Faith's suspicion that he hadn't expected her to still be there at all.

She handed him three glasses from the cupboard behind her. "I'm sure we'll be able to work something out. I'm glad you were pleased with tonight."

One of the men, who looked vaguely familiar, took the cigar from his mouth, tapped some ash in the sink, and said, "Have you got a card? A good caterer is worth her weight in gold these days. Business all right?"

"I can't complain." Faith found herself relaxing under his gaze. He was either genuinely interested or awfully good at faking it. She handed him a card.

"My name is Michael Stanstead, by the way," he said, tucking her card into his wallet.

Of course he looked familiar. Assemblyman Michael Stanstead. Stanstead Associates law firm Michael Stanstead. Society page Michael Stanstead. Husband of Emma, Michael Stanstead.

"I'm a friend of your wife's. Emma and I were at school together," Faith said. A firm believer in conveying minimal information, especially to someone's nearest and dearest, Faith didn't mention their encounter in the kitchen.

The change in Stanstead was immediate. His smile vanished and his brow furrowed. The host patted him on the shoulder. "Don't worry. I'm sure she'll be better tomorrow."

"Emma wasn't feeling well and left the party early,"

Michael told Faith. "It's probably just this flu that's been going around, but . . ." He paused. "Well, I am worried about Emma. Very worried."

That makes two of us, Faith thought.

Two

Emma Stanstead was not in disguise, as her cryptic, surreptitious words the night before had suggested. Dark glasses. Garbo hat. Nor was she on time. It was terribly busy for Faith at work. Only the memory of Emma's frightened face and Faith's own curiosity had torn her from her vol-au-vents. She was on the point of returning to them when Emma rushed up, starting her apologies from a few feet away.

"These stupid, stupid meetings. They go on and on. Nothing gets accomplished, except a few people get to hear themselves talk. I wish they'd just call me up and tell me what they want me to do. It would be so much simpler." Her Ferragamo heels clicked on the museum's stone floor, punctuating her words. "Let's go sit in the courtyard in the new American Wing. It's so peaceful there. Oh, unless you want lunch?"

Faith didn't. The food at the Museum Restaurant had always been nondescript. Now that they'd remodeled and done away with the wonderful fountain in the middle, replacing it with a kind of sunken pit for diners, she preferred Sabrett's hot dogs with everything on them from one of the vendors on Fifth Avenue in front of the main entrance. Progress. New York was always acting in haste and being forced to repent at leisure. Think of Penn Station.

The Engelhard Court in the new wing was filled with plants and an assortment of statuary. Emma by-passed a bench opposite a protective panther and her cubs, selecting instead one beneath towering fronds and art collector/financier August Belmont's fixed gaze. He had been immortalized in bronze wearing a long fur-lined overcoat, and Faith realized she was feeling slightly chilled. The entire city had entered a state of deep freeze, temperatures plummeting at night to the very low teens. It had put to rest the frightening talk the previous summer about global warming, though. Or maybe it was all part of what the future would bring—fiery summers, frigid winters. Some kind of judgment.

Emma seemed to be having trouble beginning. She sighed heavily, opened her purse, took out a handker-chief, and blew her nose. After her tirade about meet-ings, she hadn't said much as they walked through the museum. Her steps did slow as they passed the famous Christmas tree decorated each year with the Met's col-lection of intricately carved eighteenth-century Neapolitan crèche figures. She'd murmured, "Re-member?" And Faith did. As little girls, the appear-ance of the tree had marked the beginning of the holiday season for them and they haunted the museum until it appeared like magic. Each had a favorite orna-ment. Emma's was an angel with rainbow wings and trailing silken gold robes; Faith's one of the three kings, in royal robes astride a magnificent white

21

horse. Emma's single word had reminded Faith how much time they had spent together and how much they had shared.

It was time for Emma to start sharing now. With one job tonight and two on Saturday, Faith couldn't sit around watching her friend get a cold.

"Okay, what's going on? Much as I love seeing you—and it's ridiculous that we've been so out of touch—I do have—"

"I'm being blackmailed, Faith," Emma said quietly, handing her an envelope. It looked like the one she'd been holding at the party. "One of the other guests found this in the hall last night and gave it to me. He must have thought I'd dropped it. Of course, I'd never seen it before."

Emma being blackmailed! Faith had rehearsed a number of scenarios for this tell-all rendezvous, most of them involving a philandering husband or Emma herself in love with another, but blackmail! This didn't happen to people Faith knew. This didn't happen to people her age, for that matter. Blackmail was old guys caught with their pants down or hands in the till or whatever.

Faith took the card gingerly. She had some notion that they should be preserving prints for the police. She also felt a primal repulsion—who knew where it has been?

The card displayed a Currier & Ives sleigh scene, *Central Park in Winter,* one of those cards charities send in the mail as a "gift." You don't ask for them, don't want them, yet it seems a shame to throw them away. Except you can't use them unless you send a donation; otherwise, you'd feel too guilty—or cheap. Inside the card a message had been pasted over the greeting. It had been typed on a word processor, impossible to trace.

> We know everything, and if you don't want Michael to
> know, get ten thousand dollars in unmarked bills and wait
> to hear from us. Keep quiet or you'll be headlines, too.
> P.S. Remember your "mono"?

It could not have been an accident that the blackmailers had left the card's original bright red "Merry Christmas" greeting showing. There were no signatures.

After she had turned the card over to Faith, Emma's anxiety had abated. She was leaning back on the bench, her face turned toward the sun streaming in from the park through the wall of glass. Faith was again struck by Emma's beauty. She looked like a model for one of the Pre-Raphaelite painters, Jane Morris—an ancestress?—in an outfit by Donna Karan.

Like the Emma of old, this Emma was more than slightly fey. Sentences trailed off into some region known only to Emma herself. One classmate had described carrying on a conversation with her as "walking into a maze without a ball of yarn." Faith had never been troubled by Emma's sudden flights. She always came back, and anyway, it was a wonder she wasn't worse, given her family. Given Poppy.

Pamela Morris, "Poppy," had been a similar beauty at her daughter's age, and even now, in her early fifties, she was stunning. Her hair was a darker red than Emma's, and if art was helping nature, it was doing a very good job indeed. Not a single wisp of gray invaded her sleek chignon. Unlike her daughter, however, Poppy was never out of touch. She'd been in touch with—and in charge of—an elite segment of New York society since she'd come out. During the sixties and early seventies, Poppy was credited with initiating "radical chic." You were as likely to be sitting next to Bobby Seale as Henry Kissinger at one of her dinner parties. Now Bobby was promoting his new book, *Barbeque'n with Bobby,* and Henry—well, Henry was still keeping secrets, or looked as if he was.

Having Poppy for a mother meant never having to say you were sorry, because she didn't have time to hear your apology, or even notice if you'd erred. Larger than life, she sucked all the air from a room, to the delight of her adoring, reticent husband, who viewed her as his own personal exotic pet. He was content to sit back and watch the show. Faith could barely recall what Jason Morris looked like—or did to pay all Poppy's bills. There were several buildings and large parts of others named for his family. Faith had always assumed he was in the world of finance—certainly not a mere broker, but perhaps a brokerage.

Emma had an older sister, Lucy, or rather Lucretia, named by Poppy for Lucretia Mott during Poppy's intense Betty Friedan/Germaine Greer feminist period. Faith and her own sister, Hope, privately joked that Lucy would more aptly have been named for that other Lucretia—Borgia. Lucy Morris was a classic bully, adept at finding closely guarded chinks in one's armor, then thrusting her lance in with deadly precision. Emma was, of course, easy prey—too easy, and Lucy turned her attention to her schoolmates, where she used her position as a leader to make many a girl's life a living hell, all the while maintaining an untarnished reputation with the faculty. Because kids never tell. She'd been at the party, too, Emma had mentioned, and Faith was glad she'd avoided her fellow alum.

At present, Lucy was studying for the bar. Poppy continued to give unabashedly elaborate parties, still daring, but now mixing new money with old and adding a liberal dash of celebrities—and liberals—to Knickerbocker society. Jason was still paying the bills.

"Remember your 'mono'?" the card said. Faith remembered Emma's mono. It had been close to the end of junior year, and Emma had had to be tutored at home. But it wasn't something to keep from your husband. It wasn't worth ten thousand dollars. And what did "headlines, too" mean? Michael was in the news a lot; maybe that was it.

"Emma, what are they talking about? How could someone blackmail you for having mono all those years ago? I mean, it's not something anyone would be ashamed of, even if we did call it the 'kissing disease.' "

Emma seemed engrossed in the folds of Belmont's coat. "Why do you suppose they have this statue here?"

This was not the best time for an art history lesson.

"Emma! You asked me to come, you show me a very real and very threatening blackmail note— "

"All right, I know. I'd just rather not think about it. Any of it. To start with, I didn't have mono, I had a baby."

"What!"

"Well, I miscarried, but I was pregnant. That's why I dropped out of school."

"Oh, Emma, I'm so sorry. I wish I had known. It must have been terrible for you."

Emma nodded and two perfectly round tears oozed

from the corners of her eyes and slowly made their way down her smooth cheeks.

"Still, this happens all the time. It's not something to be blackmailed about," Faith persisted.

"It's—it's a little more complicated than that."

Faith was not surprised. She decided to sit back herself and let Emma tell her story. She didn't expect a torrent of words, but perhaps this method would induce a steady trickle.

Emma tucked her thick hair behind one ear. A large square-cut emerald flanked by equally impressive diamonds on her ring finger flashed in the thin winter light.

"It was a pretty crazy time. I mean, life was always a little hyper around my house, but I was used to it. I was pretty caught up in my dancing." Faith remembered. Emma had studied ballet since she was a small child, snaring an occasional part in *The Nutcracker.* She'd been talented. "But that spring, things got really insane. It's hard to talk about it, Faith. I've tried not to even think about it. That's why the card was such a shock. I've been pretending nothing ever happened, or that it was all a book I read, not my life."

Faith nodded. If you could manage it, this didn't sound like a bad idea. Her problem would be in the blotting-out department.

"I was supposed to spend the night at a friend's after a party, but I didn't feel well and went home. Nobody heard me come in. My mother and Jason were quarreling. I stopped outside the library door. It was so unusual. I don't think I had ever heard them fight—not with each other. Mother was constantly screaming about one thing or another, but Jason never responded, which would make Mother rave on. I think he got a kick out of it. Anyway, that night he was shouting, too. 'She's your bastard; you take care of her,' I heard Jason say. 'Why should your little by-blow get anything from me, and certainly not the same amount as my own daughter!' "

Emma stopped. Faith knew where they were going now. She knew why Emma wanted it to be someone else's life.

"I had no idea what they were talking about. At first I thought my mother must have had another child and given it up. Then Mother started in. She didn't raise her voice, but I could hear every word. It was ten times scarier hearing her talk this way. A dead kind of voice. 'You told me it didn't matter,' she said. 'You told me that Emma would be like your own child. What happened, happened. I should have known your precious genes would mean more than common decency. You've never been good to her. But this is it, Jason. You either make her equal to Lucy in your will or I'm leaving.' I heard something break. Poppy has always liked to throw things, and when I went in, I saw pieces of glass on the floor in front of the fireplace."

Faith was openmouthed and immobilized. She couldn't even reach for her friend's hand. The trickle of words had become a torrent. She saw it all as Emma described it. The hall in their town house, thickly carpeted with Oriental runners. Emma's footsteps muffled. The voices from the library, Jason Morris's private domain. Then the crash of crystal on the marble surrounding the large fireplace.

"What did you do? Did you confront them? Oh, Emma, I can't believe this!" She grabbed her friend's hand now and squeezed hard.

"I wasn't thinking. I couldn't think. I just walked in

27

and looked at them. They stared at me as if they couldn't believe that I was there; then Mother said, 'You were supposed to be at the Auchinclosses'. I remember thinking what a stupid thing it was to say. I mean, I've just learned that my father isn't my father and she's blaming me for not being somewhere else.

"Jason just looked at me and left the room. He couldn't handle it. I told my mother that I didn't care anything about any money. I only wanted to know the truth. Who was my father? She didn't want to tell me, said it didn't matter, that he was long gone and I couldn't see him. It was really strange. Finally I went to bed and stayed there. After two days, she cracked. I wasn't eating and wouldn't get up. She'd come in and yell or cry. I didn't see anyone else. Lucy was in college, thank God."

"Who was it?" Faith asked gently.

"Nathan Fox."

"Nathan Fox!" Faith said. Her voice was too loud and she clapped a hand over her mouth. "Nathan Fox!" she said more softly. How to offer condolences in a situation like this? Emma's father has been murdered, but presumably he had not been much of a presence in Emma's life, since she'd only found out about him when she was seventeen and since he hadn't exactly been accessible. She blurted out what was foremost in her mind, "*The* Nathan Fox, the one who was just— that is, the one who wrote *Use This Book to Wipe Your*—"

"Yes, yes," Emma said, cutting her off a tad impatiently. What other Nathan Fox was there?

"I was furious at Mother for never having told me, and things in my life that hadn't made sense before suddenly did. You know Jason had always favored

Lucy, and I thought it was because I was a disappointment to him. I never did that well in school and I was, you know, shy. He likes women like my mother, like Lucy. Women with personalities."

That's an interesting way to put it, thought Faith.

"Emma, you have more personality—and a better one—in your pinkie finger than either of them." As Faith hastened to reassure Emma, her thoughts were racing in several directions. What a thing to do to a child! And how devastating to discover your father was not your father! She felt a cold fury at Poppy's total lack of responsibility. At the same time, a voice was saying, Poppy Morris and Nathan Fox! So the photograph had not been misleading. Handsome and, by all accounts, extremely charismatic, he wasn't just coming for the food and witty conversation at the Morrises'.

But it was the blackmail note that dominated. "We know everything," it stated. Emma's pregnancy. Emma's parentage. And what else? Faith knew right away. Knew what she'd have done herself. Obviously, Emma would not have been satisfied simply to know her father's name.

"So, you got out of bed and tried to find him?"

Emma nodded. "I got out of bed and ran away. Mother swore that she didn't know where he was. That she hadn't heard from him since he went underground. I did get it out of her that he knew about me, though. They named me Emma after Emma Goldman—and all those years I had assumed it was Emma Woodhouse. Mother has a weakness for Jane Austen. *Pride and Prejudice* meets *Bonfire of the Vanities*."

Faith had forgotten Emma's sense of humor—it was as unexpected as the rest of her.

"Where did you go?" Faith was beginning to think they should get some lunch. She was getting hungry, and they still had a great deal of ground to cover. The bench was also getting hard.

"I didn't know any radicals, or Communists, or even socialists. Not personally. But I figured there would have to be some in the Village, so I took the subway downtown and started going from one bookstore to the next. Bookstores with the right titles in the window. Nobody seemed to think it was strange that I was trying to find out about Fox. I met a woman, the owner of Better Read Than Dead, who told me that someone named Todd Hartley knew everything there was to know about Fox. She gave me his address. He was living in a collective with a bunch of other people. One of them had money and had rented a huge loft in SoHo. Todd and the rest of them took me in right away. I thought it was perfect. Nobody had ever paid much attention to me at home, except to make sure my teeth got straightened and I didn't put on weight. The comrades—that's what they were called—wanted to hear what I had to say. They were all such dears and so serious."

"Would you mind if I sat here?" A young mother with a stroller, infant asleep, answered her own question by plopping down next to them. "I'm exhausted. She only sleeps in motion. I've pushed her through every museum, and, when the weather was better, from here to Battery Park and back."

This was news to Faith. She assumed normal babies knew enough to go to sleep in their cribs. An innate reflex. You put them in, they closed their eyes, and voilà. This baby didn't look like something out of a Stephen King novel, yet clearly she was an aberration, tormenting her mother. The woman's hair needed a trim and her lipstick was crooked. The baby, on the other hand, looked great. She had softly curling dark hair and her tiny lips pursed in a perfect little O. However, the poor woman's problem was not of great interest to Faith. Children were something that happened to other people.

Obviously, they couldn't continue their conversation.

"Let's grab some dogs from Sabrett's and walk through the park," she suggested.

"I'm supposed to be having lunch with people important to Michael. I'm already dreadfully late," Emma said desperately. "Except you haven't told me what to do yet."

"Call them and cancel," Faith advised. "This is more important."

Leaving the young mother, who was nodding off herself while the baby tried to eat her toes, they went in search of a phone. Faith called Josie, too.

Outside in the sunshine, deceptively warm, Emma picked up the threads. The Sabrett's hot dog had satisfied Faith's physical hunger; now she was longing for the rest of Emma's story.

"Anyway, they were so nice to me, you can't imagine. Trotskyists. You know, you're not supposed to say Trotskyites, they don't like that. They were all getting ready to go into factories to mobilize the working classes. They said the movement in the sixties and seventies had concentrated too much on students and the antiwar movement. Todd used to stand up and shout, 'If every student broke a pencil, what would you have? Splinters! If every worker shut down his machine, what would you have? Revolution!' It was one of his favorite quotes from Daddy—Nathan Fox, I mean. It was wonderful to learn all about him."

If this represented Fox's rhetoric, Faith had to wonder about the man's intellect, but perhaps you had to have been there. So much depended on context: hundreds of thousands of demonstrators in front of the Capitol building, for example. Nursery rhymes declaimed would have sounded portentous and inspired.

"Todd had dropped out of NYU to work full-time in the movement, and he was collecting Nathan Fox's speeches into a book. He promised he'd help me find Fox. He'd met him once someplace in Minnesota the year before. He wouldn't tell me where Daddy was then, but he said he'd let Fox know I wanted to see him. Todd thought it was pretty cool that I was Fox's daughter. He made me feel proud. I'd never felt anything like that about Jason, even when I thought I *was* his daughter. All the comrades had adopted Russian names as nicknames. While they were waiting to go into the factories, one girl, Olga, was teaching herself to set type. She had a little printing press. They would write all these pamphlets and go to some factories in New Jersey and pass them out at the gates. I used to fold and staple."

"I think they'd been setting type by computer for quite a while by then," Faith observed, acutely aware that while she was going to various cotillions, Emma had been experiencing a very different sort of life that spring. Certainly one less boring, although folding and stapling might have become somewhat repetitious.

"Well, nobody told Olga." Emma pulled her mink closer as they walked briskly across the park toward the West Side. There wasn't any snow on the ground, although flurries were predicted. The trees looked cheerless, their branches gray spikes against the leaden winter sky. "I got pregnant with Todd. It seemed like the thing to do—sleep with him, I mean. The comrades were all terribly chummy that way. They explained to me that sex was merely a physical act and monogamy was a bourgeois institution, though Todd didn't want me to sleep with anyone else, fortunately. I'd graduated from folding and stapling to working on a little article about Emma Goldman for a pamphlet when Poppy found me. She told everybody how old I really was, and Todd was pretty scared. I'd said I was twenty-one."

"And they believed you!" Faith said incredulously. Emma didn't look twenty-one now. A horse-drawn carriage clip-clopped past them. An elderly couple was bundled up in lap robes, clearly enjoying the ride.

"They look so happy," Emma said wistfully. "It must be nice to have normal parents. They look like some-body's parents, don't they?"

Faith steered her back to the conversation. "And when Poppy got you home, you found out you were pregnant."

"Yes. She'd been very nice to me until then. I think she felt guilty; plus, she was truly worried about what had happened to me. But you know my mother. She's so used to people doing whatever she says that she to-tally freaked when I said I wasn't going to have an abortion. I was going to keep the baby. I mean, she'd had me out of wedlock, although technically she was in it, but you know what I mean?"

Faith did. What better way to get back at your mother—and Jason—than first to get pregnant and next plan to raise the baby yourself? She also had a sneaking suspicion that Emma may have wanted to have someone she could well and truly call her own.

"She told me we were going to Dr. Bernardo for a checkup, just to make sure I was all right. You know who he is, right?"

Dr. Bernardo had been taking care of inconvenient problems for New York ladies in Poppy's circle for years, and Faith had indeed heard of him.

"When I got to his office, it turned out she'd scheduled an abortion, so of course we had a huge scene, but I did go home again. The comrades hadn't exactly been into solidarity after Poppy had talked to them. I called them, told them what had happened, but they were sort of 'See you later,' and I didn't have anyplace else to go."

Again, Faith told her, "I wish I had known."

"I wish you had, too. Poppy yelled at me all the way back to Sutton Place and half the night. It worked. I'd finally fallen asleep, and when I woke up, I realized I'd lost the baby."

Years later, there was no mistaking the grief in Emma's voice.

"I was in pretty bad shape after that and couldn't go back to school. They got a tutor for me and things calmed down. It was hard to stay mad at Mother. You know how she can be so . . . well, Poppyish. I still felt betrayed, but I caved. Let her take care of me. The one thing I insisted on was going to boarding school for senior year. I just couldn't go back with all of you and pretend nothing had happened."

"Come to work with me and I'll make you the best hot chocolate in the city." It was getting too cold for much more walking. Faith had on one of those Norma Kamali OMO sleeping-bag coats, which made you look like an army-surplus number. Normally, it verged on too much warmth; today, it might as well have been mosquito netting.

"I'm sorry," Emma said regretfully. "I said I'd join them for dessert. You know Michael's running for the House next year, and these ladies are very important to his fund-raising campaign. He was *very* insistent that I go. There was a Post-it on the mirror to remind me this morning." She stopped speaking and flushed slightly. "Sometimes I mean to go to these things, then forget until it's too late. I can't blow this off when he's made such a big deal out of it. But I can't leave until you tell me what to do," she said imploringly.

Faith was surprised. It was the second time Emma had said this. It seemed so clear.

"You haven't committed a crime or done anything anyone could remotely blackmail you over. I suggest you and Michael take the note to the police and let them deal with it. They can help you figure out who might be doing this. There can't be too many choices. Who would have known both about Fox being your father and the fact that you got pregnant?"

"But I can't do that." Emma stood absolutely still on the path, as rooted as the massive oaks to either side. "Michael would find out."

"Michael doesn't know!" Faith gasped.

"Of course not. It really didn't have anything to do with him, and the Stansteads might have been funny about it."

Given the reputation of the Stanstead family—they considered William F. Buckley a flaming, and traitorous, liberal—Faith could understand that Emma might not want her parentage known to her in-laws, or the early pregnancy. But her husband? Wasn't marriage supposed to be about sharing—you're your husband's best friend and all that? It was one of the reasons Faith had ruled out matrimony so far. She preferred her best friends. They were easier to talk to and made her laugh.

"Emma, this is *not* a secret you can keep from your husband. He wouldn't want you to. Blackmail is very, very serious." Faith thought of Michael Stanstead's concerned face. Emma had to tell him and together they could decide what to do next. She couldn't believe he wouldn't be anything but supportive of his wife and upset at what she had gone through at such an early age. She told Emma about Michael coming into the kitchen.

"He is so sweet." Emma appeared to be swayed, but then she stiffened. "You don't understand, Faith. It can never come out that Nathan Fox was my father. It would completely destroy Michael's political chances. He'd be the laughingstock of the party—that he didn't know his wife's father was one of the most notorious radicals of the century. And it's even worse now that Daddy's dead, don't you see?"

Unfortunately, Emma made sense. She *would* be headlines and the tabloids would effectively destroy Stanstead's chances—for the next election anyway. "Our Man for the Nineties"—thirty-year-old Assemblyman Michael Stanstead was being touted as the brightest young star in the New York Republican firmament. He would be running for Congress in a favorable district, and after some time in the House, who knows where he might end up.

"I feel so much better. I think it was meant that you were there last night. But I must dash." Emma gave Faith a quick hug and a smile crossed her face, fears allayed. A slight shadow: "You do promise not to tell anyone? Oh, I'm being silly. Of course I know that you wouldn't."

Faith was glad that Emma, having spilled her guts, now considered her blackmail problem solved, and she hated to spoil things. But blackmailers tended to follow up on threats.

"What are you going to do about the note?"

Emma had her hand up for a cab. She turned around.

"Absolutely nothing at the moment."

A taxi pulled up to the curb and Emma waved goodbye.

Faith crossed the street to the bus stop. Business was good, but not cab versus bus fare good enough yet. As she waited, she realized she was exhausted—and worried. She'd have to try to get Emma to tell her husband. There was no other way. Faith couldn't go to the police herself and betray Emma's trust. She wished she could talk about the situation with her sister, Hope. Hope moved in Young Republican circles and might have picked up something about Michael that would help convince Emma—that his position was so secure, nothing short of an intrigue with farm animals would hinder his campaign, for instance. Faith also admitted that she was dying to tell somebody about Poppy and Nathan Fox. She wished she wasn't so good at keeping secrets.

The bus came and, mercifully, she got a seat. It was crowded with holiday shoppers, bags making the aisle difficult to negotiate. An elegant elderly woman was occupying two seats with aplomb—one for herself and one for an enormous Steiff giraffe, the head craning out of the FAO Schwarz bag. The sight of the incongruous pair was causing the whole bus to smile. It was still early enough in the shopping season for New

Yorkers to feel the holiday spirit. Outside, the whole city was decked out in its finest. Faith was sorry she wasn't walking. Each shop window rivaled the next in glittering offerings. If you can't get it here, you can't get it anywhere—that's what the song lyric should say. The bus stopped, and through the open door, she could hear the Salvation Army Band's rendition of "Good King Wenceslas." The man next to her was humming along, and at her look of pleasure, he began to sing in a surprisingly strong tenor:

> *"Good King Wenceslas looked out,*
> *On the Feast of Stephen,*
> *When the snow lay round about,*
> *Deep, and crisp, and even;*
> *Brightly shone the moon that night,*
> *Though the frost was cruel,*
> *When a poor man came in sight,*
> *Gathering winter fu-oo-el."*

"That's as far as I go by heart," he said apologetically.

"Me, too," Faith said. "It's something about ' "Hither, page" ' and ' "Bring me flesh, and bring me wine." ' I'm a caterer, so I tend to remember the food details. I can do all the verses of the 'Wassail Song.' "

"A caterer. That must be hard work, especially at this time of year," he said. Faith was mildly impressed. Usually, she heard inanities like "That must be fun" or "How do you stay so thin?" He wasn't bad-looking—and he had to have terrific circulation. The only concession to the weather he'd made was a muffler on top of his tweed sports jacket. She looked at his hands. No gloves. No wedding ring.

"It is a busy time, thank goodness. I've only been in business since the fall, and it's been going well."

"Great. Well, this is my stop." He dug in his pocket. "Want to trade cards? I might suddenly remember the rest of 'Good King Wenceslas' and wouldn't know how to find you."

"True." Faith laughed as she fished a business card from her purse. "Or you may need a caterer."

"Absolutely," he said. "Take care."

She watched him out the window before the bus pulled away. Not bad-looking at all. "Richard Morgan," his card read. The address wasn't far from her apartment. What does Richard Morgan do? she wondered. It wasn't anything on The Street. Financiers didn't wear tweed jackets. A professor? The bus started with a lurch and he was lost to sight. Without the distraction of carol singing, Faith's thoughts reverted once more to the problem at hand. The major problem at hand.

Emma, Emma, Emma. Presumably, she was now at her luncheon, breathlessly apologizing for her lateness as the crème brûlée was served, only to be politely nibbled or politely refused by the ladies present. Eating dessert in public was a no-no. Bingeing on Mallomars at midnight and throwing up was not. Much as everyone exclaimed over Barbara Bush's inner beauty and lack of pretension, it was Nancy Reagan's size-four red suits that set the standard. This was a crowd that didn't need the Duchess of Windsor's maxim—"You can't be too rich or too thin"—embroidered on any of their pillows as a reminder.

It was difficult, almost impossible, to imagine Emma Stanstead as an increasingly high-profile politician's wife. Yes, she had the beauty and grace—and figure. Yet, she was quite shy. Growing up with Poppy—and Lucy—Emma preferred candlelight to limelight. When they had traveled in the same circles during adolescence and occasionally later, Faith recalled the change that would come over her friend when she was thrust into uncomfortable social situations. More often than not, Emma would say the first thing that came into her head, and it was often the last thing that would have come into anyone else's. At ease only with her most intimate friends, she would certainly find the campaign trail and the glare of publicity torture. *Emma as a politician's wife is almost as ludicrous an idea as my being married to a minister,* Faith said to herself as she reached up and swiftly pressed the strip for her stop.

There were moments over the next several days when Faith wondered if she was cut out for the two jobs totally occupying her life—professional caterer and amateur but increasingly expert worrier. She'd leave a message on Emma's machine, one sufficiently circumspect so as not to raise any suspicions on Michael's part, then turn to yet another tray of chocolate mousse cakes or yet another pork loin stuffed with winter fruits—the two most popular dishes of the season. She fretted over not being able to leave as many messages as she wanted—one every hour—and she fretted over Emma's not calling back. She knew Mrs. Stanstead was alive and kicking—although since it was Emma, Faith amended it to "alive and meandering"—because there had been a picture of her in the paper attending the premiere of Wagner's *Der fliegende Holländer* at the Metropolitan Opera House.

"Is there a particular reason you're so jumpy, or does

being in business for yourself do this to a person?" Josie asked after Faith made a mad and fruitless dash for the phone. It was yet another liquor supplier wanting their business.

Faith had thought she was presenting a markedly calm exterior to the world around her and was surprised at Josie's words.

"Jumpy? I'm not jumpy. Okay, maybe I'm a little strung out. But if we weren't getting steadily busier, I'd be even worse. I mean, I haven't particularly noticed anything myself, but if you say so . . ." She stopped. Josie was right. She was jumpy—and incoherent. Damn Emma's soap-opera life. And would it hurt her to call?

The phone rang. Josie answered, "Have Faith, taking care of all your catering needs. Josie Wells speaking."

She looked at Faith and raised an eyebrow. "No, she's not particularly busy. She's right here."

As Faith walked over to the phone, Josie covered the receiver. "Someone with guilt to spare. 'Please don't bother her if she's busy. Are you absolutely sure I'm not interrupting her work?' "

It was Emma.

"Emma! How are you? What's been happening?"

"I'm so sorry I didn't get back to you sooner. It was sweet of you to leave all those messages, but I'm almost never home; then when I am, it's to get ready to go to another party or opening or some other stupid thing. I shouldn't say that. Some of them aren't, but then most of them are. I don't know how Mother has done it all these years. And anyone who doesn't think Brooke Astor has energy to spare . . . well, I'd like a little of it, that's all."

Emma did sound exhausted, yet Faith was not interested in her friend's social schedule.

"But what's going on? You know, the issue we discussed late last week."

Josie was busy layering phyllo dough, but her hearing was excellent.

"Not a thing to worry about anymore. I would have called you as soon as everything was settled, but it's so hard to find a phone, and then there's always someone waiting right next to you."

Faith wanted to scream into the phone, "Get to the point!" but, mercifully, Emma kept talking and returned to the matter at hand.

"We can forget all about it. It's such a relief."

Faith was confused. "You mean it was a hoax? A bad joke?"

"Oh, no, it was real enough, but I gave them their money. Too complicated about where to put it and when."

"You gave them the money!" It hadn't occurred to Faith that Emma would simply pay them off. First of all, where does one lay hands on that kind of dough so quickly, and second, didn't Emma realize they would simply keep asking for more?

"It was the only way. Michael was beginning to notice that something was bothering me. I was even having trouble sleeping."

Trouble sleeping! Faith thought about the previous few nights, when she'd been tossing herself, exhausted from work, yet worried about her friend. It had been impossible to put it out of her mind. Every newspaper in the city screamed headlines about Fox's murder and now the magazines were coming out with their indepth analyses, complete with cover photos.

"I'm not sure that was the best way to go," Faith said as evenly and calmly as she could manage. "These events have a way of repeating themselves. You know, as in coming back for more."

Emma got the message. "Of course I thought of that," she reassured Faith. "I enclosed a very stern note and told them it was simply too much and this was the end. That should do it, and I haven't heard a peep out of them since. No nasty cards. No calls. Now all I have to do is think about what to get my dearest Michael for Christmas."

Ten thousand dollars poorer, Emma might want to head for Crazy Eddie's, Faith thought. It was so typically Emma to do what she had done. And who knew—maybe these were ethical, or one-shot, blackmailers. Faith sighed. She did want to hear all about it, though. How had they contacted Emma and where had she made the drop? And again, how had she come up with a bundle like that so easily? She couldn't exactly have asked her husband for it—tips for the doorman, the mailman, the maid. Just as she was trying to think how to phrase her queries in a form intelligible to Emma, but Greek to Josie, Emma said, "Oops, sorry, have to run. Lunch soon? I will call. I promise. Couldn't have done it without your help!"

Big help, Faith thought somewhat despondently. She hadn't even figured out who was blackmailing Emma. Didn't even have a list. Probably her evil sister. Faith brightened at the thought. It made sense and it was fun to consider. Lucy, the girl you loved to hate. Lucy had been at college when all this was happening, but it was possible she'd have heard about the pregnancy. Emma had made a scene in Dr. Bernardo's office, and that was the kind of gossip that got around.

Faith was surprised she hadn't heard about it at the time herself. Lucy had also been at the party and could have dropped the card in the hall where it was certain to be found. The blackmailer had to be someone who'd known that Emma would be there.

She turned back to her work. She was chopping apples for the pork loin. It wasn't for a party—or rather, not one that she was catering fully. The hostess had ordered it cooked as a full main course. Josie would deliver it with instructions for reheating late in the afternoon. It *was* a good dish, and when the meat was sliced, the apple and prune stuffing made a tasty little circle in the middle of the juicy meat. [See the recipe on page 280.] She served it with two side dishes: red cabbage, more apples, with a hint of onion and new potatoes that had been quartered and steamed, then sautéed in butter until brown and crispy on the outside. A city tired of *cuisine minceur* had been tucking into this comfort food with a ferocity. She paused and asked Josie, "Why is it New Yorkers always do everything in extremes? Fads, fashions, foibles—we're so intense."

Josie answered promptly, "That's easy. You put way too many people in one place and they have to start moving fast just to keep from getting stepped on, bumped around. The rest of the world has opinions, too, but they're operating at play and New York is fast forward."

Made sense to Faith. They worked in companionable silence until the phone rang again. It was Hope.

"I'm in like, maybe love," she announced joyously.

"And who might the lucky object of your affections be this time?" Faith asked, crooking the phone between her chin and shoulder while she continued to work. It could be a long conversation.

For a sophisticated New Yorker, Hope Sibley was extremely naïve when it came to men, Faith had always found. In high school, her sister had gravitated toward the misunderstood loners, the unrecognized geniuses, the substance abusers. A budding Dr. Joyce Brothers, she was always on the phone saying "Uh-huh" and nodding so constantly that Faith had begun to envision her sister as one of those rear-window car ornaments, heads bobbing around like crazy on a spring. This phase had passed, yet still Hope often failed to vet a new beau with the same thoroughness, obsessive at times, that she turned on a potential stock option. Never one to intrude in her sibling's life, and therefore ensuring a lifetime of closeness, Faith had felt compelled to have a little chat with Hope after observing her last heartthrob stuffing his pockets with the host's expensive cigars at a party Have Faith catered in early November. She'd been discreetly hidden from his notice, gazing through a slight opening in the kitchen door. "So tacky, sweetheart," she'd told Hope. "So not you."

Now Hope had found someone new. "Who is it and what does he do?" In a city where you were what you did, Faith tried to make a point of remembering to at least ask for a name first.

"His name is Phelps Grant and he's a commodities broker. I met him at a party last weekend. We started talking and things just clicked, Fay."

For years, Faith had been vowing to tell Hope how much she disliked the nickname, but for years she'd been putting it off.

"Phelps—prep school, right? You don't do that to your kid unless you're very sure he's going to be surrounded by Bancrofts and Chadwicks."

"Choate, if you must know. Anyway, he can't help his name, and I like it. Very traditional. We played squash together on Sunday and had brunch afterward. We're going out again Friday."

Faith wanted to ask, "Why not Saturday?" The prime spot. But she didn't wanted to rain on Hope's parade. Maybe Phelps had a prior commitment—passing around the drinks tray for Mater. Or maybe he was seeing another woman.

"He looks like Tom Cruise. Very hunky."

Once Hope was out of her missionary period, appearance mattered a great deal, and Faith hadn't seen her with a homely short guy in years. Tall, with thick brown hair and deep green eyes that were the envy of her blue-eyed sister, Hope turned plenty of heads. When both sisters went out together, the effect was more than doubled. Faith was as fair as her sister was dark, but their faces were just similar enough to proclaim a family connection. Fortunately, their mother, Jane, had never considered dressing them alike. Not even the same style in two colors.

"I ran into Emma Stanstead the other night at a job on the East Side." Faith threw out the line, hoping for some kind of bite.

"Her husband's going to be president someday. We'll have a friend in the White House, although it's hard to imagine Emma there. But he's a very smart cookie. He'll get all sorts of people to keep her on track. She'll just have to smile and produce a few kids, of course."

Faith hadn't thought of this, yet political dynasties meant offspring, and Michael Stanstead seemed like a dynastic kind of guy. Most of the Michael Stansteads of the world were.

"Emma didn't look pregnant. In fact, she's thinner than she was the last time I saw her, but she's still beautiful."

"I see them in the paper all the time. Where have you been? They're one of New York's golden couples."

In a kitchen of one sort or another, Faith thought, answering Hope's question silently.

"So, he really is being put forward by the party as a serious contender for future presidency?"

"Absolutely. That's all I've been hearing, and he wouldn't be bad."

Faith and her sister studiously avoided discussing politics, but each was aware that in many elections they were canceling out each other's votes.

"Get a date and have dinner with us next week. I'm dying for you to meet Phelps." Hope tried to sound plaintive. She knew it was a busy time for her sister.

"I'll try. I did meet a cute guy on the bus the other day. He was singing carols."

"On the bus! Are you crazy?"

"Not all of us can afford cabs, sweetheart."

"You know very well I didn't mean that. I take the bus sometimes myself. I mean getting involved with a total stranger—a stranger who's singing to himself."

"I'll be careful." Faith was smiling. There were any number of men who'd be happy to get her call, yet the idea of someone new was appealing. For months, she'd been telling her friends—and herself—that she was too busy to get involved with anyone, but New York during the holidays was so romantic. She pictured the older couple in the horse-drawn carriage that had passed by when Emma and she were in the park. Nice to take one of those carriages under a starry winter sky after a long, leisurely meal at one of those bistros on the East Side with a fireplace.

"So, you'll let me know when?"

She hadn't been listening to her sister. She hadn't been dicing apples, either.

"I'll try. If we can't get together before then, bring him to Chat's party."

"But you'll be working."

"And socializing. I plan to do both. It's the last one she's giving in the apartment. I'm really going to miss that view."

Chat's apartment in one of the San Remo towers on Central Park West had been a fixture in the Sibley girls' childhood—and adulthood. They'd watched every New Year's and Fourth of July fireworks from Chat's windows high above the city and every Macy's Thanksgiving parade from one of Chat's neighbors' windows in an apartment closer to earth. It was a ritual.

"Got to go. Call me," Hope said before hanging up.

Faith put the phone down.

"Phelps," Josie said, having eavesdropped expertly, as usual. "Sounds like money. Think he'd be interested in investing in a restaurant?"

"Not unless you have plans to franchise in all fifty states, I'd imagine," Faith said wryly.

Josie had gone to deliver the order and Faith was about to leave when the phone rang. She debated letting the machine pick up, but she shut the door and crossed the room instead. It was Emma. And she was frantic.

"I just got another Christmas card!"

Three

"Where are you? Are you home?" Faith asked tersely. Of course Emma had received another demand. It wasn't a question of waiting for the other shoe to drop. This was Imelda's whole closet. She had to make Emma realize what a dangerous game she was playing.

"Yes, I'm at the apartment." Emma was speaking quickly, breathlessly. "The card was in the newspaper. The doorman leaves it on the mat, and usually Michael gets it first thing, but he left for Albany early this morning. I left the back way when I went out and didn't think about the paper. Then when I came home, there it was. I picked it up and the card dropped out."

"I'll be right there. Are you sure you don't want to call the police while you're waiting for me? I'll be there with you," Faith pleaded.

Emma's voice lost its tremulous quality. "I'm sure. And I'm also sure I don't want to stay here one minute more. Meet me at Rockefeller Center. At the café. That's halfway for both of us. I'm leaving as soon as I hang up."

Faith agreed and headed for Fifth Avenue. Emma was safe inside her apartment, but Faith could understand how frightening the large, empty, silent rooms were at the moment. The bustle—and anonymity—of the city's crowded sidewalks would be infinitely preferable.

It didn't take Faith long to get to Rockefeller Center. Strange to think it had been open pastureland until the early 1800s. Now herds still gathered, but human herds intent on snaring tickets for a Letterman taping, the sight of the tree, a blowout at the Rainbow Room, or some very expensive shopping. She pushed her way through the crowds gathered around the Channel Gardens, those huge raised beds running from Fifth to the ice-skating rink. Tourists were posing for pictures next to the wire angels sounding their horns, poised in the masses of greenery. This whole business with Emma is definitely putting a damper on my Yuletide spirit, Faith thought sadly. Normally, it was her favorite time of the year. She looked straight ahead at the towering seventy-foot Norway spruce rising toward the winter sky, the GE Building behind it. Oddly, the tree seemed to grow smaller as she moved down the promenade and the view widened to include the incongruous forest of skyscrapers to either side, the rink below. Garlands of lights hung from the tree's boughs, tossing flickering colors over the skaters and Manship's huge statue of Prometheus, the gold leaf thinning in places, the fountain beneath stilled until spring. She turned to go down the stairs to the American Festival Cafe, still gazing at the tree. The ultimate Christmas tree, befitting the city that was, in Faith's opinion, the planet's shiniest ornament at any time of year.

Despite the urgency of the situation, she couldn't

stop herself from watching the skaters for a minute. As usual, they were all ages, all shapes, all sizes. Stumbling, laughing beginners, ankles wobbling. Serene-faced experts gracefully gliding in perfect time to the "Skater's Waltz." Around and around they went. If she hadn't been meeting Emma, Faith would have joined them.

But she was meeting Emma, and surprisingly, Emma was inside already, a pot of steaming tea and two cups on the table in front of her.

"They're bringing some scones and tea sandwiches. I thought you might be hungry."

Emma was paler than Faith had ever seen her. The faint sprinkling of freckles across her nose had emerged and her hair was more red than gold, in contrast to the flat white of her skin.

Faith took off her coat, hat, and gloves, then sat down, extending her hand across the table. "Let me see the card."

Emma had it ready in her lap and silently gave it to Faith. Once more Faith had a vague feeling that she shouldn't be touching it. That it should be dusted for prints. She shook her head. The whole situation was insane, and the way Emma and Faith herself were handling it was even crazier. What did they know about crime?

It was another card from the same pack, a Currier & Ives snow-covered barn this time, and like the first missive, it got right to the point. But this one was scarier. Much scarier.

You see we know where you live. We're getting closer. We have very expensive tastes and we'll be needing some more cash. Don't worry. We'll be in _touch_.

"When is Michael getting back?" It was abundantly clear why Emma didn't want to stay in the apartment alone now. There was no mistaking the threat implied by underlining the word *touch*.

"Tonight. He just has time to change before we have to go to some fund-raiser."

The waiter came with the rest of the order and fussed about with the scones and sandwiches. The delay was maddening. Finally, he left, but not until both women had thanked him profusely and falsely.

"You do see that they'll just keep upping the ante. Blackmailers don't stop, especially when they get what they want. This could go on for the rest of your life— or until you run out of money. And how *did* you come up with that much cash so fast?"

Emma looked down at her untouched plate. "Well, I do have rather a lot." She sounded apologetic. If giving into these demands was some sort of perverse rich girl's guilt over her assets, Faith could think of any number of better recipients for her largesse. "Poppy was worried that Jason would figure out a way to cut me off without her finding out, so she set up a trust for me out of her own money. It's supposed to be a secret." Emma looked even more mortified, if that was possible.

"Don't worry. I'm not sure I would even recognize your stepfather if I saw him, let alone tell him anything at all. You know that."

Emma nodded absently, smiling slightly. "Then when I was twenty-one, I came into the money left by my grandparents. A good bit of it is real estate. They thought Poppy had enough—and so did she—so everything went to Lucy and me."

Real estate. Nothing like putting your money into

land. Especially on the island of Manhattan. Faith dimly recalled hearing from her own mother, who could tell you the owner and price of virtually every building in the city, that Poppy had been born not with a silver spoon in her mouth, but a platinum one. By the time her two daughters were shoveling in the Pablum, the utensil had apparently become encrusted with diamonds.

But back to the issue at hand. It was nice for Emma that she had such bushel baskets of money, yet there was no reason for her to watch it all get dumped out.

"Even so, you can't keep paying," Faith said firmly. "And what about your safety? They were able to get into your building, past the doormen, and up to your floor!"

Tears came into Emma's eyes and she poured the tea with an unsteady hand. "Yes, I'm scared. Terribly frightened, in fact, but I'd rather die than betray my husband, and that's what it amounts to." She offered Faith the cup.

Faith took it, noting that Emma had been worrying the cuticles on her thumbs. Reflexively, she began to pick at her own, then stopped in annoyance. There was really nothing she could say after Emma's impassioned declaration, but Faith gave it a try. "You can't live like this. It's only going to get worse. Think about it! You have got to do *something!*"

Emma poured herself some tea, peered into the cup, and, despite the lack of tea leaves, announced her decision. "I'll tell Michael everything when things calm down. After he's elected next fall." The matter dismissed, she moved on. "You've seen the papers?"

Faith had. She'd been buying all of them, even and especially the tabloids, since Thursday. Fox's murder was still all over the front pages and the press had been pulling up file photos from Nate's radical salad days. In one of today's papers, there had been a large blowup of Fox leading chanting demonstrators in front of the Federal Building. A young woman linked to his arm, someone who could have been Emma's twin, was obviously Poppy Morris. So far, however, there hadn't been a word connecting either Poppy or Emma to Fox.

"I'm learning all sorts of things about my father from the articles," Emma said wistfully. "Mother would never talk about him. But I've read all his books."

If ever anyone wanted proof of filial devotion, here it was. Faith well knew that Emma's favorite book had always been *Charlotte's Web,* and even in adulthood, her reading, other than periodicals, tended toward idyllic—and usually bucolic—fiction. Family sagas with happy endings.

Faith had been learning things from the papers, too. She'd wondered how Fox had gotten his books published without either revealing his whereabouts or implicating his publisher. An extensive interview in Sunday's *Times* with Arthur Quinn, his longtime agent, had provided the answer. Quinn claimed not to have seen or talked with Fox since his disappearance. The manuscripts and various instructions would arrive in the mail with postmarks from several different South American countries and no return address. Quinn might get one a year, then nothing for two or three. As per Fox's wishes, all the royalties went to charities that he would update from time to time.

Faith tried a new tack. "Your father would never have put up with blackmail, and think how upset he would have been to know he was the cause of so much

54

unhappiness for you." It was the right button. Emma immediately burst into heartrending sobs that people at neighboring tables professed not to notice. It was New York City, after all. Besides, most of the café's customers were weary shoppers close to tears themselves.

"Don't you think I've thought of all this? There's no choice but to wait and see what happens. I can't tell Michael and I *really* can't tell the police. Oh, I wish Daddy hadn't died! He'd know what to do."

If Daddy hadn't died—and it certainly wasn't Daddy's idea—Emma would be in only a slightly less awkward position. Faith sat up suddenly. There had been something in Emma's tone that—

"You did find him, didn't you!"

Emma took out a handkerchief trimmed with an inch of the kind of lace that took French nuns a year to create. She dabbed her eyes. Her nose didn't get red when she cried, Faith had noted with some envy, but her whole face was pink now. Emma had never been a good liar.

"Todd took me to him. Before my mother found me and made me return home. My father was living someplace upstate. Neither he nor Todd told me the name of the town. For all our protection. Before that, he'd been out in Oregon, then Minnesota. He moved around a lot, of course. But if I hadn't found him through Todd, I would have kept looking. I *had* to see my real father—and he wanted to see me. It was his dream, he told me."

"Did you know he'd moved into the city?"

Emma nodded.

Faith blew at a strand of hair that had fallen into her eyes when the door to the frigid outside opened. One thing was clear. Whether it had occurred to Emma or not—and possibly not—if she went to the authorities now, she could be charged. Concealing the where-abouts of a wanted felon was itself a crime. In any case, she'd certainly make the headlines. And no one would be happy. Not the Stansteads, not the party—and, most especially, not Michael.

"He thought he would be safe enough after all this time, and he'd changed his name."

Yeah, Faith thought, to Fuchs, German for Fox. She began to wonder just how clever a man Fox had been. One would have thought that number one—or at most, number two—in the *Instructions for Going Under-ground Manual* read, "Do not assume a name resem-bling your own. Avoid the same initials." So, Nathan Fox decided to become Norman Fuchs. Maybe he had luggage.

" 'All old Jewish men look alike,' Daddy said. He'd grown a beard and cut his hair. It was very gray. I would never have recognized him from the old pic-tures. He was terribly good-looking back then, don't you think?"

Outside the large windows, the skaters endlessly circled the rink, leaving sharp trails and occasionally tracing intricate figures in the ice. A group of schoolkids sent a spray of chips flying up against the glass as they came to a sudden stop before racing off again.

"Very good-looking. Handsome as all get-out, but Emma, weren't you afraid someone would see the two of you together?"

"We never went outside. He never did go outside much anyway. He thought too much fresh air was bad for people," Emma smiled reminiscently. "I used to bring him bialys. There's a good place near where he lived. He liked to eat them when they were still warm.

56

His grandmother made the best ones, ones you could really sink your teeth into, he said. That was my great-grandmother."

Faith wasn't sure she could stand the pathos. And it was true: Like a real bagel, it was hard to get a good bialy these days.

"I'd have brought him more food, but there were some weeks when I couldn't come, and I didn't want him to depend on it. So he stuck to his own shopping. He went out to shop once or twice a week. Daddy didn't care about what he ate."

Faith knew there were people like this, but she preferred not to hear about them.

"I couldn't call him. He didn't have a phone. We arranged that he'd be home at three o'clock on Tuesdays. Not that he had other places to go, but this way, we'd be sure. If I could make it, fine; if not, fine. Daddy was very nonjudgmental."

Of his daughter, perhaps. Few others, apart from some of the working class, had escaped his scathing view of the world. Fox had once put the entire United States of America on trial in a mock version staged in Central Park. Since they didn't have a permit, the trial ended before a verdict could be reached.

Emma was buttering a scone. We seem to be developing a pattern here, Faith observed to herself. Emma unburdens herself, feels better, perks up, and I inch closer to prematurely adding Nice 'n Easy to my shopping list.

"They didn't name the amount of money they wanted in the note," Emma pointed out. "And my name hasn't been in any of the papers, or someone would have told me by now, so there really is nothing we can do at the moment."

She took a bite, swallowed, and added, "The police would certainly have been in touch with me already if they had been going to." She laughed at her own illogic—and perhaps the awkwardly dangling infinitive.

"Why are you so sure about that?" Faith asked suspiciously. Grammar or no grammar, she knew what Emma was hinting. She took a bite of the scone on her own plate and put it down. Too much baking powder.

"I always sent Daddy postcards when I was traveling and couldn't get to see him. Besides, he did so miss leaving the country. He'd hitchhiked all over the world when he was younger."

"And he saved them?"

"One was on the fridge the last time I was there."

Ignoring the homey image this conjured up—hammer and sickle refrigerator magnets?—Faith pressed. "But how would the police have known who you were? Granted, they could check up on people named Emma who'd left the country for those destinations near the postmarked dates, but it wouldn't be easy."

"They would have recognized Michael from our wedding picture," Emma answered matter-of-factly.

Faith's head began to reel as she envisioned the Spartan studio apartment described in the media filled with nothing but books, an ancient Underwood on a card table, a bed, and a file cabinet—envisioned the apartment complete with an eight-by-ten glossy of Emma and Michael, the bride and groom, in a silver frame from Tiffany's.

But Emma was right. The police would have been onto her immediately. Fox's murderer had taken the photo and the cards. Fox's murderer. Emma's blackmailer?

Emma stood up. She looked out at the tree and said

pensively, "I'm madly behind with my shopping. I'd better go to Saks."

Faith pulled on her coat. "What about Todd? What happened to him? Don't tell me you see him at three o'clock on Wednesdays."

"Don't be silly. I never saw him again after that, but I did get a card in the mail a couple of years ago from some real estate firm on Long Island. You know the kind. 'If you're thinking of buying a house, think of me.' And it had his picture on it; otherwise, I would never even have read it. It was right after we got married, and he must have seen the announcement in the *Times*. Maybe he thought we wanted to move out of the city. City—that's where he was—Garden City."

So, Todd Hartley had not assumed a blue collar— and he knew what had happened to Fox's daughter. And that she'd been pregnant by him. Faith put his name on the list of potential blackmailers.

"Was there anybody else who knew who Fox was and knew you? Anyone else around when you went to see him the first time?"

"He was living with some woman. Daddy always had women," Emma added ruefully. Faith was glad to see it. All this Daddy Fox worship was getting to be a bit much. "I didn't meet her, though. I think he didn't want her to know about me."

Faith made a mental note of this woman. The list could use a few more names. At the moment, it consisted of Lucy Morris and Todd Hartley. Poppy Morris knew about her daughter's pregnancy and parentage, but it strained credulity to think she would be blackmailing her own daughter. Still, Faith made another note to try to find out if Poppy was paying her Bergdorf's bills on time. Some of the veteran sales force who had been outfitting Jane Lennox Sibley's family forever could be counted on to spill a few beans.

Jason Morris obviously knew about Nathan Fox and his wife's affair, yet he may not have known about Emma's pregnancy, although Emma had mentioned that Poppy was carrying on about it all over the house. The only reason he'd have to blackmail his—what, stepdaughter?—would be pure spite. To get his hands on the money Poppy had set aside for Emma behind his back? Faith added Jason to the list. From what little she recalled, he'd never struck her as a terribly nice man, and at the moment, that was enough to fit the profile. Then there was Fox himself—he knew Emma was his daughter and she may have told him about the pregnancy during one of their parent-child bonding visits. But Fox was already dead when the first card turned up. Even if he'd written it, he couldn't have orchestrated the delivery of the money or composed the second from the grave. He'd been a vocal force when previously underground, but this time around was decidedly different. Whatever one's beliefs concerning the hereafter, none included the postal service or even faxes.

"I know I have no right to ask you to do anything else, Faith, when you've been such an angel, but there is one more thing. A big favor."

Emma was putting some money down on the table, over Faith's protests that they split the bill. "Women aren't good at this. No one ever has the right change or can figure out who owes what, so it's easier for me to pay, and besides, I want it to be my treat." Emma had interrupted herself to settle the question of the bill. Faith put her coat on and waited to find out what this favor might be. It could be anything from helping her find that perfect little something for sister Lucy—some desk models of guillotines, "conversation pieces" leapt to mind—to breaking into Fox-Fuch's apartment to be sure the photo and cards were gone. This had already occurred to Faith. And if Emma had a key, it would even be somewhat legal.

"There, that should be right." Faith looked at the money tucked next to the teapot. If everyone tipped the way Emma did, the waiter could go to Acapulco for Christmas *and* Easter.

Emma pulled on her long suede gloves and put one hand on Faith's arm.

"Will you go to the service for me? Daddy's service? Knowing that you're there will be the next best thing to being there myself, and you can tell me all about it. I wish I could go, but I can't. There could be pictures, and soon everybody would be asking why I went."

"Of course I'll go. The *Times* had said Quinn, his agent, would be arranging a memorial service soon. Tell me once you know when it is, in case I miss the notice." This was not a big favor. This was nothing.

The big favor that Faith had already taken on—in her mind anyway—was finding out who was black-mailing her old schoolmate.

And going to the memorial service would be the first step in her investigation.

Emma left and Faith made her way to the rest rooms. There had been talk of placing public conveniences like the coin-operated kind in Paris at various locations throughout the city, but at present one had to grab at any opportunity or go into a department store, which

invariably cost much, much more than any pay toilet—
in Faith's experience anyway. The last time she'd
dashed into Bloomies, she'd come out with a Jil
Sander jacket—it had been on sale—and a Mary
McFadden scarf for her mother—it hadn't. The cubi-
cles on the streets in Paris had occasionally failed to
open, trapping the occupant, and Faith had resolved either to avoid them until foolproof or always carry a
very long book—something like Proust—that she'd
been meaning to read for years.

Returning, she again noted a man with his face
buried in the *Wall Street Journal* a few tables behind
where they had been sitting. The few other men in the
café at this hour were older with, presumably, spouses
or were younger with families. She looked back at
him. He was leaving. There was something familiar
about him, yet it could just be that they'd been on the
subway together, or he could have been at any number
of dances and parties over the years. Parties. That was
it. He'd been at the party she'd catered last week. He
was with the host and Michael Stanstead when they
came into the kitchen. He must not have been a close
friend of Stanstead or he would have said something to
Emma today. Unless he was so intent on his reading
that he didn't see her. Or unless he felt he'd be intrud-
ing. His presence continued to disturb Faith. What was
he doing alone at the café at this hour? The market had
just closed.

She walked out into the bitter cold and took a soft
wool cloche out of her pocket, pulling it down over her
ears. The hat made her look like a Gatsby girl and
filled her hair with static electricity, but it was warm.
She stood on Fifth Avenue, glancing back over her
shoulder at the huge tree at Rockefeller Center. It was

even more dramatic as the day drew to a close, its lights glowing like jewels against the dark branches.

On the other side of Fifth stood Saks on one corner, Saint Patrick's Cathedral on the other. God and mammon. The front windows at Saks were filled each Christmas with ever-more-elaborate moving figures— scenes from *The Nutcracker,* Dickens, the *Arabian Nights*—glimmering, glistening fantasies. Shoppers filed by in long lines behind the velvet ropes, funneled at the end of the oohs and aahs into the Palace of Goods.

Worshipers at other altars across the street—those dedicated to Saint Anthony, Saint John, Saint Theresa—also moved in lines, walking slowly up the nave to gaze back at the rose window and ahead toward the lady chapel. Today, Faith decided to join this crowd. She crossed, darting between two cabs, only one of which, miraculously, honked at her, and climbed the stairs into Saint Patrick's marble interior. Instantly, she knew she had picked the right place and she walked quietly up the side aisle toward the altar, banked with row upon row of brilliant red poinsettias. The cathedral was filled with a golden glow—tiers of flickering votive candles and interior spots created sudden pools of light against the early dark. The smell of incense mixed with that of burning candle wax and hung in the warm air. She slipped into a row and took a seat on one of the hard wooden pews. She had yet to be in a church—and she'd been in a great many of them over the years—with comfortable seating. She'd mentioned this to her father a few times, commenting that penance of this sort seemed at odds with modern religion. "We don't beat ourselves with sticks, wear hair shirts, or put pebbles in our shoes. Why do we have to sit on such unforgiving surfaces?" Once, he'd told her that if the pews were too deeply cushioned, he'd put his parishioners to sleep. Another time, he'd answered that it was simply a matter of economics. Something else was always more pressing—disaster victims, the homeless, the poor, the leaks in the church roof. He'd got her there, yet she continued to secretly hope for a bequest from some eccentric who would stipulate the money could be spent only for the betterment of congregational buns.

She closed her eyes for a moment, and when she opened them, the altar blazed before her. It was truly beautiful. She didn't like poinsettias, opting instead for amaryllis, cyclamen, clivia, and hydrangea during this festive season, yet she would have been the first one to protest the absence of the traditional plants from Saint Patrick's. Protest. That brought her back to Nate Fox— and Emma.

It was difficult to sort things out. This last conversation with Emma had made one thing clear, however. She had adored her lost and found father. What's more, he seemed to have cared for her, displaying the postcards, her wedding photo—though in that case, Faith was sure Fox also got a kick from the irony of conservative Michael Stanstead in full nuptial regalia posed next to, say, Fox's autographed copy of Trotsky's *History of the Russian Revolution.*

Yet Fox, the devoted dad, had never tried to get in touch with Emma, although he certainly knew where she was all those years. Granted, he was on the lam, but if it had been his dream to see her, wouldn't he have done something about it? Watched her incognito at the park with her nanny? Impersonated a waiter at her coming-out ball? Faith could think of all sorts of soppy grade-B movie plots. Maybe he had had a deal with Poppy. Obviously, they'd decided it would be better for the child to believe Jason was her father. Only Jason didn't love her. All those years of never pleasing him, never being what he wanted—and never knowing why. Emma had been physically abandoned by her real father, and the man she'd thought was her father had abandoned her emotionally and in a more tangible, economic way, although she wouldn't have learned that until Jason's death. Faith shuddered. She thought of her own father—and she was sure he was, since she had his clear blue eyes. Lawrence Sibley had been an impoverished divinity school student when Faith's mother, Jane Lennox, had met him and been uncharacteristically swept off her feet. The two opposites had forged an indissoluble union. That's a hard act to follow, Faith reflected as she heard the soft murmur of whispered prayers around her. No wonder I'm not married. Because when I am, it's got to be for keeps.

Like Emma. Emma and Michael. In Emma's mind, revealing to her husband what she was going through, had gone through, would be an act of betrayal, equal to something like adultery—a sin. Finally, in Michael, Emma had found a man who would not leave her. Someone she could trust and she would literally die rather than destroy or even jeopardize that.

Once again, Faith was back at the beginning. There was only one thing to do. Find out who was blackmailing Emma. Put a stop to it—note to self: Have to work on this angle. Then Emma can live happily ever after and Michael will remain in blissful ignorance.

Faith stood up and walked toward the altar. She was starting to think like Emma, she realized with dismay.

* * *

Someday when things are so busy that I don't even have a chance to catch my breath, I'll look back at this time and regret I didn't enjoy it more. This was Faith's advice to herself after she checked the messages at work and found nothing urgent. No emergency calls from Gracie Mansion to whip up a quick mayoral dinner for two hundred. Not even a call for a dinner party for twelve. She did have a party to do the following night, and she decided to make another hors d'oeuvre, although there were already several selections. They'd prepared phyllo triangles stuffed with a proscuitto and ricotta mixture and others filled with diced mushrooms and smoked turkey. Then there was gravlax with plenty of dill and mustard sauce on rounds of thin dark rye and toasted brioche. She'd do some spiced nuts and put bowls of them next to the bowls of various kinds of olives she'd already planned. Before she got started, she decided to check the messages at her apartment. Emma would be getting ready for her fund-raiser— Faith had forgotten to ask her where it was—but there might have been further instructions from the black-mailers. Emma would leave some sort of message, Faith wanted to believe.

She punched in the code—and beep, "Faith, love, it's Granny. I'm totally distraught and can't understand why someone didn't tell me sooner! I suppose they were trying to spare an old lady."

Whatever it is, it must be bad. Faith felt a flicker of anxiety. When her grandmother started referring to herself this way, it meant she'd lost another friend or received some other devastating news. Normally, she made a point of ignoring the aging process, and she still had the legs to prove it worked.

"Altman's is closing! B. Altman! They're having a

gigantic sale and simply gutting the place. I can scarcely take it in. I'd like you and Hope to come to lunch with me at the Charleston Gardens. Remember all those times we used to go there before the ballet? Humor an old lady and call me, dear." Two mentions of "old lady" in one message. Faith hated that Altman's was closing, too, although she hadn't been there in years. It had furnished her grandmother and mother's trousseaux—and first apartments. When Hope and Faith were little girls, Altman's was de rigeur for party dresses, white gloves, navy blue Sunday school coats, and, of course, Easter bonnets. She felt a sudden nostalgia for the Charleston Gardens' rendition of chicken à la king. (And which king was that? British, surely, not French.) The memory was complicated by an equally strong one of Hope losing her lunch in the final moments of *Romeo and Juliet,* when sister and grandmother took her tugs on their sleeves to mean requests for information—Hope had been a great one for questions like "Why can't she climb down the balcony and leave?"—rather than the urgent need for the bathroom that it was. The image of mopping Hope up, as well as three ladies from a women's club on Long Island who had been in the row in front of them, had stayed with Faith as clearly as if it were yesterday. It was the first time she'd ever seen what she later learned was called a "merry widow." Yes, she'd have lunch with Granny and they could all mourn the passing of yet another treasured New York institution and bemoan the shortsightedness of the philistines responsible—but Faith would stick to the BLT.

Beep: " ' "Hither, page, and stand by me,/If thou know'st it, telling,/Yonder peasant, who is he?/Where and what his dwelling?"/"Sire, he lives a good league hence,/Underneath the mountain,/Right against the forest fence,/By Saint Agnes' fountain." ' "

Richard Morgan! Things were looking up. "I can sing some more verses, too. If you'd like to hear them, meet me for dinner tonight. I know it's short notice, but I thought I'd still be out of town. Give me a call. Five five five, eight nine four seven. I'll even not sing, if you'd rather."

The last message was from Hope. She was at work and had her work voice on. "Please let me know some times when you're available for dinner, so we can arrange a date and place to meet. Best call me at work. I won't be home until late all week." Hope got to the office well before dawn and seldom left until it was time to tumble into bed. It wasn't until all the Michael Milken stuff came out, revealing, among other things, that, like many in the business, he rose at 4:00 A.M., sleeping only four to five hours a night, that Faith conceded her sister wasn't seriously disturbed, simply seriously lacking perspective.

She shook her head and dialed Richard. He answered on the second ring.

"Hi, it's Faith Sibley, and as it turns out, I am free, and trying to remember all those verses has been driving me crazy. Your call came just in time."

"One so rarely has the opportunity to be of service. I'm delighted. Now, what's your pleasure?"

That awkward moment had arrived. Where to eat? And she had no idea how fat his wallet was. Did the absence of an overcoat mean good circulation or an unhealthy cash flow?

"I dunno. What do you want to do, Marty?" Faith had been brought up on black-and-white classic movies. Apparently, so had Richard.

"If I remind you of Ernest Borgnine, we may have a problem."

Faith laughed. "Okay. What kind of food do you like to eat, and if you say everything, I'm hanging up."

"Don't do that! Let's see, there's wassail. No, how about I dare the impossible and choose for the caterer. They make great margaritas at Santa Fe on West Sixty-ninth, and the food is pretty good, too."

Faith had been there a few times and liked it. The warm brick-colored walls and soft lighting were any girl's best friends. "Done. Meet you there at eight?"

"Meet you there at eight. And Faith, I'm looking forward to moving on to the next topic."

"Me, too. See you soon." Frankly, at this point in her life, she wasn't the least bit curious about the forest fence or Saint Agnes's fountain. She already knew how it turned out.

Richard Morgan was a freelance journalist, and Faith now recalled seeing his byline in a wide variety of publications—*The New Yorker,* the *Village Voice, The New Republic*, as well as the *Times.* She was going to have to be very, very careful. But she brightened at her next thought. She'd be able to pump *him* for information. First, it seemed that they needed to find out what each other thought about everything from Leona Helmsley's trial—"Anyone who goes on record saying, 'I don't pay taxes. Only the little people pay taxes' has to take her knocks," said Richard—to Paul McCartney at forty-seven—"Can he still cut it?" "*Flowers in the Dirt* has some great moments, but it's mixed," said Faith.

Richard had been at Tiananmen Square and Faith listened spellbound as he described what it had been like to stand shoulder-to-shoulder with the students as the tanks rolled in.

"Enough about me," he said.

It had been awhile since Faith had heard these words. Maybe he had a brother for Hope.

"Tell me about Faith Sibley. I want to know everything. All your secrets." His grin was disarming. There's nothing like charm to extract information. He must be very good at what he does, Faith thought, beginning to realize writing wasn't his only talent.

She gave him the Cliffs Notes version of her life to date. He smiled again at the vehemence with which she declared she would never, ever marry a man of the cloth.

"Good news for the rest of us."

"Unless you've grown up as a PK—preacher's kid—it's hard to understand. We never gave the parish anything really juicy to comment on, like running away to join a cult or shaving our heads and piercing our noses. But there were plenty of annoying day-to-day remarks. 'Isn't she a little young for makeup?' 'Did I hear the girls were going to Europe by themselves this summer?' 'Has Faith decided on a career yet, like Hope?' You get the picture."

"Yeah, might make a good article. Don't worry," Richard said, seeing Faith's look of alarm, "another PK. I don't take advantage of my friends—or try not to, anyway."

If one of them was sitting on a story as big as the one she was, Faith was sure Richard's scruples would vanish before you could say "Pulitzer Prize."

They were waiting for their main course—they'd both ordered a pork dish with green chili. It would make splitting the bill easier, but Faith wouldn't be able to find out how comfortable he was about sharing food. She firmly believed "Do you promise to share what's on your plate?" should be worked into the traditional marriage vows. Forget *sickness, health, love, honor,* and especially *obey.* Most divorces could be avoided by a simple test. Order something you don't particularly want in a restaurant and urge him to get something you adore. Ask for a taste and take careful notes. A cousin of Faith's reported her fiancé's reaction: "If you wanted it, why didn't you order it?" Faith advised caution, was not heeded, and they were splitsville less than a year after the honeymoon. But tonight she was really in the mood for the pork. Maybe next time?

Inevitably, the conversation turned to food, which then led to travel. Richard had been all over the world and even expressed a desire to hop aboard a space shuttle should the chance arise. Faith was drawn to space travel in theory—the extraordinary sight of earth from far, far away, that big blue marble. Yet, lurking beneath her adventurous spirit was a tiny voice insistently whimpering, But what if you couldn't get back? For the moment, she wasn't taking a number. She definitely *did* want to go to the Far East, and she listened intently—and enviously—as Richard described his journeys. The margaritas were drained and they ordered dark Dos Equis beer to go with the rest of dinner. Faith was feeling more relaxed than she had been all week.

"But you haven't told me any secrets," he said suddenly.

"You haven't told me any, either," she countered. Two could play at this game.

"All right. I'm secretly writing a book that is going

to blow a certain southern town sky-high. A best-seller for sure." '

Faith looked at him scornfully. "Every other person in this city—and probably the rest of the country—is writing some kind of explosive book. That's not a real secret."

He leaned forward. He really was good-looking. Deep brown eyes and lighter brown hair—wavy, not curly. He was thin, but not skinny; his chin and cheekbones well defined. Kate Hepburn's cousin, without the voice.

"While I was doing a story on something else, I stumbled across a mystery. I met the principals and haven't been able to stay away. It's one of those situations in life where nothing you could dream up as fiction could match the bizarre and byzantine nature of this reality."

Faith was with him there. She found herself nodding. Nothing one could imagine . . .

"So what's yours?"

She came to with a jolt.

"I stole a ceramic animal from the gift shop at the Museum of Natural History when I was nine years old, never told my parents, and kept it." She didn't add that she had felt so guilty, she was unable to look at the little lion. Too afraid of the questions that might arise if it was discovered in the trash, she had stashed it in a shoe box in her closet until two years ago, when she donated it to a local thrift shop as a collectible.

"So, keep your secrets. My nose for news, and experience with sources, tells me you're a complicated woman and one extremely capable at keeping things hidden, Faith. And how did you end up with a name like that? I've never met a Faith before. Funny, though, it seems to suit you."

Faith told him the family story and they moved on to discuss an article about the eighties he was finishing up for the *Times* magazine section.

"This could get depressing," Faith remarked. "I keep thinking of people like Mark Chapman and John Hinckley. And the Ayatollah putting a price on Salman Rushdie's head. So much craziness."

"The *Challenger* tragedy, the savings and loan crisis, Black Monday . . ."

Faith began to chant, "Nancy Reagan's china, Beemers, 'Whoever Dies with the Most Toys Wins,' Malcolm Forbes's two-million-dollar Moroccan birthday bash . . ."

"But there were also all those KILL YOUR TELEVISION bumper stickers, and we weren't involved in any major wars during the entire decade, although there's still time."

"Not much. I read a wonderful quote from that British novelist Angela Carter the other day commenting on the heavy pronouncements we've been reading almost all year: 'The *fin* is coming early this *siècle*.' "

They both laughed.

"I'll track it down and use it. It would make a terrific title."

The only dessert Faith ever wanted at Tex-Mex places was flan. It was the perfect counterpoint to the spicy main dishes, and she recalled that Santa Fe's was perfect—rich, creamy, yet not cloying. They both ordered coffee. Richard didn't seem to be in any rush to get back to his article, and though Faith was tired, it was pleasant to linger. Besides, she realized, she'd been having such a good time, she'd forgotten to work

Fox's murder into the conversation and see if she could get any further information. She had to act fast before the evening ended.

"How about the murder of Nathan Fox? Do you intend to use it in your article?"

"It's worth a mention. A lot of what's happened in the eighties—the excesses—was what people like Fox were predicting in the sixties. It hasn't simply been a case of the rich getting richer and the poor getting poorer. That's always been true. But in the eighties, the rich got *much* richer. Even after the 1987 crash. Last year, in '88, Milken made five hundred and fifty million dollars—ironically fifty million more than the Gambino family, crime apparently not paying as much as it used to, or their kind anyway—and I *am* using that. Fox and his cohort believed that the widening gap between rich and poor would lead to revolution. Well, it hasn't. At least not yet, and I don't see it happening anywhere in the near future, but the seeds of the eighties were sowed in the sixties. Ironically, Fox liked nothing better than schmoozing with wealthy New York intellectuals and socialites. He was a regular at certain dinner parties, delighting the guests by telling them what decadent leeches they were. That all the finger bowls in the world wouldn't be enough to cleanse the blood of the workers from their effete, uncalloused hands—that, or something very similar, was one of his lines."

Faith thought again that Fox wouldn't have lasted long at Aunt Chat's Madison Avenue ad agency if the tired, trite slogans she'd been hearing were any indication of his acumen.

"So you haven't really heard anything. But why murdered? Why now? What's the 'bottom line'?" She injected the eighties buzzword to keep things light—and keep the conversation going.

Richard thought for a moment. "There has been some talk that Fox's murder was tied to his politics—that it wasn't just a robbery by some cokehead—but I haven't been able to come up with an angle. Unless he's been keeping some pretty heavy stuff under wraps all these years. Maybe about someone else in the movement. Or let's say he was about to get a pardon and write a tell-all book. If Reagan could get a seven-million-dollar advance, Fox could certainly have hoped for half that—or more in hush money! But I jest. He wasn't into material goods. More to the point, he's not the pardonable type. Wrong haircut. Besides the politics theory, there are a lot of rumors about where he's been all these years, and maybe there's a motive there. Someone he crossed. A woman? And from all accounts, in Fox's case there were always lots of ladies."

"Where do people say he was?"

Richard signaled the waiter for more coffee. "If Fox was everywhere I've heard he's been, he would have racked up enough frequent flyer coupons to last through the next millennium. California, the Pacific Northwest, the Dakotas, Minnesota, Maine, Florida—oh, and Cuba, to name a few. Apparently, he was all set to spend his golden years with Fidel, but Nate got kicked out when he said, 'Thank you for not smoking' to the big guy."

"And what about the murder weapon? According to the papers, he was shot at close range and the weapon hasn't been found."

Richard rubbed his chin. He was in slight, very slight need of a shave.

"It would have been pretty stupid to leave the murder weapon behind as a calling card. If it was your average B and E, they'd have further use for it. If it wasn't, but, rather, someone Fox knew and let into the apartment, then all the more reason to get rid of it, say in that big Dumpster known as the East River."

"The papers haven't said what kind of gun it was. The police would know from the bullet. Have you heard anything?"

Morgan shook his head and then looked sharply at Faith. "Why so much interest in Fox? He wasn't a well-known food connoisseur, to my knowledge. Don't tell me—your parents were in the Weather Underground and you're actually a red-diaper baby."

"Sorry, my father never even remembers to carry an umbrella and my diapers were as snowy white as the diaper service could make them. Mother has always believed some things are best done by others. Now come on—that business with Fox in Cuba, you were making that up."

"I kid you not."

Faith made a face and, terrierlike, held on to the subject. "Why do you think he wasn't caught?"

"At first, probably because no one squealed on him, and it's not so easy as you might think to find someone who doesn't want to be found, even if you're the feds. Especially when he disappeared. Pre–cyber spying. Then later, they had more important things to do. Better ways to spend taxpayers' money. They probably unloaded a bunch of dusty file folders on all those Weathermen, Yippies, pinkos, et cetera, on one poor slob and he'd make a few calls every once in a while. Check the taps on their parents', siblings', old lovers' phones. Reel somebody in by chance now and again."

"Then Fox wasn't taking much of a risk moving into the city."

"Well, it did get him killed."

"So you *do* think his murder is tied to his past?"

"Isn't everything?"

Four

Almost everybody was wearing black at Nathan Fox's memorial service, which was exactly what Faith had expected. It was not from a deep sense of propriety, but because this was New York City and everybody, especially women, wore black most of the time. It wasn't timidity; it was the acknowledgment of a universal truth. You always looked good in black—and in style.

Fox was going out in style. Going out on the Upper East Side at Frank E. Campbell's, where anybody who was anybody had his or her service. Faith walked in under the marquee and quickly went into the building. There was a basket of yarmulkes at the door to the chapel. They seemed at odds with the bland, goyish entry room, complete with an Early American grandfather clock. But Fox had been, if not Jewish, a Jew, and many of the men were covering their heads.

Faith slid into a seat far enough back for a good view of the audience—the mourners, she corrected herself—but close enough to hear the lines—the eulogies, that is. It had felt like a performance from the moment she'd pulled up to the entrance, her cab nosing out one limo and pulling up behind another. The service was private, the paper had said, and no time or place was given, but Emma had called Campbell's, posing as her father's cousin—"He has some," she'd told Faith—and received the information. She'd called Campbell's because, Faith realized, it would never have occurred to Emma that there might be other possibilities. So here Faith was—waiting for the curtain to go up, or down—after getting the message from Emma the night before.

The night before. Faith had been tired, but pleasantly so. After finishing dinner at Santa Fe, Richard and she had gone to Delia's, a newish downtown club on East Third Street. The owner was Irish, and Delia's had a slightly Celtic air, enhanced by books on the "auld country" scattered about. But its main charm was in its unabashed romanticism. The interior was the color of raspberry silk sashes on little girls' party dresses. There were vases crammed with fresh roses. A vintage bar and minuscule dance floor completed the decor. Prints of elegant long-ago ladies hung on the walls.

They hadn't danced, not this time, but talked for hours more. Then Richard had taken her back to her apartment building. At the front door, he'd asked, "When can I see you again?" "When would you like to see me?" she'd answered, slightly muzzy from fatigue and a large cognac. Richard asked, "Tomorrow?" It woke her up instantly, a dash of cold water. This is going fast, she thought, half in fear, half in delight. "That's too soon. Besides, I have to work. The next day?" He kissed her, and it was a good one, not too dry, not too wet. Her purse slipped off her shoulder into the crook of her arm. He slid it back into place. "I'll call you."

" 'To everything there is a season . . .' "

Faith opened her half-closed eyes. The service had started.

It was plain by the third tribute that if she had hoped to get any clues as to Nathan Fox's true nature, it would not be here. But she had not harbored any such hopes. Funerals and memorial services are only venues for truth in fiction, where scenes of bereavement might dramatically reveal hitherto-undisclosed feelings. In reality, most people keep their private opinions private and eulogized. True, she'd been to heart-wrenching services where the naked grief of those left behind laid bare their hearts, but it was never a surprise. The same for those stoic occasions where not a single tear was shed.

There were no tears at Fox's service, but a great deal of talk. The dinosaurs—the remaining larger-than-life figures from the radical sixties—needed to weigh in and be counted. Radical lawyers, radical professors, radical clergy, radical writers, professional radicals. The chapel was packed. People were standing.

Faith began to feel fidgety in the warm room. Outside, it was cloudy, with gray skies. A light snow had begun to fall earlier in the day. It was bitterly cold. Inside, the smell of wet wool, designer perfumes, the single floral arrangement of oversized stargazer lilies, and furniture polish commingled. The temperature crept up, increased by the crowd. Faith began to feel slightly nauseated.

She took off her coat and tried to concentrate on what the speaker was saying. There was no casket, no urn. The only sign of Fox's mortal existence was a large framed photograph next to the flowers. It was the same picture that had been in the *Times*. His smile looked less smug and mocking now, more self-deprecating, sadder. But that could just be the place getting to her. She leaned over to look directly toward the man who was sonorously droning on, and for the first time she spied Poppy, who had turned around, presumably looking for someone, or counting the house.

Poppy Morris was sitting in the middle of a row. Protective coloration? Unlike most of those Faith could see, Poppy looked genuinely stricken. There were deep circles under her eyes that even carefully applied concealer didn't mask. She turned her head back, face-forward. Noting the woman's distress, Faith seriously doubted that Emma was the only one to know that Fox had been back in town; the only Morris to have seen him in all these years.

Two more pundits spoke, and Faith did not even attempt to concentrate after hearing the beginning of the phrase "This is the end of . . ." It was all so impersonal. What was she going to tell Emma? There was no wailing, no gnashing of teeth, no rending of garments. Not that Emma herself would have behaved with such primitive lack of control, but Fox's daughter was bereft. She'd want to hear that others were also. That her father would be missed. That her father had been cherished.

Faith turned around, as much to stretch her neck as to see how many people were behind her. A middle-aged woman stood against the wall, her eyes locked on the speaker, hanging upon every word. Tears streamed down her cheeks. Faith would have liked to stare longer. Not only was someone besides Poppy exhibiting signs of loss, but the woman was hard to categorize. She was wearing a drab mustard-colored parka, which she'd unzipped, revealing a white cotton turtleneck. Her hair, light brown with as much again of gray, was parted in the middle and worn in a long braid, snaking down across her shoulder toward the waistband of whatever was completing her uninspired outfit. There was some sort of button pinned to the jacket. Faith could not read the slogan from this distance, but she was sure it expressed solidarity with someone—or something like whales or redwoods. It wasn't hard to imagine her in the sixties, fist raised, hair blowing in the wind, finding answers in Fox's diatribes—and maybe more. Emma, and Richard Morgan, had spoken of Fox's women. Faith had a hunch that the lady in brown was one.

The man who had read the lines from Ecclesiastes at the start of the service stood up again and addressed the group.

"Aside from his cousins Marsha and Irwin"—he nodded toward two elderly people sitting close together in the front row—"Nathan Fox leaves no survivors but his words. As his agent and friend, I watched his words transform a generation. Nathan was cruelly, barbarically struck down in an act we cannot comprehend, but he is not dead. Not while his words live."

This looked to be the finale and Faith tuned back in. "No survivors." Well, she knew that wasn't true. She looked at the back of Poppy's head. Besides the two of them, who else in the room knew that Arthur Quinn's words were false? Knew the whole story, knew enough to blackmail Emma?

"He was a skinny kid when he came to me with the first book. How could I not take him on, even when he called me a parasite?" He paused for the laugh, which came. "Yeah, I told him, I'm a parasite, but an honorable one." More laughter. "He liked that." Quinn stopped again, seeing that Nate Fox in his mind's eye, or assuming that was what people would think. A sensitive parasite.

His voice grew louder as he continued his speech. "How could I not do everything to spread those words? He wrote with passion, conviction, and a monumental sense of injustice. There's been a great deal of talk these last days about Nathan Fox's life underground—a wasted life. But Nate loved being on the run. He was on the run all his life—from the establishment, and maybe from himself. Certainly"—he smiled with studied ruefulness and a twinkle in his eye—"from every woman who tried to keep up with him." During the laugh that followed, Faith darted a glance at the woman in the rear. Her cheeks were flushed and her mouth was closed in a tight line.

"How shall we mourn Nathan Fox? Not at all. He wrote to me once that he had no regrets, and how many men can say that?"

And how many should? Faith said to herself. No regrets. They'd entered the chapel to Mozart; was "My Way" going to see them out?

"How shall we honor Nathan Fox's memory? By reading his books and making his thoughts a part of us—living his words and by our acts, he will be with us always. He has left us this gift—and there is another yet to come. The last letters I had from him spoke of 'the big one.' A book that was to be published only after his death 'far in the future, Artie,' he wrote, advising me not to count on the 'shekels' for a 'long, long time.' Inutterably sad words now. So, I watch the mail. It may come tomorrow, next week, next year. It will be his monument, one, to quote him again, 'That will blow the fuckin' lid off.' This, ladies and gentlemen, was Nathan Fox's purpose in life. May he rest in peace, but not too much. He'll get bored."

The music, Mozart again after all, started immediately, and everybody rose at once, cramped or moved by Arthur Quinn's startling eulogy. It had been a performance and people immediately surrounded him, waiting to pump his hand. Faith wanted to see him, too.

When Emma had first asked her to go to the service, Faith had already realized that Arthur Quinn was someone she needed to see. The relationship between author and agent is complex—a business agreement, but of a personal nature. An agent holds an author's ego, as well as an author's advance, in his or her hands. Agents find themselves functioning as critics, confidants, shrinks, and sometimes friends. What was the bond between Quinn and Fox? Faith guessed from the interviews she read that it was strong. Quinn's words at the service confirmed the impression. Did he know about Emma? Forget about the "no survivors" rhetoric. Quinn had better hope that Fox's words survived—and stayed in print. She almost laughed out loud. Clever, clever man—essentially putting Fox's posthumous book out for bid at the man's funeral. She imagined what Richard would have to say about Fox's speech, then realized she couldn't tell him she'd been at the service.

Quinn was still mobbed by well-wishers. Faith had worked out her approach. She would pose as a graduate student contemplating a book on the radical movement as typified by Fox. Quinn, she hoped, would be interested in the book as well as the subject matter. But she wanted to talk to him alone and could make an appointment by phone. She'd hoped to at least introduce herself today. She'd picked a nom de plume, Karen Brown—something easy for someone like Quinn to forget and far removed from Faith Sibley. It was unlikely their paths would cross, except perhaps at an event she was catering, but she was usually out of sight in the kitchen. She looked at the number of people between Quinn and her. It would take too long to wait.

No, what "Karen Brown" needed to do now was find out who the woman in the rear was—and how much she knew about Nathan Fox's life above and under ground.

It wasn't hard at all. Following at a discreet distance, Faith wormed her way out of the chapel behind the woman, who stopped only when Quinn reached out for her hand over the shoulder of someone who looked like or was Norman Mailer. "I'll call you," he promised, and gave a sad smile. Faith couldn't see the woman's face or note her response, but her shoulders relaxed visibly and perhaps her lips, which had tightened at Quinn's throwaway reference to Fox's love life, did as well.

Passing into the front room, Faith saw the two Fox cousins standing to one side with an air of patient waiting. There must be a gathering somewhere, she realized, and someone must be taking them. A postmortem on the service. She could hear the voices, congratulatory, self-congratulatory, and the whispered asides, the sotto voce digs. She envisioned drinks gulped, some spilled, and the platters of shrimp, finger sandwiches rapidly depleted. Poppy and her crowd would be there—but it wouldn't be at the Morrises'.

"Well, of course we haven't actually seen Nathan for

many years," his cousin Irwin was explaining to someone. "Marsha might know better than I. I'm in the dry-cleaning business and don't have much time for reading."

What was the question?

"No," Marsha said firmly, "Nathan Fox never wrote a novel." She looked at Irwin. Can we get out of here? was written all over her face. Her questioner persisted and she replied edgily, "Yes, I would know. We're family."

Faith couldn't hear the rest, but presumably Fox's cousin was continuing to reiterate her statement. And what need did cousin Nate have for made-up lives when he was so busy working on his own?

Out on the sidewalk, the crowd was thinner, scurrying into waiting cars or flagging down taxis. The woman in the mustard-colored parka, hood up now, was heading for the bus stop. Faith walked rapidly until they were side by side.

"Did you know Nathan Fox well?" Faith asked. It was the right thing to say.

"Better than anyone," the woman answered, her face revealing the aching need she had to talk to someone—anyone—about him. It almost wasn't necessary to recite her story, but Faith did it anyway.

"My name is Karen Brown and I'm considering writing a book about his life. I've been doing some work in graduate school on the sixties and got interested in him."

"I was a student when we met—a long, long time ago." Suddenly, the woman seemed tired.

"Would you like some lunch?" Faith asked. "There's a coffee shop on the next block that's not too bad."

"Yes, yes, I would. I don't have to be home yet."

They walked quickly, without speaking. The snow had stopped, leaving a thin, crusty layer on the ice that had built up at the curbs and around the traffic lights. It was grimy; the soot on the top looked like a sprinkling of black pepper. The cold wind brought tears to Faith's eyes and stung her cheeks. The woman didn't have to be home yet, but she did have to be home sometime. A husband? Kids? She'd find out soon.

The coffee shop was tropical in comparison to the weather outside, and Faith led the way to a booth at the rear, far from the opening door. The windows were outlined with colored lights and garlands proclaiming MERRY CHRISTMAS and HAPPY HANUKKAH, and HAPPY NEW YEAR had been looped uncertainly behind the counter. A plastic poinsettia stood next to the cash register. Each table sported spiky evergreens, with smaller versions of the poinsettia shoved in the glass vases normally reserved for limpid carnations. But the attempt managed to impart the same air of holiday festivity that was filling every corner of the city with a vengeance as the countdown to Christmas continued.

After sitting for a moment, contemplating the decor and thinking how best to begin the conversation, Faith realized it was one of those places where you ordered at the counter and served yourself.

"Come on, let's get some coffee right away and order."

It wasn't long before they were settled in. The woman—Faith realized she didn't know her name—had ordered pastrami—clearly not a maven. Coffee shops were not the place for pastrami. Katz's was, the Carnegie Deli was.

Faith took a sip of coffee, enjoying the feeling of the

hot liquid traveling down her throat, past her rib cage, restoring her circulation. She held the paper cup in both hands for warmth—a blue-and-white cup with Aegean decorations, Greek keys on top and bottom. "We're Happy to Serve You." All New York coffee shop paper cups looked like this. How did it start? A supplier in Athens?

"Sad that the only ones left are his cousins," Faith commented. It was an opener.

The woman nodded vigorously and put her thick sandwich down. Under her parka—the button had urged people to continue to boycott lettuce—she'd partially covered the turtleneck with a loopy beige crocheted vest. She tossed her braid, almost long enough to sit on, back over her shoulder and started talking intently.

"When he was in college, first his mother died, then his father. Sophomore year. The year we met. He took it very hard, and later he used to say how much he regretted they never knew what a famous son they had. 'Lorraine,' he'd say—oh, I'm sorry. I haven't introduced myself, Karen." She looked genuinely stricken.

Faith instantly quelled the impulse to look over her shoulder for "Karen" and instead said, "It was pretty cold outside, not the place for introductions."

The woman smiled. She'd taken her glasses off, which had steamed up when they entered the restaurant, and was wiping them with a tissue. She must have been, if not beautiful, at least pretty when she was younger. Even now with a good haircut, losing the gray, a little makeup, new clothes . . . It would be a big job.

"I'm Lorraine Fuchs."

"Fuchs?" Faith was surprised.

Lorraine blushed. She was a lot better-looking with some color in her face.

" 'The wife of his heart.' That's what he always said. Of course, we never believed in the bourgeois institution of marriage, created solely by men to ensure that property would be transferred to a legitimate male heir and to further subjugate and humiliate women."

This is going to be heavy going, Faith realized dismally. But "wife of his heart"—that was sweet.

"I'm so pleased that someone, especially a woman, is writing an account of Nathan's life, and I'm happy to help in any way I can. I've been with him since the day we met."

"You mean you went underground with him?"

"Of course. He needed me. Maybe I'd better start from the beginning."

"That would be wonderful. You're the only person I've interviewed so far, and it certainly seems you've been the closest."

Again, it was the right thing to say. Obviously, Nathan Fox was Lorraine Fuchs's entire reason for being—or so Faith thought.

"We met at City College. He was in my poly sci class and knew more than the professor. They were always having these big fights." She sighed blissfully. "Nathan started to offer his own course. He was living in a tiny apartment on Morton Street. The rest is history. We became his cadre. I don't know why people always say the fifties were dull. Believe me, there was never a dull moment for us!"

"So you all stayed together as a social-action group?"

"Yes. For a while, we were in the Socialist Workers party, but that didn't work out. Nathan felt the party wasn't sufficiently committed to the working class. We formed a faction and published a paper, but eventually we left. Then Nathan wrote the first book and started giving talks all over the country. He was one of the first to speak out against the war in Vietnam," she related proudly. "You've probably seen him in the documentaries. There was no one who had as powerful an effect on a crowd as Nathan."

Faith hadn't seen Fox in action, but she planned to soon. She'd heard about his charisma, though. The peculiarly mesmerizing, yet galvanizing, effect he'd had on great masses of people.

"Of course, my parents disapproved terribly. I'm an only child," she said apologetically, as if her mother and father's failure to produce a sibling were somehow her fault. "They thought Nathan was using me. That's what my father used to say. They didn't understand that even without Nathan, I would have chosen the life I led." She began to eat her potato chips, one at a time. She had long, slender fingers unadorned by any rings.

"They never cut me off. They weren't like that, and my mother always made a nice meal for us when we'd visit, but Nathan said it made him uncomfortable to be there, even if the pot roast was good. He always had his little jokes. He told them their phone was probably tapped and to be careful. My father was pretty upset at that. It was the last time Nathan went with me to the house. Harvey was a baby, so it would have been around 1964."

"Harvey?"

"Harvey's my son."

Faith swallowed hard. A piece of her pita pocket lodged in her throat and she reached for her coffee. Not only did Emma have two—what would Irwin and Marsha be, first cousins once removed? Second cousins? It was one of those things she'd never been able to keep straight—but a half brother around her own age!

"So, Arthur Quinn was wrong." And where was Harvey? Why hadn't he been at his father's service?

"Harvey isn't Nathan's child, although Nathan was the only father figure he ever knew. Nathan worried that any child of his would be persecuted by the police, the foot soldiers of the ruling class. We made a decision not to have any children. I'm not proud of what I'm going to tell you next, but things happen in life."

And how, Faith thought.

"I left Nathan briefly at one point. I needed to get my head together. He'd become very well known. The first book had been published and he was traveling in pretty high circles. I felt excluded and wrongly assumed it meant he didn't love me. He tried to reason with me, and deep inside I knew I was the only woman for him. My jealousy was an indication of my own weakness and lack of commitment to our goals. But I went out to California for a while and lived in a collective in San Francisco. Somehow, I got pregnant."

Somehow? Surely Lorraine wasn't that naïve, although Faith had quickly realized that Naïveté could be Lorraine's middle name.

"It was very difficult to get a safe abortion in those days—women had not won the right to choose, a right imperiled now. But thank goodness I didn't. Then I wouldn't have my Harvey. I'd have nobody now."

"What does your son do?"

"At the moment, he's seeking employment." Lorraine managed to sound proud. "He's an expert mechanic, so good that many of the employees and even the bosses where he's worked get envious of his skills."

Mouths off and gets fired was Faith's hasty analysis. She was beginning to feel very, very sorry for Lorraine Fuchs.

"We live in Brooklyn. My mother passed away recently and my father has been gone for some years now. I inherited the house. I know I'll eventually have to sell it and give the money away, but it's been wonderful having our own place. We've moved so often. I grew up there," she added wistfully. "And it's good for Harvey to have a real home. I mean to come to. He's got an apartment with some friends. They grow up so fast."

Before Lorraine could go off on a Harvey and motherhood tangent, Faith slipped in a question.

"Had you been living with Nathan Fox in the city?" It would have been cramped in the studio apartment with the three of them.

"No, he was working on a very important book and wanted to be completely alone. Of course, I knew where he was. He got sick once and called me to take care of him, which I was only too happy to do, but that was just one of two times I was ever there. The second was the day before he died. When he said good-bye, how could I have known it would be forever? You'll have to excuse me." Tears were streaming down her face. She took off her glasses and wiped her eyes with another tissue.

"I'm so sorry," Faith said.

"Well, that's life, isn't it? Anyway, he didn't have a phone, but he'd call once in a while. We were going to move back together when the book was finished. In any case, it would have been hard to live together when he decided to move to the city, because I was taking care of my mother. I guess I secretly hoped he'd move to the house after she died, but people would have known who he was. The neighbors are . . . well, they like to keep track of what's going on. So he stayed where he was and I stayed where I was."

Lorraine, clinging to Fox as they got older, would have had to play by his rules—always his rules.

"And Harvey? Were they close?"

"Well, not to say close, but Nathan was a very accepting man. That was what was so special about him. He didn't judge. When Harvey was a little boy, Nathan explained to me that it wasn't a good idea for the child to get attached to someone who might have to disappear, and there were long stretches when Nathan was in a safe house that only had room for him. I've always been able to find secretarial work and supported us that way."

Us being Harvey and Lorraine, or all three of them? Faith wondered. Probably both at different times.

Time! She didn't have time for this—unfortunately. There was much more to be learned from Lorraine. And she now had two more people who knew where Fox lived. Faith had no doubt that whatever Lorraine knew, her son knew—if he wanted to, and she'd have to meet him to judge that. Had Lorraine seen the Stansteads' wedding picture when she went to care for Fox, seen the postcards on the fridge? Somehow, Faith thought not. Fox would have tucked them out of sight. But still the question remained. Did Lorraine Fuchs know about Emma?

And what about the bank job?

"Were you involved when they tried to rob Chase Manhattan?"

"No, I'd been away for a few weeks helping my mother sell my grandmother's house. She'd died a month earlier and there was a lot to do to get it ready to put on the market. It was in New Jersey, out in the country near the Delaware Water Gap. It would have been a nice place for Harvey. He loved it there." Lorraine sounded wistful. It had probably been one of the happiest times in her life, and Faith imagined the two women going through drawers, closets, boxes in an attic, reliving old memories while the little boy played outside in the sunshine. But it was time to get back to business.

"When did you find out about the robbery?"

"Right away. I had called Nathan the night before and told him I'd be back the next day, but I still had to help my mother unpack the things she'd decided to keep. I couldn't just leave her, no matter how much I missed Nate. She gave me a beautiful set of dishes— Nippon—that had been my grandmother's. Nate, Harvey, and I were living in a tiny apartment in the Village then, and I thought I'd just bring a few plates. They're still in a box. I really should get them out and use them at last. But anyway, about that night. Nathan knew where I was, of course, and showed up there. He tapped on the kitchen window when he saw I was alone." Obviously another blissful memory. "He was really annoyed with himself for making such a mess of it. Two were arrested right away, but Nate and the driver of the car got away. He would never tell me who the driver was, but I have my guesses. I sometimes wonder what would have happened if I hadn't gone away. I would have been there, too, and things would have been a lot harder. About keeping Nathan safe, I mean. The authorities weren't looking for me. I mean they were, but not like with Nathan. I changed my name to Linda Fuchs and called my parents only once a year for a long time. That part was hard. But things got better after a while. I think the FBI had better, or worse, things to do."

Fox had found the perfect helpmate. She didn't even seem to be much of a worrier, yet she was obviously intelligent. Faith wished she had more time to talk. She wanted to find out about the other men involved in the robbery attempt. Close comrades. Did they know about Nathan's personal life? Where were they now, and were they in need of cash?

She grabbed the bill, over Lorraine's protests that going Dutch was only fair. "You've been such a help, so please let me get this. I'm sorry I can't stay longer, but I have to go. I have to be at work. Maybe we could arrange a time to meet again?"

Lorraine was clearly delighted at the prospect. "Why don't you come to the house and look at my scrapbooks? I've kept every news article, every review over the years."

"That would be fantastic. I'm so glad I met you today," Faith said.

"Me, too." Lorraine had eaten everything on her plate, not wasting a crumb. The older woman seemed so lonely that Faith felt a stab of guilt at the way she was using her. But when this was all over, she assured herself, Emma could meet Lorraine and they could engage in mutual Fox worship.

"I'm not sure what my schedule is, so could I call you?" she asked.

"Sure," said Lorraine, digging out a ballpoint pen and writing her number on a napkin.

Faith tucked the napkin in her purse and put on her coat. She hesitated before asking one last question, but knew if she didn't, she'd be kicking herself later. "I

95

know it must be upsetting to think about, but who do you think killed Nathan Fox?"

Lorraine's washed-out blue eyes filled with tears. "I wish I knew. I wish I knew."

When Faith got to work, Josie was up to her elbows in *coulibiac* of salmon and muttering to herself, "Why folks can't eat a good old Brunswick stew, I'll never know. Just wait 'til Josie's comes along."

"We're not behind, but we're not ahead," she told Faith, who was hastily changing into some work clothes.

"Any calls?"

"About ninety from someone named Emma. Left them on the machine, and we've chatted a number of times since. I believe it to be the concerned lady who didn't want to bother you at work. You recall?"

Faith did and raced to the phone.

Emma was home and picked up on the first ring.

"Emma, hi. It's Faith. I don't really have much—"

"Tell me everything. Were there a lot of speakers? Was it crowded? Oh, I should have taken a chance and gone. How about the press—were they there?"

"Yes, yes, and yes. I'll tell you everything tomorrow. We have to do a dinner tonight on Gramercy Park and—"

"Faith, I got a call. From them."

"Oh God, Emma. You have *got* to tell Michael! What did they say? When was it?" If it was during the time of the service, that eliminated a whole bunch of people.

"I don't know when. It was on the machine and I didn't get back until around two o'clock. I left about ten. Hair, manicure, Christmas shopping, a lunch meeting—it should be one or the other, a meeting or lunch."

She was rambling on, her distraught voice making the prosaic words a litany of fright.

"Emma! What did they say!"

" 'We'll be in touch.' That's all. 'We'll be in touch.' " Her voice was dead calm now, leaden.

"A man or a woman?"

"Impossible to tell. Strange, kind of squeaky, high-pitched."

"Take the tape out and put a new one in. If I can convince you to go to the police, they'll want it, and meanwhile, I want to listen to it."

"I erased it," Emma said softly. "I'm sorry. I didn't think. I just hit the delete button."

"Look, we'll meet for breakfast, okay? Don't worry about it. It was a natural response. What are you doing tonight? Is Michael home?"

"Yes, he's not going away again until January, and I'm going with him. Someplace in the Caribbean. And tonight? I think it's the opening of *Tru*—you know, Robert Morse doing Capote. No, wait, that's not right." She sighed heavily. "I can't remember, but something. Michael knows."

"Just don't go anywhere by yourself. Stick with him," Faith knew that Emma wasn't going to take any solitary walks—not in this subzero weather and not when she was this terrified—but Faith was nervous. Easy enough to get the Stansteads' number. It was listed. At breakfast tomorrow, she'd try again to convince Emma to tell someone—maybe even Poppy. Meanwhile, Faith had many hours to fill with trying to figure it all out. A murderer and a blackmailer, or two separate crimes?

After arranging to meet at 8:30 the following morning at the Maximilian Cafe at Fifty-eighth and Seventh Avenue, Faith hung up and turned, to find Josie staring at her, a guarded, worried expression on her face. "Is this something you want to talk about? Because, girl, it sure sounds like something you *should* be talking about," she said.

Faith pulled a stool from under the steel countertop and sat down, cupping her chin in one hand.

"I wish I could, but it's not my story to tell, and I've sworn that I won't."

Josie came up alongside. She looked straight at Faith. "Remember I'm here. And I thought I had heard it all, but apparently . . ." She smiled and coaxed one from her boss. "Apparently, I was wrong. Just don't go starting something you can't finish. I need this job."

"Me, too." Faith gave her a hug. "Now, what are we doing for dessert? French apple cake? [See the recipe on page 283.] The host's allergic to chocolate, right?"

"Now, that's someone with a real problem."

Yes, thought Faith—and Emma, uptown, opening her closet, laying out what to wear tonight for yet another dinner party, gallery opening, or benefit, would be ecstatic to trade for a problem like this.

Faith was drinking coffee, sitting by the window at Maximilian's, drumming her fingers impatiently on the red-checkered tablecloth. Like the coffee shop yesterday, the creperie was bedecked with garlands spelling out good cheer—except JOYEUX NOËL had been added, and here the poinsettias were real. Outside, a Salvation Army Santa was vigorously ringing his bell, the little red collection pot swinging merrily on its tripod. Saint Nick had a boom box and Faith could hear "Santa Claus Is Comin' to Town" faintly through the glass. Every once in a while, someone would stop and slip some money in the pot. But only once in a while. Most people were streaming out of the subway and off the buses, single-mindedly heading straight for work, not so eager for the day's toils as to escape the freezing cold.

There were less than two weeks until Christmas. Faith wished the events of the last week either far into the future or far into the past. It was *Christmas*. She should be spending what precious little free time she had at Carnegie Hall listening to Handel's *Messiah*, going to see *A Christmas Carol* somewhere, hearing the Vienna Boys Choir sing "pa-rum-pa-pum-pum," shopping and more shopping, *The Nutcracker* for the umpteenth time, of course—and not embroiled in crime.

"Sorry, sorry, sorry. No cabs." Emma ordered coffee immediately, then glanced at the menu, adding, "An English muffin, butter on the side." She looked at Faith. "I know it's a French place, but I like English muffins."

"I'll have a plain omelette and whole-wheat toast," Faith said. She had the feeling she was going to need sustenance today.

"Any more messages?" she asked her friend as soon as the waitress left. The sidewalks were packed, but the restaurant was almost empty.

Emma shook her head. "If there's another, I'll save the tape."

"There'll be another," Faith said pointedly. "Do you have any idea, any idea at all who could be doing this?"

Emma looked woebegone. "I've thought and

thought, but the only person I can think of is Lucy. You know what she's like, and she's been even more horrid since I got married."

"Jealous, of course. I would be more than happy to confront her with you." Faith brightened. Something concrete to do.

The food arrived. Emma put a millimeter-thick coating of butter on her muffin. "But if I'm wrong, then she'll know things she didn't know before. We can't just say, 'Are you blackmailing me, Lucy, and if so, cut it out,' without her wanting to know why, and then I'll never have a moment's peace again for the rest of my life."

"Which you might not have unless you ask her," Faith pointed out logically.

"But it's likely that if it isn't Lucy, she'll blackmail me over having something someone could blackmail me about." Emma broke off a tiny piece of her muffin and raised it halfway to her mouth. "How can this be happening to me?" she asked in despair.

She was right—on several counts. The Lucy plan needed more thought. Faith patted Emma's hand, the one without the muffin. Her cuticles were even more ragged than before. "It's not about you, remember? Now, I need to know some things; then I'll tell you all about the service. It was everything your father would have wished." Faith was sure of that.

"How did the blackmailers—although we don't know if it's more than one; the 'we' could have been put in to lead you astray—anyway, how did you find out where to leave the money, and where was it?"

Emma sat up straight. She could do this. "I got a call. I was home. It was Sunday afternoon, and as soon as I answered the phone, a voice said, 'Put the money in a green plastic trash bag and leave it in the Dumpster at the construction site on Forty-eighth and Lex at five o'clock today. Take a cab and have it wait. Then leave. If you screw up, or tell anyone, Christmas won't be merry this year.' "

"Was it the same voice as the voice on the machine?"

Emma flushed. "I should have thought of that. No, it wasn't, but again, I couldn't tell whether it was a man or a woman with one of those Lauren Bacall-type voices, husky."

"So, you took the bag and went to the spot."

"Yes, first I had to go buy some trash bags. I couldn't find where Juanita keeps them."

Faith was struck by something. "Wait a minute. This was Sunday. How did you happen to have ten thousand dollars in cash lying around?"

"I know you said paying them wasn't a good idea, but it seemed the simplest way to me, so I'd taken money out on Friday. Just in case."

"Who could have known about it? Michael? Someone at the bank?"

"Not Michael. It's my own account. Technically, it's joint, but his name isn't even on the checks. It's just for my expenses. Anyway, I put the money under my lingerie, and of course I didn't mention it. It was a very busy weekend, lots of parties, and he had some kind of fund-raiser upstate that I didn't want to go to. I keep telling him 'I think I'm coming down with the flu.' He's been very worried and made an appointment for me with our doctor, which I guess I'll have to keep, but I feel like a fraud."

Once more, Emma digressed. The stress was loosening her hinges—hinges that weren't too tight to start.

Faith persisted. "Did you see anybody you knew at the bank? Was it a teller you'd recognize?" She couldn't picture Michael Stanstead rifling through his wife's panties. She had another thought. "Was Lucy—or anybody else—at the apartment during the weekend?"

Emma started with the first part of the question. "I remember saying hi to a couple of people, and I think it was at the bank—or it may have been on the way. The teller just looked like a teller. A man. He had to go and get some kind of approval. I think he was new. I brought one of those Coach saddlebags someone gave me once. Somehow, I thought it would be a bigger bundle. Anyway, I put the money in that. I was so nervous, I went straight home. And Lucy? Yes, she, Mother, and Jason came for drinks Saturday night with some other people. We were all going to watch Michael cut a ribbon at a YMCA. He cuts a lot of ribbons. I think this was a new media center for an after-school program. Poppy and Jason gave some computers or something, so that's why they were there. A darling group of children sang carols; then we all went on to a party at La Côte Basque."

"Why was Lucy there?"

"Well, she's always around this kind of thing. She's very interested in the campaign. Of course she'd love to be married to someone like Michael, and it just makes her worse. She was with this man who works for Michael."

"Okay, now was there anything unusual about the cabdriver? And what about at the Dumpster? Was there a car near it? There must have been people on the sidewalk." It seemed like a very risky drop, and whoever had planned to pick it up would have had to be seconds away, watching Emma.

"The place was deserted. Remember how cold it was? And there wasn't even much traffic, not the way it would be on a weekday. The doorman got me a cab, so that was complete chance, unless this is all a gigantic conspiracy. The driver was from Haiti. I know because he was complaining about the weather. It's his first winter in New York."

Maybe not such a risky drop after all. Social-service agencies had been sending vans around to move the homeless into shelters. One poor man had been found lifeless, huddled in a box over a nonfunctioning heat vent that had probably provided some warmth when he'd first discovered it. Not only would no one be working at the site on the weekend, but no one would be camped out there, either. And five o'clock was a dead time in the city on a Sunday, a lull between the day's activities and the night's festivities. Easy enough to stand in the lobby of one of the buildings nearby, or to duck down in a parked car, racing out to pick up the money as soon as Emma's cab turned the corner.

"No cars you recognized?"

"No, and I did look. The Dumpster was on Forty-eighth and there were NO PARKING signs all along where they're working."

Faith finished the last scraps of her omelette.

"I really have to get to work," she said, and signaled the waitress for some more coffee.

"I have a ton to do," Emma agreed, lifting her cup for a refill.

Realizing she'd been remiss in not giving a full account of the service, Faith described the event. Hesitating slightly, she told Emma about Lorraine Fuchs. As she'd suspected, Emma wanted to meet her at once and talk about her father.

"When things are a little more settled," Faith advised, not wanting to muddy the waters any further. It was impossible to see bottom now, and if Lorraine was to learn of Emma's existence, not having known previously, the waters might well silt up to deltalike proportions. For, if Lorraine knew, then Harvey would, and so forth, until the paparazzi outside Emma's apartment building would be more numerous than at Jackie O's and Princess Di's combined.

"In detective stories, they always try to figure out who benefits from a death, which should be fairly simple to figure out. If Fox made a will—and I'm not sure Communists do this sort of thing—it would have to be probated, and some lawyer—or Arthur Quinn, if he has it—will be coming forward one of these days."

"But Daddy didn't have any money, not much anyway. Just enough to pay his rent, buy food, books, typing paper."

Faith suddenly had a whole bunch of questions and didn't want to forget. "Remind me about the books and paper, but we've been overlooking something. How did he even get the small amount he needed to live on? He wasn't getting any royalties. Lorraine has always done temp work, which can't pay much. I suppose she must have supported them before they came to New York, and sympathizers may have sent her money. I'd like to get a list of those charities Fox stipulated as the recipients of his earnings. Could one have been Lorraine, a way of funneling the money back to himself? But the FBI would have checked each one thoroughly, so that's out."

"How about Poppy?"

How about Poppy, indeed? Easy enough for her to supply her ex-lover with cash now and then. It made a great deal of sense. Faith had left Fox's service with the distinct impression that Poppy Morris had been carrying a torch of Olympic proportions for Fox all these years.

"It's a thought," she said slowly.

"Now, what about the books and typing paper?" Emma had a hectic flush on her cheeks and asked this eagerly. It was just like the old days, when they'd tried to get locked in the Metropolitan Museum after reading *From the Mixed-Up Files of Mrs. Basil E. Frankweiler.*

"At the service, his agent talked about a book, one that was to be published only after Fox's death. Lorraine mentioned that he was working on an important book, too. What do you know about it?"

"A couple of times when I visited him, he was typing. I could hear it through the door. It wasn't a very safe building—the buzzer didn't work and anybody could get in from the street door. I really wanted him to move, but he always said no one would bother an old man like him. He gave me a key, 'just in case,' he said, but I'm not sure what he meant, what the case would be. I always knocked, since there wasn't an intercom and I didn't want to disturb his work. That's how I heard the typing. He was pretty good at it."

"The book, Emma, what was the book about?"

"Some political thing, I imagine. He told me it was his magnum opus and the most fun he'd had in years. He kept it in a fireproof metal file cabinet. He *was* afraid of fire—said the building would go up in a flash. I gave him one of those small extinguishers, and he was very pleased. But he never said anything about when the book was going to be published."

"Did he ever talk about being afraid of anything else, particularly anyone else?"

Emma shook her head. "It's not the greatest neighborhood and, as I said, the building wasn't secure. He was afraid of fire because of his books and papers, not because he was worried about himself. I always thought he liked living on the edge—in a funny way, liked being a wanted man, hiding out."

Which was what Arthur Quinn had implied. Well, thought Faith, whatever gets you off—although in this case, it was permanent.

"It just doesn't make sense. Without much of an estate, Nathan Fox was certainly worth more alive than dead to anyone who knew who he really was. Why kill him? Why not simply turn him over to the feds for the reward money?"

"But only a handful of people knew who he was— me, this Lorraine Fuchs, Todd, but that was years ago."

Emma was right. It was a short list—so far. Faith could already add several names: maybe Harvey Fuchs—she hadn't mentioned him to Emma yet— maybe Arthur Quinn, maybe Poppy Morris.

"You better watch out . . ." The Salvation Army Santa's tape was starting from the beginning again. This time, Faith put the money for the check on the table and they put their coats on.

When she passed him, Faith shoved a five-dollar bill in the pot.

They were rolling out pecan shortbread cookies for an office party at one of the publishing houses when the phone rang. Faith grabbed it, hoping it was her grandmother, with whom she'd been playing phone tag since receiving the plaintive message about the closing of

B. Altman's—or "Baltmans," as Hope had called it when she was little.

But it wasn't Granny; it was Emma. Emma sounding more frantic and flat-out terrified than Faith had ever heard her.

"I don't know what to do! You've got to help me!"

"What's wrong! Where are you! Emma, if you're in any danger, you *have got* to call the police!"

"No, no! Faith, I'm at my wit's end!"

"What! What is it!"

"The caterer I hired for the Stanstead Associates holiday party tomorrow night has been shut down by the Board of Health!"

Five

This *was* serious.

"Michael thinks everything's all set, and besides people from the firm, he always invites extras—people he wants to impress, important people. I've been calling every caterer in the city and everybody's booked. I'm desperate!"

Trying extremely hard not to feel slighted as a caterer, Faith worked to sound sympathetic. The important "extras" would no doubt be people essential to Michael's political ambitions, and a wife who muffed a simple thing like an office party was not going to present herself as a strong candidate for pulling off state dinners.

"I know Have Faith won't be able to do it. Of course you're booked, but do you know anyone who could possibly step in? It could even be an outfit from Jersey." Emma's voice trembled.

Faith was enormously relieved. She should have had more faith. Emma assumed she was busy, as all the hot—and even not so hot—caterers in town were. And

Faith *was* busy. She was doing a lunch tomorrow and an after-theater dessert buffet in the evening. Saturday night, she had two dinners and a cocktail party.

"What time is it scheduled for, and is it dinner?"

"Six o'clock, supposedly after work, but no one's going to be working much on a Friday this close to Christmas. What we'd arranged was hors d'oeuvres, then a buffet of more substantial food and desserts. But it can all be scaled down. The most important thing is to have a lot to drink. At least that's what Michael always says."

"I have a job, but not until later, and I think we can do both."

"You! But that would be heaven! I never dreamed you might be able to do it. Come over and take a look at the place. I don't think you've seen it. I'll give you a key and then you can come and go when you want. Oh, this is too good to be true! We'll keep it simple— things everybody likes: foie gras, caviar, festive things."

Foie gras and caviar with toasted brioche and blinis being the Triscuits and Wispride spread of this crowd, Faith reflected. Obviously, money was no object, and it certainly did make things easier. She took down the number of expected guests and a few other details from Emma, then began calling her suppliers. By the time Josie returned from a lunch break of Christmas shopping, Faith had the Stanstead party pretty much under control. She was happy to be helping Emma out, but even happier to have the opportunity to get a good look at some of the guests.

Emma and Michael Stanstead's rich young urban professional apartment, up in the Eighties between Fifth

and Park in a grand old prewar building, owed more to
Mark Hampton than Pottery Barn. Faith looked around
the spacious living room. The walls had been covered
in heavy damask silk with a slight woven stripe that
was the color of bittersweet in autumn. In addition to
the grouped collections of botanical and architectural
framed prints, there was a striking modern oil by Wolf
Kahn over the fireplace. The seating was chintz, but
comfortable. Couches to sink into and curl up on.
Large easy chairs next to skirted round tables piled
with books. The lighting from the ceiling was soft and
supplemented by table lamps. Another painting, a por-
trait of Emma as a child by Aaron Shikler that Faith
recognized from the Morrises' living room, hung between the front windows. The entire apartment had
been tastefully bedecked for the season. Swags of
white pine and holly and pots of deep crimson cyclamen trailed across the mantel. More pine was fes-
tooned over the doorways with shiny red ilex, gauzy
silk ribbons floating from the boughs. There were
flowers everywhere. She went to adjust one of the
blooms—a white amaryllis, faintly edged with red—
that had fallen slightly to one side, away from a profu-
sion of blossoms and greens in a large silver Georgian
wine cooler. The flowers were replacing a Dale Chihuly
glass bowl, normally on the pedestal. "Too horrible if
someone knocked into it," Emma had declared,
cradling the fragile piece in her arms and putting it in
one of the cabinets under the wall of bookshelves,
which contained burnished leather-bound volumes,
complete with an antique mahogany library ladder.

There were small white French lilacs in the arrangement and their fragrance suggested spring sunshine,
not the slate sky outside. Looking up, searching the

heavens anxiously for signs of more snow, Faith pushed one of the drapes farther aside. The pale gold silk fabric was so fine, it slipped through her fingers like molten metal, not woven threads. She let it drop back into place.

The room was perfect. There wasn't a single jarring note. Usually, she thought of rooms as backdrops for the food, settings in which a meal, the main event, was served. This room refused to be relegated. Soon it would be filled with people. You wouldn't be able to see the intricate pattern of the huge Oriental rug almost covering the parquet. The bowls of Christmas roses and other more elaborate bouquets would be shoved to one side, displaced by plates with scraps of food, empty glasses. Yet, the room would still dominate. Josie came in with a pyramid of fruit and stopped in the doorway.

"Yes, I could live here. Oh yes. Wouldn't ever have to leave. Could sleep on the sofa. I'm definitely going to have to get me a place like this."

They both burst out laughing.

"Where do you want this?" She held the fruit on top of her head and did a passable Carmen Miranda.

"On the buffet, next to the fruit knives. It's meant to be consumed. The comice pears are perfectly ripe— delectable. I had one for lunch." Besides the foie gras, caviar, and champagne, Faith had added a buffet with roast sirloin of beef with two sauces—creamy horse-radish and portabello mushroom—garlic mashed pota-toes, roasted winter vegetables, a pesto pasta frittata, and the obligatory salad of mixed baby greens. The desserts, an assortment of cheeses, the fruit, cham-pagne, and dessert wines were at one end of the table; the main course occupied the rest. Howard, bless his heart, would tend the bar, set up in Michael's study. Jessica, a graduate student at Columbia who was on Faith's list of part-time help, would take care of serving the buffet. Josie and Faith would alternate keeping an eye on things in the kitchen and circulating with a few platters of hot and cold hors d'oeuvres. Josie had offered to do all the serving, knowing that Faith preferred to stay in the background, but Faith had refused. This was one party where she planned to circulate.

Emma was thrilled. She dashed into the kitchen before the first guest arrived, looking spectacularly pretty in a lacy Geoffrey Beene slip dress. The lingerie look was big for evening wear this year, and some of the events Faith had catered recently looked more like slumber than dinner parties. But Emma didn't look ready for bed—or rather, not ready for sleep.

"Thank you, thank you, thank you! I told Michael about the catastrophe but that I was able to get a great replacement, and he says he remembers a party you did and you'll be even better than Henri, whose food was getting too predictable. I wonder why he was shut down? I never thought to ask, but it doesn't matter. Michael thinks I've done a terrific job, and now I have to fly. There's the door!"

Emma's speech was delivered at the speed of light and she was in and out of the kitchen before Faith had time to ask if they should start serving the hot hors d'oeuvres right away. She made the decision herself and popped a tray of coconut shrimp in the oven. Emma's kitchen contained state-of-the-art equipment—Viking range, Sub-Zero refrigerator, Calphalon pots and pans—but showed absolutely no signs of use. Faith was accustomed to this, but she noted that the

Stansteads did stock some food—DoveBars, of course, milk, English marmalade, and orange juice. Somewhere, there were probably English muffins, too.

Faith walked from the kitchen down the hall, past the front door and foyer, and into the living room, which was already buzzing with conversation. The holiday season was adding glitter to what would be a sparkling group at any time of the year. Well dressed, well coiffed, they did indeed look like beautiful people. A subtle smell of expensive perfume filled the air. The women were wearing more jewelry than usual. Just as their sisters under the skin pinned a rhinestone Christmas tree to a coat collar or hung tiny Christmas ball earrings from their earlobes, these ladies had unearthed their Judith Leiber minaudières and Tiffany diamonds by the yard. They formed a seamless whole with their surroundings, and Faith felt as if she were watching an exceptionally well-staged and -costumed play.

She started passing the tray and dispensing napkins. Michael's study was off the main room. Setting up the bar there seemed to be working, freeing up space in the larger room for mixing and mingling.

Looking about, she was reminded that her role as employee made her virtually invisible. All her senses were heightened—particularly sight and sound. She was acutely aware of everything going on in the room. Her first thought was that there were no surprises—yet.

It was no surprise to see Poppy holding court, back to the fireplace, bathed in what was the kindest light of the room. It was no surprise to see Jason Morris, either, who was sitting in a large wing chair off to her side, watching his wife with an expression of tolerant amusement. Faith remembered him now. A large, florid man in bespoke suits, with patrician good looks that had once been much, much better. He looked all of his years tonight, especially compared with his wife. Faith remembered Emma's recent description of her mother's current attitude toward Jason, "But now she *is* fifty and he *is* seventy."

It was no surprise to see Lucy, dressed in those dreary lawyerlike clothes from Brooks—navy blue suits, skirt not too short, white blouse, maybe a fabric rosette at the neck. No jewelry except a very expensive watch. In deference to the hour and occasion, Lucy had chosen a black evening suit and the rosette was black satin. She'd inherited little in the way of appearance from her mother, certainly not her glorious red hair. She was a wheat-colored blond, thanks to Daddy, tall and large-boned, but with the athletic body of a would-be partner who regularly hits the squash court, letting the boss win, but not by much.

And there were no surprises in her greeting to Faith.

"You must all be so proud of Hope. I hear she's taking the city by storm. And what are you doing with yourself these days? Waitressing?"

Resisting the temptation to tell the bitch to take a flying leap, Faith smiled and moved the shrimp just out of Lucy's reach. "I own the company that's catering the party tonight." She took a step away.

"How, well, how very unusual," Lucy said, smiling nastily. "And here I thought you were merely one of the help, but then again . . ." She let her words hang in the air like industrial waste. She didn't need to finish. She didn't need to say, "But then again, you are." Letting it hang there was so much more fun.

Faith moved sister Lucy to the top of the list of people who might be blackmailing Emma, as well as to the top of the list of those who might have murdered Nathan Fox. She'd happily move Lucy to the top of more, but two was all she had at the moment.

She went back for another tray, and when she returned, studiously ignored Lucy on her rounds. It was impossible to escape the voice, though. "I'm sorry," Faith heard her say without a note of regret, "I really can't get worked up about where to put the homeless. Long Island, wherever—so long as they're not in my face."

No surprises. But yes, surprises.

First, Hope walked in and sister bumped into sister. She was looking particularly gorgeous in an ivory satin blouse and short black velvet skirt, her dark hair loose. The hose on her shapely long legs had little rhinestones at each ankle. Hope must be in a whimsical mood tonight, Faith noted.

"What are you doing here?" Hope asked.

"I was about to ask you the same thing. You haven't started moonlighting, working for Stanstead Associates, have you? Where would you get the time? And I'm catering this thing. Just ask Lucy."

"Of course I'm not working for them, but it might be fun someday. They're an exciting bunch. No, Phelps invited me. He's a good friend of Adrian Sutherland. They were at school together. You do know who Adrian is, don't you?"

Faith had heard the name but couldn't place it. "Remind me," she said, looping her arm through her sister's and pulling her in the direction of the kitchen. "I have to get some more food. They're eating like locusts."

"Adrian is Michael's campaign manager and has also been with Stanstead Associates since it started.

115

He's Michael's right-hand man. He was born here, but his father is British, so he has that cool accent. I've never actually met him, but I heard him on the news once. Everything he said sounded so terribly believable, so terribly important. He wants Phelps to work on the campaign, which is why he got invited."

A bell went off, and it wasn't the oven timer. "Did you tell your new beau that you went to school with Emma?" Faith asked her sister.

"I might have. Why?"

"No reason, I just wondered. Now we'd better get out there before this gets cold. Plus, I want to meet your charming friend."

A friend who might be looking to use Hope to ingratiate himself with the party powers that be. Why else would he invite her to come along, especially when he was already a step removed himself from being asked by the host and hostess?

The crowd in the living room had increased substantially and, unlike many parties Faith had attended, nobody seemed in a rush to go on to the next—and at this time of year, there were plenty of nexts. But this tended to happen at the parties she catered. Josie was sure it was the food. "They want to scarf down the good stuff and then they won't be stuck with greasy buffalo chicken wings and limp crudités wherever they're going. They can just get loaded."

It was a possibility. They were even eating the fruit now.

"Phelps, I'd like you to meet my sister, Fay. Fay, Phelps Grant." The young man turned from his conversation and shook Faith's hand—she'd put her empty tray down—with every indication of pleasure. Yes, preppy, but definitely attractive. Very attractive.

Hope knew how to pick them—at least in this department.

"Hope tells me your catering business is doing very well, and after making a total pig of myself on all this, I'm not one bit surprised. I'm out all the time, but I haven't had such good food in ages."

"Thank you. That's one of my problems—that New Yorkers eat out so much and at such great places. It's a hard act to follow—or complement."

"Well, you've certainly succeeded where others have perished." He then proceeded to tell a mordantly funny story about a friend who had opened a restaurant down in SoHo and went bankrupt before opening. "He had no idea he'd have to think of anything but dishing out his grandmother's secret spaghetti sauce recipe. That was going to be the key to fame and fortune. He never got past the lighting fixtures."

Faith found herself liking him, but there was something about his polished delivery, and polished self, that still warned her to keep her guard up. Hope, of course, was looking at him the way a kid looks at her first puppy.

"Phelps, sorry, didn't mean to interrupt." The man with whom Phelps had been in conversation before had turned away from a small group of people.

"You're not interrupting at all. This is Hope Sibley—she's with Citibank—and her sister . . ."

"Faith Sibley, the caterer. I knew the food was unusually good." It was the man who'd come into the kitchen with Michael Stanstead the night Emma had made her panicked exit after receiving the first blackmail demand. "I'm not sure we were properly introduced the other night. My name is Adrian Sutherland."

Here was surprise number two—and three. Adrian

Sutherland was also the man who'd been sitting alone, reading the *Wall Street Journal,* at the American Festival Cafe at Rockefeller Center.

Lucy chose this moment to join the group. "Adrian, you'll never guess. My glass is empty." She held it out in front of her.

"Now, that will never do. Phelps here—you remember Phelps Grant—was just about to fetch a whole bottle of bubbly, weren't you?" Phelps left instantly. So it was like that. Gunga Grant. Faith realized that as the caterer, she should be seeing to the libations herself, but her job as investigator was more important at the moment. She wanted to watch Lucy and Adrian. What was going on between the two?

"I see you know the Sibley girls," Lucy continued in her slightly nasal, well-bred voice. She managed to make it sound as if Faith and Hope were still in braces, allowed to stay up for the party as a special treat.

"Not as well as I plan to. Especially you, Faith. I see many Stanstead events in your future."

Lucy looked piqued, and she moved closer to Adrian, leaning her head on his shoulder in a proprietary gesture.

Adrian made no acknowledgment of her more intimate presence, nor did he shake her off. He looked older than the rest of them, and Faith wondered if he had been ahead of Phelps in school. Or maybe he was one of those people born looking old. He was attractive, but not handsome. However, his suit, his hairstyle, the way he carried himself, and even his shoes suggested wealth—and power. He didn't need to be handsome.

Hope was asking about some party-sponsored event

on New Year's Day, whether Michael would be speaking and, if so, officially announcing his candidacy for the House seat, about to be left vacant by the incumbent's retirement. Stanstead would get the nomination. That was a given. Winning the election was another matter.

"Come and find out. Ah, help is at hand!" Phelps was back with the champagne and pouring it for everyone. Faith incongruously found herself with a glass. "I don't mean to be coy, but we, or I should say he, really haven't decided yet. I do know one thing, though." He held his glass up as if toasting. "I'm sorry we already hired a caterer."

On that note, Faith excused herself with thanks and rushed back to the kitchen to maintain her reputation and to escape the lethal glances Lucy was slinging her way.

The fourth surprise was Richard Morgan.

Faith had returned with Josie to replenish the buffet table, where Jessica was still busy serving. He entered the room, made a beeline for the food, and stopped when he saw Faith.

"Terrific!" he said. "I assume you're catering this affair, and I assume it's delicious. Nobody who can dissect a menu the way you can could have impaired taste buds. Not to mention my delight at seeing you again so soon." The night before, they'd eaten at a noodle place and gone to see Woody Allen's new movie, *Crimes and Misdemeanors*. It had had a bit too much resonance for Faith at the moment. Richard had loved it.

"This is my assistant, Josie Wells. Josie, this is Richard Morgan." Faith was beginning to feel less and less like the anonymous help, what with all these introductions.

"Pleased to meet you. I have a thing for your boss."

Josie laughed out loud, shot Faith a look as she left, and said, "Get in line."

"She's loyal, very loyal," Faith countered.

Richard was eating a large amount of caviar on a blini. "This does not shock—or deter—me at all."

"I would love to stay and chat longer, but I have to get back in the kitchen," Faith said. "But first, please, quickly satisfy my insatiable curiosity and tell me why you're here. Did the Stansteads hire you to sing carols?"

"And well they might. No, my dear Faith—and I mean that—I am here in a reportorial capacity. I'm doing a profile on Michael Stanstead for *The New Yorker* and I'm trying to get as much done as possible before I have to leave town next week. Stanstead invited me here. To see him at home, just your average guy with your average multimillion-dollar apartment."

Faith was dismayed. Not that Richard was doing a profile on Michael. That should be interesting. But that Richard was leaving town so soon. If he was gone, how was she going to find out how she felt about him?

"Harry Connick Jr.'s at the Algonquin. Want to catch him after you finish here?" Richard had moved on to the foie gras.

"I'd love to, but I have another party to do," Faith was already getting a bit panicky about the dessert buffet and planned to send Josie and Jessica on ahead as soon as possible, even though it wasn't scheduled to start for another few hours.

"Another time, another place," he said, kissing her swiftly. Again, he was on the verge of needing a shave. Her cheek felt warm, ever so slightly scratched.

"Yes," said Faith.

*   *   *

Josie and Jessica had gone. The party was winding down at long last and Howard came into the kitchen to say he was leaving the wine and champagne on the buffet table but was packing up the bar. There was another door to the study and he could do it without going through the living room.

Faith had done everything she could do until everyone left, so she sat down at the kitchen table to think about the evening. No one had been waving those Christmas cards around or making menacing gestures in Emma's direction. In fact, it was hard to find Emma in a crowd, even when she was the hostess. Contrary to convention, she didn't circulate. She'd greeted everyone at the start of the party, then gravitated toward a corner with some of the people she'd invited herself: neighbors in the building, a distant relative who was teaching at the Little Red School House, and her godmother, Madeline Green. Nobody knew how old Madeline was, and she wasn't telling. She was Poppy's mother's best friend and the closest thing Emma had to a grandmother, since neither her mother's nor Jason's parents was still living. A grandmother of the Auntie Mame variety. Faith found herself wishing they could tell Madeline everything and let her handle things. She probably already knew about Poppy and Nathan Fox, maybe even about Emma's birth. Madeline knew everything. Tonight, she was wearing a gorgeous sapphire blue Zandra Rhodes caftan, which set off her white hair—and sapphires—perfectly. In a room filled with people wearing a great deal of black, an occasional white or splash of red, Madeline stood out—as usual.

Faith thought about the party some more. What little she had seen of Emma, after the first glow of having solved her catering problem had worn off, convinced her that something new had happened. Emma was even quieter than usual. She looked worried until occasionally, remembering she was supposed to be a fun hostess, she replaced the guarded expression with a frenetic smile. What was she keeping from Faith? Did she know who the blackmailer was? Did she know the murderer? One and the same? Eating Faith's *gougères* this very night?

The door to the kitchen opened and Hope came in.

"Does it look like people are really leaving?" Faith asked her sister. "I want to get over to Sixty-ninth and be sure everything's all right. Emma's cleaners are coming to put everything back in shape, but I still have to pack up my stuff."

Hope pulled out a chair and sat down. "I think you could start clearing the buffet in a few minutes. A lot of people are putting on their coats and saying goodbye to Emma. She's in the foyer giving out the party favors. Very classy. Those Angus McDougall glass apples from Steuben. You've seen the ads, right? 'Give the Big Apple for Christmas,' something like that. I put mine in my briefcase." Of course Hope was one of those who had worked late today.

"*Very* classy—and very expensive. Emma does have good taste, especially since she doesn't need to read price tags. Those apples run about three hundred dollars apiece."

Hope nodded. She picked up a metal strainer that looked like a dunce's cap and started fiddling with it, twirling its sharp-pointed wooden pestle against the sides. Faith had used it for the mushroom sauce. She took the equipment away from her sister and shoved it on the counter behind the table. These things were expensive.

"Why aren't you out there making merry with your honey?" Faith asked. "Or home reading a good book. You look bored."

"Phelps, Adrian, Michael, and some other people are in the study smoking cigars, talking politics. I would have stayed, but the combination of the smoke and the sight of Lucy draped on the arm of Adrian's chair and the arm of Adrian's bod was more than I could handle."

"What's with them? Have you heard anything? She was certainly crawling all over him tonight, which I haven't seen her do with other men—and he wasn't exactly pushing her away. Somehow, I've never thought of Lucy as that interested in sex—except as a bargaining chip. Plus, she'd always want to be on top."

After Hope stopped laughing, she said, "Phelps mentioned we might be going to dinner with them, and from the way he said 'Lucy and Adrian,' it sounded as if they were an item."

Lucy and Adrian. The plot sprang fully formed into Faith's head like Athena from Zeus's. Emma had said Lucy was even worse to her after her marriage to Michael. What better, and more evil, way to express what was so obviously a lifelong resentment of your sister (half sister, in reality) than first to blackmail her, then expose her, wrecking her husband's chances for success? Lucy would then emerge the winner and marry his aide-de-camp, who would then proceed to take his old boss's place. Lucy and Adrian. More than a couple—say a partnership?

"Fay! Fay! Hello!"

"Sorry, I'm a little tired."

"The bus pickup?" Hope asked.

"His name is Richard Morgan, and he's here. I should introduce you. He's writing a piece for *The New Yorker* about Michael."

Hope brightened. The man had credentials. "Okay, let's go."

Entering the foyer and looking at the small crowd left, Hope whispered to her sister, "Your journalist friend could have a field day writing about most of the people here tonight. All the secrets, and I don't just mean Moira over there, who, according to rumor, has no original body parts left."

The svelte woman in what appeared to be a long red satin nightgown, the kind Jean Harlow wore with mules to match, was smiling at her companion's remarks. The skin on her face was as tight as a drum.

Secrets. If Hope only knew . . . "There's Richard, and he has his coat on, so we'd better hurry."

While Faith was making the introduction, Phelps Grant appeared from the study. His eyes and nose were slightly red, and Faith wondered whether he was allergic to cigar smoke or hitting the bathroom down the hall, which had proved popular with the "White lines" crowd.

He tapped Hope on the shoulder. "We've been invited to go out to dinner with Lucy, Adrian, and the Stansteads. Ten minutes. Okay?"

"As for myself, I couldn't eat another bite tonight. I felt it my sworn duty to make sure the Stansteads didn't get stuck with a lot of leftovers. My name's Richard Morgan, by the way." He put out his hand. Phelps took it halfheartedly, said, "Phelps Grant; nice to meet you," and turned to go back to the inner sanctum, where all the important people were. Faith couldn't resist.

"Richard's a writer. He's doing a profile on Michael for *The New Yorker*."

Phelps swung around instantly, and Faith left him in earnest conversation with Richard. The word *quintessential* pronounced with great intensity reached her ears, and she laughed to herself at serious little Phelps. She headed toward the kitchen for the large trays and rolling cart she needed to clean up. She'd liked Phelps earlier, but less and less as the evening wore on. Why on earth couldn't her sister see what a sycophant this guy was? That was such a good word. She'd drag it out again when she talked about the party with Richard. Soon.

By the time she emerged from the kitchen, Richard was gone. She was glad. For a moment, she'd thought he was going to offer to help, and that would not have worked at all. She liked to keep her work life and private life nicely separated, although tonight it had been difficult.

Poppy came out of the study.

"Faith, I haven't had a moment to talk to you all evening. Wonderful party, dear. You are fabulous. Everyone is saying so. I tell them I taught you how to make s'mores, obviously starting you on the road to success." Poppy laughed. Faith had forgotten how completely charming she was. And yes, she had taught Faith how to make s'mores—at a sleepover. It had been terrific fun. Poppy had seemed like a kid herself. Faith also remembered Poppy's saying they would do it again. She was still waiting.

"It's a perfect place for a party. A beautiful room. Hard to go wrong."

"Emma does have a knack this way, I'll say that for her."

And what else, Mom, what else do you have to say about your daughter?

"We're all going out to dinner. Not that I can eat anything. Maybe a little salad."

Suddenly, Poppy seemed distracted. She was looking toward the study, where all the others were.

"What are you doing for the holidays?" Faith asked politely to fill the gap in the conversation. So many topics were off-limits. Too bad.

"Jason isn't interested in skiing anymore, so that means Mustique again. We've taken a house. You should come down," she added with such sincerity that Faith could almost believe she meant it.

Emma came out of the study. She looked exhausted, ill even. She read the fear in Faith's eyes and immediately said pointedly, "Everything's fine. It was all perfect. And Mother, Faith has another party to do, so you mustn't keep her."

"*Another* party. You're working very hard, Faith. I hope it's not all too much. Everyone seems to be getting that ghastly flu that's going around. Emma, you should stay here and get into a bath and bed. You know you haven't been feeling up to par lately. You look a little feverish." Poppy's maternal concern extended to stroking her daughter's hair, which meant she must be very worried indeed; then she gave Faith a slight wave and went off toward the study.

"I wish I didn't have to go, but I do." Emma's eyes filled with tears. She slumped down in one of the chairs by the fire, which was going out. "Are you all right for the next party? Shouldn't you be leaving?"

"The rest of my staff is taking care of it, and I'll be finished here soon, anyway. But the question is, Are *you* all right? And I don't mean the flu."

126

Emma answered in a slightly manic torrent of words. "I thought it was a coincidence, so I didn't mention it before, but now I'm not so sure. I've been getting a million hang-up calls since all this started. It's horrible, Faith. I've been going crazy. The phone rings ten or twelve times in a row, and every time I pick it up, there's no answer. Just breathing. At first, I kept asking who it was, but now I don't say anything, either, and after a while, there's a click. I tried letting it ring, except then the machine would pick it up, and I don't want Michael to think anything's wrong. Besides, they just keep calling—whether I answer or not. Over and over and over again. It's getting so that every time the phone rings, I'm afraid to pick it up." She shuddered and wrapped her arms together.

And exactly how does Emma think she is going to hide the current state of her emotions from her husband? Faith wondered. Emma was close to the edge now, about to burst into frightened sobs.

"I don't think it's a coincidence. And if you went to the police, they could have the phone company trace the calls. You can't keep this up! You really will make yourself ill!"

Emma shook her head; her hair fell over her face, a curtain of red gold. "No police," she whispered.

Several people were coming out of the study, Michael Stanstead among them. The party was definitely over. "We'll meet you there, then. Sign of the Dove, in half an hour."

At the sound of her husband's voice, Emma hastily blotted her eyes on the insubstantial lacy hem of her dress, tossed her hair back, and sat up.

"Everything was perfect," she said loudly to her friend. "You saved my life, Faith."

                                *   *   *

Saturday was a blur of work, and when Faith locked
the door of the catering company's kitchen in the wee
hours of Sunday morning, she vowed to hire more help
in the New Year—and, more immediately, sleep until
noon.

The phone rang at nine. Fighting her way to con-
sciousness, leaving behind what was possibly a pleasant dream involving Richard and a beach—she
couldn't quite grab on to it—Faith picked up the receiver.

"Um," she said.

"I didn't wake you, did I?" Emma asked anxiously.

"No," Faith lied, wondering why people always lied
about being awakened and why no one ever simply
said, "Yes, I was happily comatose until the damn
phone rang." Then suddenly, she was wide-awake.
Emma. Anxious.

"What's happened?" Something had to have happened.

"I got another card. It was mixed in with the mail,
but it didn't have a stamp. I've been dropping all the
cards into that big bowl on the table in the hall until I
had a chance to open them."

"And you just did," Faith said, finishing for her, now
agitated herself. She knew the blackmail wouldn't
stop, yet there was always the faint possibility that she
might be wrong. "What does it say this time?"

Emma lowered her voice. She'd been practically
whispering to start, and now her words verged on in-
audible. "I can't tell you."

Faith managed to catch the phrase. "You're afraid
Michael will overhear or you just plain can't tell me?"

"Both," she whispered.

"Look, Emma, tell Michael you're going to church, or shopping, or whatever you do on Sunday mornings and get yourself over here immediately."

Faith took a quick shower. Normally, she did some of her best thinking under the strong, warm spray, but today her mind was on autopilot. She lathered, rinsed, and got out, then dressed and made a pot of coffee. She was looking at the toaster with a slice of bread in it when she realized she had virtually no memory of her previous actions. She focused on the matters at hand, first pushing the toaster control down, then thinking about this latest blackmail attempt. The card could have been in the pile for days—*or* someone could have slipped it in on Friday night. Someone at the party.

The buzzer sounded, and in a few moments Emma was sitting at the small table Faith had placed between the two front windows overlooking West Fifty-sixth Street.

"Are you hungry? English muffin?" Faith asked, pouring coffee. She firmly believed that food enhanced mental processes.

"I don't want anything to eat, thank you. I'd probably throw up."

"You're not . . ." Faith began. Why not complicate matters a little further.

"No," Emma said sadly. "I wish I were. You have no idea what it's like getting your hopes up every month. We've been trying for over a year now. The doctor says I need to relax. Michael has been an angel. Did I tell you he's taking me with him in January for this business thing in the Caribbean someplace? He says he just wants me to sit in the sun on a beach. I know he's as disappointed about not having a baby as I am, but he never shows it—or blames me."

It was on the tip of Faith's tongue to ask why their infertility was necessarily Emma's "fault," but this was not the time. Of course Michael would need heirs—a bunch of little Stansteads to cluster round for the family Christmas card sent to constituents. Oddly enough, politicians still seemed to think that the way to win the hearts and minds of the electorate was by sending these yearly missives with wife or husband, progeny, and dog posed in front of a fireplace. Cards most voters promptly tossed out.

"I'm sure you'll get pregnant; you did before." Faith blurted the words out, then realized that what she had meant to sound reassuring hadn't quite come off that way.

Emma didn't seem to notice. "That's true, but it's why I feel so guilty. It's like this is a kind of judgment on me for all of that."

"Oh, Emma, come on! You were pushed into a terrible situation. None of it was your fault."

Emma was staring out the window. New York was in a deep freeze. Records were being shattered. On the corner, a man and his wife from Maine had set up a Christmas tree lot, as they did each year, she'd been told. The whole neighborhood had adopted them, greeting them as the first harbingers of the season, their reappearance each Christmas something you could count on—a grown-up city dweller's version of believing in Santa. They offered the couple showers, a bed when the temperature dipped below zero. The gaily trimmed tree they'd set up on the roof of the dilapidated camper they lived in for these few weeks was a welcome sight against the dreary morning sky.

"Look," Faith said, "let's take one thing at a time. Your doctor is probably right. God knows, you've been under enough stress lately. Why don't you show me the card and tell me all about it. *All,*" she repeated.

Emma dug the card out of her bag. It was from the same series. A Victorian child with blond ringlets was holding a huge present. "Season's Greetings" was printed on the large red bow. Inside, the greeting was grim:

What do you think Michael's chances of getting elected will be when people find out he's married to a murderer?

Six

Obviously, this was yet another item on Emma Stanstead's "Things I May Not Have Mentioned" list. A major item.

"Don't tell me," Faith began as Emma started to sob. "You were in Fox's apartment the day he was murdered."

"I was there, but I didn't kill him!" she shrieked.

"Of course you didn't!" Faith grabbed a box of tissues and moved Emma over to the couch. Faith hadn't imagined Emma could ever make a noise like the one that had just issued from her mouth. She'd finally flipped out.

Emma began to shake. Just shake, soundlessly now. Faith threw the down comforter from her bed around Emma's shoulders and went to get her a cup of fresh coffee. Emma held it tightly, slowly moving it to her mouth, taking small sips. Faith felt as if there should be a dog sled nearby.

"He wasn't dead. I didn't see that, thank God, but I could have. If the killer had come sooner." She closed her eyes and drank again. Her pain, moving in waves from beneath the quilt, was searing.

"You went to his apartment at three, the way you always did, right? And left when?"

Emma opened her eyes, looking directly at Faith. "I only stayed an hour. I've felt so guilty ever since. I had to be back uptown for a cocktail party. A cocktail party! If I had stayed longer, my father might still be alive."

"Or you might be dead, too," Faith said briskly. She was beginning to understand why hysterical people get slapped across the face. Anything to bring them back. Since she'd seen Emma that first night in the kitchen, Faith had had the same impulse. Anything to ground her in what passed for reality—and what seemed to work best was the verbal equivalent of a slap.

Emma came to—for the moment. She sat up straighter.

"I never thought of that." She put the cup down on the low table in front of the couch.

"But it wasn't likely," Faith pointed out. "Whoever is blackmailing you knows you were at your father's apartment that day, which means he or she saw you. Saw you leave and then went in. Don't you see? The killer *waited* until you left. You were meant to be kept alive. You'd be no use to anyone dead. How would they get the money?"

"That's a relief—I think," Emma said, kicking off her shoes and curling up on the couch with the quilt pulled over her. She was looking a whole lot better.

"Someone was watching, yet how would they know you'd be there? It couldn't have been a coincidence. Someone has to have been watching you for a while." Someone knew Emma's schedule, her every move.

Faith didn't give voice to the rest of her speculations. Emma had all she could take for now. But suppose someone, say Lucy, knew or had found out about Emma's real parentage and either knew or supposed that Emma was seeing Fox. Easy enough to follow her. New Yorkers are street-smart, but in a heads-down sort of way. You don't make eye contact. And Emma, whose thoughts tended to be very far away from the immediate, would not have been paying attention to what was going on around her anyway—like someone following her. And New York is a big, crowded city. Following someone, particularly Emma, would not have been hard.

"Did your father seem any different from usual? Apprehensive?"

"No, if anything, he was extremely cheerful. Maybe he'd finished that big book, the one you were asking about the other day. I remembered after I talked to you that I hadn't heard any typing that day. And there weren't any papers on the table. Usually, it was pretty messy. When I gave him the bialys, he said they would be a perfect celebration."

"So, the two of you clinked breadstuff and made merry?"

This continuing picture of Nathan Fox the doting father was far removed from Nathan Fox the flaming radical.

"I didn't eat anything. I wasn't hungry. Besides, I wanted him to have them. I'd brought some cream cheese. I made him a glass of tea. He'd taught me how. He drank his tea in a glass. He said his father always did." Emma said in wonderment—at the custom and maybe a little at her startling culinary accomplishment.

Nathan Fox, Norman Fuchs, wasn't disguised as an

old Jewish man. He was an old Jewish man, Faith thought.

"Did you ask him what he was celebrating?"

Emma looked downcast. "No, at the time, I kind of thought it was because I was there. I'd missed the week before."

"And I'm sure that's what he meant." Maybe, Faith thought, qualifying to herself. "What did you talk about?"

"Daddy always liked to hear what I'd been doing. Where I'd gone. Who I'd seen. He knew quite a lot of people. Michael and I had been to the opening of 'The Age of Napoleon' at the Met's Costume Institute the night before. It really is a wonderful show. If you haven't seen it yet, you should go. I told him about dancing with my Michael by the Temple of Dendur. It was a lovely evening, although terribly crowded. Anyway, that got us talking about Napoleon. Daddy was very big on him and planned to write a book about whether he'd subverted the goals of the French Revolution or not, which of course he'll never do now—Dad, not Napoleon. Although, I suppose both. Daddy was always quoting him, history was 'a set of lies agreed upon,' that kind of thing. He thought Napoleon had been misunderstood in many ways."

This was all very interesting. It didn't surprise Faith in the least to discover that Fox had had a Napoleon fixation. And about the Met—she had heard both the show and the opening were spectacular, but she had more questions. More pertinent questions.

Emma's prints were spread over the apartment, what with the tea making and all, but the police wouldn't have had anything to connect her with them. And surely the killer hadn't left any. But getting back to the business of the book—Emma *must* know something more.

"Did he show you a finished manuscript?"

"No, he must have put it somewhere. In his file cabinet, probably."

A logical deduction.

Emma continued. "I told you before that he never actually said what it was about. I merely assumed it was like the other books. Political. The masses being oppressed. That kind of thing."

Had it occurred to Emma that Nathan Fox the revolutionary regarded her as a class enemy? Probably not, since it was Nathan Fox, the radical chic darling of the Upper East Side, who was pumping her week after week for details of the life he obviously very much missed. It was all going on without him—the repartee, the gossip, the affairs, the beluga.

"And then you left?"

"Then I left." Somehow the three words uttered in this completely flat tone sounded more tragic than all of Emma's earlier outcries put together. There was very little to say after this, and during one of the silences Emma dozed off, exhausted by the surfeit of emotion.

Faith stood up and went to the window. The Christmas tree sellers, in bright red stocking caps and down parkas, were doing a brisk business. She'd planned to get a small tree herself. It was her first Christmas in her very own place. Maybe next year. She was going to be too busy. Emma's latest revelation brought several parts of the picture into sharp focus. Faith now knew that Fox's murder and Emma's blackmail were the work of the same hands. It was highly unlikely that the blackmail operation had just happened upon the murder, which just happened to occur the day and time of Emma's habitual visits. Which upped the ante considerably. Before, Emma had been in danger. Now that Faith knew they were dealing with a killer or killers, it was mortal danger.

A family was looking at trees. The kids kept dragging out Rockefeller Center–size pines; the parents, tabletop versions. Somewhere on that lot, they'd find the perfect one, something in between—and each side would feel victorious.

Emma, Emma. Faith looked at her friend—oblivious in sleep's sweet escape. She'd been right all along. Of course she couldn't go to the police. Once they discovered she'd been at Fox's apartment so close to the time of death—the newspaper had said 4:00 P.M.—she would immediately become a suspect. Could even be charged. It would all make very good sense to the district attorney's office. Discovering her father's whereabouts, Emma kills him and fakes a burglary to protect her husband's political future. And the blackmail? She could have written the notes herself. The only hard piece of evidence was a tape—which she'd destroyed. And her motive? That was easy. Faith had known from the start Emma would do anything for Michael. Do anything to keep him from leaving her once he found out who she really was—and she'd managed to convince herself that was what he'd do, be forced to do to save his career . . . and face. No, this was not one of those times when your friend Mr. Policeman would be of much help. This was one of those times when the only person who could help was, unfortunately, you—or rather, your nearest and dearest friend.

And Faith had to move quickly. Before Emma lost

all her money, was arrested, made the tabloids, cracked up, or all four.

Outside, the family had tied their purchase on top of a child's red wagon and started off, the father pulling, one of the kids holding the precariously balanced tree steady. Faith sighed. She wouldn't be stringing any popcorn and cranberries herself this year.

Instead, as soon as Emma woke up and left, Faith would continue her investigation. Although, with this latest revelation, it seemed as if she was starting from the beginning. She decided to take a ride out to Long Island. Garden City, Long Island. People looked for houses on the weekends—and Todd Hartley was a real estate agent. Wasn't it Dorothy L. Sayers who said, "Suspect everybody?"

Faith knew how to get to Long Island. It wasn't like New Jersey. She *knew* where Long Island was. Theoretically, she knew where Jersey was, too. You could see it directly across the Hudson from the West Side. There was a tunnel underneath you could take to go there. But it wasn't like Long Island. She could find her way around the island—or rather, across the island from west to east to the Hamptons—with no stops in between. I'm not going anywhere near as far today, she thought with some relief, remembering the traffic back to the city on Sunday summer nights, exit names— Eastport, Patchogue, Islip, Amityville—passing at a snail's pace.

Garden City was at the near end of the island, close to Queens. She'd studied the map while Emma slept and planned her route. There weren't any of those little black dots AAA uses to mark the scenic roads. Those dots started at Hampton Bays, started where the money started—Southampton, East Hampton, Amagansett. It might be fun to move the business to the island during the summers. Fun and profitable.

She popped a cassette of Christmas carols into the tape deck and began singing along. "God bless the master of this house." Faith was under no illusions as to her vocal ability. A Jessye Norman, she was not. Yet, she wasn't bad in a chorus, and she certainly knew how to belt out hymns. Her father, if he did not exist, would have to have been invented. He actually got his jaded, weary Manhattan congregation to turn out for hymn sings—just for the fun of it—where he would joyfully accompany them on a very ancient and always slightly out of tune guitar.

"Let every man with cheerfulness embrace his loving wife." Verse three. Always the afterthought. If Emma didn't care so much about the master of her house, all of this would be a much more manageable problem. Not that Michael didn't seem to care about his wife, too. Whenever Faith had seen them together, and that once without, he seemed genuinely to adore her. Faith had intercepted a look he gave Emma at the party the other night. She had been greeting someone and as Michael walked over to join them, he gazed on her with something more than love, more than appreciation. It was a "Could I possibly be this lucky?" look; a "Could this amazing, beautiful creature actually be mine?" look. Faith recalled hearing when the engagement was announced how he'd pursued his intended, wooing and winning her with extravagantly romantic gestures. Can't go wrong with romantic gestures, she thought, as the flowers at Delia's and Richard slipped into her thoughts.

She came out of the Queens Midtown Tunnel into

the bright afternoon sunshine. It sparkled on the mounds of dirty snow. She had thought it best not to drive the van from work with HAVE FAITH, the address, and the phone number emblazoned on the side. So, she'd borrowed her parents' car, a sedate black Volvo—her mother's choice. Lawrence had probably driven it only once or twice, if that much. Things like borrowing the car were easy with them. They were not the kind of parents who would have to know where she was going, with whom, and why. Lawrence never asked this kind of question, period. Jane saved up her queries, hitting you on big stuff like what you were planning to do with your life, rather than day-to-day minutiae in which she wasn't really interested—or didn't want to know about. Today, however, did fall into the "big stuff" category. Yes, she was helping a friend—both parents would applaud that—but the rest was way beyond "Can you look me straight in the eye and say that?"—and she had no intention of their ever finding out. Not her parents. Not anyone. She'd sworn to Emma she wouldn't—and besides, at this point, knowledge was becoming an increasingly dangerous thing.

Not wishing to squander an afternoon driving to Garden City, which she was sure was not a garden anymore, even in clement weather, Faith had called the agency where Hartley was—after working her way down a number of them from the Yellow Pages. He was available and she set up an appointment. She was Karen Brown again, not a lowly graduate student, but Mrs. Karen Brown from Los Angeles. Mr. Brown—she decided to call him Richard just for the hell of it—was being transferred east and she was scouting communities for that perfect location. It had to be an easy commute to the city, good schools . . .

"And of course we both love the water, so maybe something closer to the North or South Shore?" Faith was sitting in a comfortable chair, drinking a cup of coffee she really didn't want and watching the lies slide off her tongue as easily as sap from a sugar maple in a spring thaw.

Todd Hartley was busy filling out her wish list. Faith was waiting for him to ask how she'd been referred to him, and she had an elaborate story involving Saint Paul's School and a cousin of her husband's and always hearing about Garden City, then seeing an ad in the Yellow Pages and his name just hitting her, because of Bob Hartley, you know the old *Bob Newhart Show*—except Todd Hartley didn't ask, not yet.

"Contemporary? Center entrance colonial? Ranch?"

"Not ranch." Faith and Karen were both positive about this. Not on Long Island, anyway. Colorado, Montana, maybe.

He nodded. There was no vestige of the radical Emma had described. No *Little Red Book* sticking out of his handkerchief pocket, no Marx and Engels tie tack. He wasn't bad-looking, although he'd be overweight soon. She'd noticed the buttons on his suit jacket straining at the midriff. His forehead was rising, too. Bald and fat someday. Not a pretty thought. She'd also noticed a fancy watch and heavy gold wedding band. Todd had apparently given in to the bourgeois institution of marriage. His wedding picture was on his desk, and from the setting, Faith surmised that Todd had been indulging in the opiate of the masses, as well. Mrs. Hartley had big hair—at least on her wedding day—and was a very attractive brunette. She was covering his hand with hers and the camera had picked up the sparkle from the rock she was wearing—something close to Gibraltar. Faith twisted her own modest wedding band and engagement ring, purchased at Woolworth's a few hours ago. She was willing to bet that Mrs. Hartley's rings weren't from Woolworth's. Todd's, either.

It cost a lot of money to be a well-turned-out Realtor. Without actually fingering the fabric, which might appear suspect, Faith guessed his suit was Brooks or Paul Stuart. Maybe on sale, but not cheap. In addition, you had to have an expensive, new—or nearly new—car. No one was going to be persuaded into assuming a monstrous mortgage by someone driving an old Pinto.

"I think the best way to start is by selecting some target communities; then we can go for a drive and you can get a feel for them. What's your timetable?"

Faith was tempted to say she wanted everything cleared up by Christmas, but she answered instead, "We'll be moving in the late spring."

"No problem. As you've probably heard, in the East, a lot of houses come on the market then, with the good weather. Things slow down in the winter, but you can pick up some real bargains that way."

"People are desperate, you mean." Faith wasn't sure why she said that. Maybe it was to try to tease out whatever personality he had. It certainly wasn't being expressed in the artwork on the walls—a framed map of the island and a generic floral still life.

He smiled slightly. "I guess you could put it that way." There was a slightly awkward pause. "Well, Mrs. Brown, why don't we—"

The phone rang.

"Sorry, could you excuse me?"

Faith nodded and sat back in the chair. She'd wanted

to dress for the part. She wasn't sure what a Californian with no winter clothes would wear on a foray to the Big Apple, but she figured she couldn't go wrong with a pair of Lauren black trousers and a white man-tailored shirt. She'd added a chunky gold-link bracelet she'd never particularly cared for that a too-serious admirer had given her last Christmas. She wanted to look as if she could afford a house, but not a mansion. She'd made a joke about having to borrow her Kamali coat from a friend and said she supposed she'd be buying things like it herself once they moved to this terrible climate. Chuckle, chuckle.

After picking up the phone and saying hello, Todd hadn't said anything other than "This isn't the best time now." The person on the other end obviously did not agree, and after saying it once more with feeling, Hartley turned toward Faith.

"Would you mind terribly waiting in the reception area? I'm afraid I have to take this."

"Not at all. My schedule is flexible. I have plenty of time." Today anyway.

Unfortunately, the receptionist was at her desk. No way to pick up the phone and eavesdrop. Faith was forced to sit down and thumb through a back issue of *People* magazine—more Donald and Ivana.

The agency wasn't on the skids, but the carpeting was ever so slightly worn in spots. It wasn't affiliated with one of the big national firms, just a small family-owned outfit, probably been around forever. Hartley's family? How had he ended up here? It wasn't that long ago that he'd been hanging out with the comrades, desperately searching for Nathan. Who or what had changed his mind? The lovely Mrs. Hartley? Or after Poppy Morris's revelation of Emma's age, had young Todd decided to retreat—fearful of statutory rape?

The agency, like much of the rest of the country, had dragged out its box of holiday decorations. A small clear plastic tree with unappetizing fossilized gumdrops skewered to its sharp branches stood on the receptionist's desk. A row of stockings with names written in glitter pen hung in a line from the mantel of a faux fireplace. Todd's, like the others, was empty. What would Santa bring? A lump of coal? A huge pot of pink poinsettias stood in the fireplace opening and tinsel garlands looped about the walls and door frames completed the festive decor.

Faith has just finished her inventory when the receptionist got up, put on her coat, and left. Creeping over to the door to Hartley's office, Faith could hear Todd's voice, but she couldn't hear what he was saying. She went over to the desk and carefully picked up the phone, pressing the button next to the line that lighted up.

"It's too soon. That's all I can tell you. Not yet. You'll have to be patient. It worked once. It'll work again. She's scared. Leave her alone for now," said a voice on the other end of the conversation. A voice Faith had never heard before. "Do you catch my drift, Hartley?"

"Yeah, yeah . . ."

"Because if you don't, you know what will happen, right?" There was no mistaking the menace in the man's voice.

And she'd been about to get in a car with Todd Hartley, a man who, given what she knew, was up to his ears in something that sounded very much like a partnership in blackmail and murder! He knew who Emma

144

was. He'd known where Fox lived before. If Fox had trusted him that much, he'd have no qualms about revealing his most recent whereabouts. But knowing Fox was in the city, why hadn't Todd turned him in? Still Red below the surface, or afraid of being outed to his new wife, his new life? Or afraid of a charge of corrupting a minor, and worse? It hadn't been that long ago.

The man on the phone was telling him to wait. Wait to ask for money again? Wait to ask for more?

"What the hell do you think you're doing?" His hand came down hard on her shoulder and she dropped the phone. "Get into my office!" he barked. She grabbed the plastic gumdrop tree—none of them moved—and shoved it in his face. Startled, he relaxed his grasp. "What the hell!" And she took off for the door. She had it partway open when he threw himself against it, overturning the coatrack. She started screaming. It was the only thing to do.

"Shut up! Shut up!" he yelled at her, reaching toward her to cover her mouth. She shut up. The notion of that big sweaty palm on her lips made her gag.

"Who are you and what are you doing here? Who sent you?"

She was trapped. Please, please let it be that the receptionist was just going out for a sandwich.

She wanted to say nobody had sent her, but she also wanted him to think all five boroughs knew where she was. She concentrated on thinking how to get away. Yet she had to be sure. "Nathan. You could say Nathan sent me," she said in a firm voice.

"Nathan?" He looked shocked. "How do you know . . . Jesus, *you* want money. That's it, isn't it?" He exploded again. Her coat was at their feet. He thrust it at her, opened the door, and pushed her out. "Just get out of here—and don't come back."

She was at the parking lot, light-headed with relief, when he came running after her, red-faced, panting. He still looked sweaty, even in the cold. There was a pad of paper and a pencil in one hand. Damn. Her license plate—or rather, Mother and Dad's. All she could think of to do was to keep going so he wouldn't know which car was hers. It was a municipal lot and almost full. He couldn't stand outside in these temperatures without a coat for long. She kept walking. At the corner, she looked over her shoulder. He was taking down the numbers of every car in the lot. "Don't worry, Mrs. Brown," he yelled after her. "I'll find out who you are. Don't worry, you bitch! I'll get you!"

She ducked around the corner and into a card shop. Thirty minutes later, with several packages of Christmas cards she doubted she'd get time to send, she went back to the lot. He was gone. She drove off in the opposite direction from the real estate agency and, as she'd been doing since she was so unceremoniously shown the door, ran through what had just happened. Of course he must have heard her pick up the phone. She'd have to get better at "overhearing" conversations if she was going to be good at this. Or maybe he hadn't bought the whole act. She doubted this, though. She hadn't done anything to raise his suspicions that she was anything other than what she appeared—a lady looking for a house.

Absentmindedly, she put on the tape again, but she wasn't in the mood for medieval merriment. She decided to check her messages. She had to bring the car back, but the evening was free. She supposed things would even out, yet so far the business had been mad rushes followed by enervating doldrums. Still, she reflected, if she was busy all the time, either Emma's major problem or Faith's fledgling business would suffer. Every silver lining has a cloud. Since when had she begun to think in clichés? Especially such tired ones. Tired. That was it. She hadn't had much sleep lately.

She reached for the car phone she was sure her father didn't know existed and called her machine at home first.

"Faith, darling. This is absolutely the last message I'm going to leave. Altman's will be an office building or whatever horrendous thing they're planning to do with it before we get there for lunch. I'll see you and Hope at Chat's party and we'll make a date then. I positively refuse to talk to this machine again." Faith could picture her grandmother's face. Amused indignation or indignant amusement. Added to tolerant bemusement and bemused tolerance, these made up the major portions of Mrs. Lennox's emotional repertoire.

"Got a gig tonight yourself, or can we catch Connick? Call me?"

It was Richard. Faith felt happy. That was unusual lately. Worried, fatigued, frightened, yes—but happy was in short supply. What was going on? It had been a while since a man's voice had caused this kind of reaction. She knew she was interested in him, but was she getting *interested?* She had a fleeting fantasy of pouring the entire tale out to him at the Algonquin tonight. They'd be drinking Manhattans while Harry Connick Jr., the boy wonder, played Gershwin and Cole Porter on the piano. It would be such a help to get another opinion. Was Todd Hartley, former radical, on the phone with an accomplice? Being advised, say, to wait before telling Emma when to make the latest drop? Or was he talking to a disgruntled home owner who was getting close to putting a contract out on Todd himself—or switching brokers—because Todd wanted him to drop the price of his house to move it? Wanted to push someone, a woman, into making an offer?

Yet Faith couldn't try to get things clearer in her own mind by picking Richard's brains. She was back at the Midtown Tunnel and plunged down the ramp. Yes, she'd go out with Richard, but she wouldn't be able to tell him a thing. Any hint of what was going on in her life and it would be "soon to be a major motion picture" time. Any reporter worth his or her salt would react the same way. It was in their genes. But yes, she'd see him tonight. Yes.

Richard couldn't meet her until nine, which was fine with Faith. Garden City had left her feeling drained, more relieved than frightened now. She was at the stage where she was imagining all the things that could have happened to her and hadn't. She wanted to take a long, hot bath and a long, warm nap—under the quilt Emma had left on the couch.

The phone rang. It was her sister. She sounded upset. A highly unusual state for her. Faith remembered with a pang that she had never called Hope to arrange a time to have dinner with Phelps. Maybe she should ask if they were free tonight? They could come to the Algonquin afterward. No, scratch that thought.

"It's about Phelps—"

"I know. I'm really sorry I didn't get back to you about dinner, but it's been crazy."

"No—or rather, I mean yes. Let's have dinner together sometime. But he just called, and I'm in a quandary about what to do. This kind of thing has never happened to me before."

It sounded like she needed more than simple advice to the lovelorn.

"What's wrong?"

"Probably nothing. It's just that Phelps has the chance to invest in—"

Faith interrupted again. It was getting to be a habit.

"He wants to borrow money?"

"Yes, rather a lot of money."

"This is an easy one. A no-brainer. You know the golden rule. Never loan money to men, especially the ones you're dating."

"I know, I know. But it's a short-term loan. With interest. His lawyer will draw up the papers."

"This sounds like more than 'rather a lot' of dough! What does he need it for?"

"He has the chance to get in on the ground floor of a terrific new software company. It all makes sense, except—"

"Except he doesn't have the money and wants to borrow it from his girlfriend."

There was silence on the other end. Faith didn't know whether Hope was enjoying the appellation or pondering her decision.

"Look, sweetie, I'm not just being flip. Think about it. You loan him the money and he can't pay it back. This places a strain on the relationship and you break up. You loan him the money and he does pay it back, but he's always aware he was dependent on you for his new good fortune or whatever. Men don't like that kind of feeling, so you break up. Now there is also the possibility that your lighthearted refusal to loan him any money—Mother always said never do things like this; you can even hum a few bars of that other classic, "Mama said there'd be days like this"—will cause him to break up with you, too. But you'll still have your money and will have saved even more on Doritos, which you know you eat when you're depressed."

"Oh, Fay, life is so simple for you!"

"What!" Faith exclaimed in astonishment.

"Well, you always know what to do."

This was a complete revelation. Faith viewed her younger sib as the one with the Filofax lobe, the life plan. Faith tended to make snap judgments, go on a gut response . . . but it was true, when it came to questions of the heart, that she was quicker to ring in than her well-programmed sister.

"True or not—and we have to talk—the question now is, What are you going to do?"

"Dunno. Stall. Find out more about the company. Might be a good investment for me, too." She perked up.

"Hope!"

"I'll think about what you said. Got to run. Love you. Bye."

If there *is* a company, Faith thought as she ran a bath. That would definitely solve Hope's dilemma—if she asked for a prospectus and none existed.

She got into the fragrant, steamy water. Phelps Grant needed money. A lot of it. She'd never really considered him a suspect, but he was always there in the back of her mind with everyone else. He'd been at the party and could have left the card. He could have been at the first party, too; Faith had stayed in the kitchen that night. Then there was the second card. The one in the newspaper outside the Stansteads' apartment door. The threatening one. Someone who looked as presentable as Phelps, particularly if he'd been there before, could easily get into the building. There were always times during the day when the doorman was away briefly. The Stansteads' building had a rear entrance and stairs next to the service elevator. She'd noted them when they were catering the party. Having evaded the man at the door, you could avoid the one in the elevator by slipping into the rear and up the stairs. Where there was a will, there was a way. And Phelps definitely aspired to riches and power. He could be in the hole for any number of reasons—rent on a tony apartment he couldn't afford, picking up the tab at Mortimer's to impress a little too often, treating everyone to lines of the good stuff . . .

She'd have to find somebody new for Hope after the holidays. It wasn't the season to break up, although from the sound of it, Hope shouldn't expect much in the way of a gift from Phelps. It *was* nice to have someone at the holidays. New York was so romantic. Twinkling lights everywhere. Red, green, gold—the city was swathed in the colors of the season. She added some more hot water.

There was no sense in going back to Garden City, even if she hadn't been literally thrown out of the real estate office. She wouldn't be able to find out anything more about Todd Hartley there. She smiled. He'd have a hard time finding her. The car was registered to Jane, age fifty something. In the last years, her mother had grown a bit vague as to the exact number. There was nothing to link Faith Sibley to Karen Brown. She had nothing to fear from the man.

She let her mind wander. Fox was killed to blackmail Emma. But did that really make sense? There was already enough to blackmail Emma about well into the next century. Why kill Fox?

The apartment had been trashed. Maybe by junkies, as both Josie and Richard had suggested. But what if that hadn't been the case? What if it had been somebody looking for something other than stereo equipment and jewelry?

Something like a tell-all book. A magnum opus. Something that would blow the lid off—blow the lid off somebody's secret. Somebody other than Emma. Richard's book was going to blow a southern town sky-high. What was it with men—success had to be measured on the Richter scale?

Faith suddenly decided she had to get into Fox's apartment. Emma had a key. Surely the police would be finished with it by now. A key didn't mean breaking and entering. She wanted to see the place for herself. See how it had been searched.

And it was time to talk to Lorraine Fuchs again. Lorraine, the faithful companion. Find out if Lorraine knew anything more about that "very important book" Fox had been working on at the time of his death.

Lorraine Fuchs had sounded thrilled that Faith—or rather, Karen—could drop by the next day.

"It's so important. I've thought of doing it myself, only I'm not a writer. Oh, maybe the odd pamphlet, but not a whole book! You were at the service. You heard Arthur. Nathan's words were his legacy. But his life was, too, and you'll be putting it into words!"

Faith arranged to be there at 2:00 P.M., took down the directions, and felt like a heel.

Next, she called Emma.

"I want to get into your father's apartment." She

came right to the point. It was the best way with Emma.

"What! You don't want me to go with you, do you?"

"No, but I do need the key." Faith thought they should assume that Emma's movements were being closely followed, and the last place she should go was to Fox's apartment. She wondered if the blackmailers had pictures of Emma on the day Fox was killed. Well, even if they did, there was no need to supply them with any more opportunities.

"It's best to do this sort of thing during the day. Less suspicious. I'd like to go over in the morning."

"You sound terribly professional," Emma remarked admiringly.

"It's common sense—and television." You could learn a lot from *Cagney and Lacey*.

They arranged that Faith would drop by Emma's apartment and pick up the key the next morning on her way downtown. "I have to go to a breakfast with Michael, and if I'm already gone, I'll leave it in an envelope with Juanita," she told Faith. "If I leave it with one of the doormen, Michael might be with me when he said something like 'Your friend got the key all right.' Then it would be 'What key?' and everything will be ruined. Michael and Juanita never talk."

Faith's next call was to Josie.

"It's about time! I've been worrying my head off about you all day," Josie complained.

"Why didn't you call? And what's going on? You just saw me last night?"

"Didn't want to bother you. Maybe was taking a little nap myself. Yeah, I know," Josie muttered.

"But what's wrong?"

"You know. That phone call you got last week. The

one we're not talking about. I'm not asking any questions—not that I don't want to—but when you're working the way we are, you *know* when something heavy is going down. One look at you is all I need."

"I'm okay." Faith wished she could add that everything else was, too, but she couldn't lie to Josie. Besides, Josie would know the minute she saw Faith.

"Any new jobs?" Josie asked.

"No, but don't forget we have a million party platters, some buche de Noël, and several main courses to do this week. I don't know which is more work—a whole dinner or assembling all those for the do-it-yourselfers."

"I'll be in bright and early. What do you want me to start on—pastries or pâtés?"

Faith felt a little embarrassed. "I won't be able to get there until later, and I have to be away for a while in the afternoon, but I plan to work late. I'm going to ask Jessica to come in. She can clean up and do some of the simple prep work—wash fruit, cut up cheese. Why don't you start on the desserts?" Faith knew Josie preferred making bite-sized pecan tarts, tiny profiteroles, and white chocolate mini-cheesecakes to putting together the vegetable terrine, pâté de campagne, duck with armagnac pâté, and others that, along with an assortment of breads, went into that offering.

They talked business some more; then Faith realized she'd better be getting ready for her date with Richard.

"I've got to meet Richard in an hour," she said.

Josie voiced her approval. "I liked him. Good appetite. You can tell a lot about a man by the way he eats. This is good. If you're with him tonight, I won't have to worry."

Faith was a little annoyed. She could take care of herself. "You don't have to worry in any case."

"Whatever you say."

Monday morning, Faith breezed past the doormen, who were getting to be old friends, and went straight up to Emma's apartment. She was anxious to get downtown, get a look at Fox's apartment, then get some work done before she had to leave for her appointment with Lorraine Fuchs. Busy, busy, busy.

It was sunny and several degrees warmer than it had been lately. People looked happier. Maybe there was something to this sunlight-deprivation business. After getting the key, Faith walked briskly to the subway entrance. Richard and she had been talking about the decade again last night at the Algonquin. Faith supposed every era had spawned a variety of popular notions—fads, even—but they seemed on the increase, and they seemed to be taken more seriously. Like the sunlight theory or the Yuppie fatigue thing. Then her own personal favorite—that an unmarried thirty-one-year-old woman was as likely to find a mate as she was to win the New York State Lottery and/or be awarded the Nobel Prize for anything.

"That's not something you'll have to worry about," Richard had said, reaching for her hand. They *were* drinking Manhattans and Connick *was* playing Cole Porter—"Easy to Love," to Faith's delight and discomfort.

"Which part?" Faith had asked.

"The married part. You'll be married long before your thirty-first birthday."

"What makes you so sure?" she'd asked.

Richard had signaled the waiter for more drinks and

the menu. "Because you're the type. Aside from being very lovely and smart, you're a head-over-heels kind of lady. And that's irresistible."

It had been on the tip of Faith's tongue to ask, "To you?" but for once she'd kept quiet. Maybe she wasn't ready to hear the answer.

Now, leaving the subway and walking along the sidewalk, she cast a longing glance at the Grand Dairy restaurant. No time for blintzes today. She passed the place where her father bought his pure English lisle black socks by the dozen and turned off into Fox's street.

The building was run-down. There was a small area in front, just big enough for a few lawn chairs, which would sprout in the spring, their elderly occupants passing time by watching what passed. The front door looked secure, but it opened with a push. Faith looked at the mailboxes. None of them had the name Fuchs. Emma had given her the apartment number. It was on the third floor, and she walked up the stairs, key in hand.

It wasn't hard to find the apartment. Not hard at all—with its bright yellow crime-scene ribbon taped across the door. And her key was worthless. The apartment had been secured by the police.

"Can I help you, dear?" An incredibly short woman who looked to be in her eighties came out of the apartment next door.

"I'm . . . I'm a graduate student and I'm doing my thesis on Nathan Fox, his life, his writings." Faith fumbled for words and quickly put the key in her coat pocket. "I thought maybe some of his neighbors might have had some contact with him."

"You'd better come in," she said. "I'm Sadie Glickman. What's your name?"

"Karen. Karen Brown," Faith didn't dare look the woman in the eye. She'd be lost if she did. It was a whole lot harder to lie to a little old lady than to someone like Todd Hartley. Fooling him had been exciting and fun, in a way—at least at the beginning. Reeling off whoppers to someone her grandmother's age conjured up Dantesque visions of what might await her in the hereafter. I'm doing this for Emma, she repeated to herself. It was becoming a mantra.

"You want something to eat, Karen? I have some nice pound cake."

"No, no thank you. This probably wasn't a good idea. The papers said he kept to himself."

Sadie sat down in a chair by the window in her tiny living room and motioned Faith into another. The largest piece of furniture was a television set. Besides its function as entertainment, it served to hold more photographs than Faith had ever seen assembled in one place. "My family," Sadie said, waving her hand. "Now that's true—Mr. Fuchs did keep to himself. The police questioned me. A very nice young man." She looked at Faith in an appraising way and Faith was tempted to pipe up, "No, I don't have a steady."

"I was here when it happened," she continued. "But when they asked, the only thing I could tell them was that I thought I *might* have heard a backfire then. Of course, I'd see Mr. Fuchs now and again on the stairs, in the hall, but Live and Let Live is my motto. There are plenty like him in the building. Stella—that's my upstairs neighbor—she used to get a little smile and a hello out of him. She's younger than I am," Sadie said pointedly.

Faith laughed.

"Are you sure you don't want some cake?"

"Why not?" Despite the photo gallery, the woman was obviously lonely, and Faith felt she owed her something for the lies she was telling.

They settled in with cake and tea. Faith heard about the achievements of various Glickmans and a great deal about Leona Helmsley, who had been sentenced the previous Thursday.

"An old lady! An old lady like me! And they're going to send her to prison for four years! When I say 'like me,' I mean, you understand, that we're in the same time of life, not the same type of person."

"I'm sure you have never been driven in your life by 'naked greed.' That's what the judge said. Why he was so hard on her. He accused her of thinking she was above the law."

Sadie nodded solemnly. "No, greed was never a problem for me. I never had enough to be greedy about. Not that I'm complaining. Abe and I had a good life. All the children went to college and are doing well. Maybe she did think she was above the law. Harry, of course Harry can't even think these days. You have to feel sorry for another human being. He spoiled her maybe. Too many fur coats. It went to her head. But above the law? There are a lot out there"—she pointed to the street—"who think that. And what about Mr. Fuchs when he was Nathan Fox?"

And what about Mr. Fuchs? Faith had momentarily forgotten her mission. A mission impossible, and she'd better get going. But Sadie was a smart lady. Nathan Fox *had* thought himself above the law. Maybe it wasn't the same kind of self-interest as Queen Leona's. Fox had used the old "for the greater good" argument to justify his actions. Always a chilling phrase.

Yet, self-interest was a good part of Fox's life, self-aggrandizing in a way not dissimilar from Leona Helmsley's ad campaigns. What about all his enfant terrible books? Dinners at Elaine's—and his society matron groupies.

Sadie was still talking about the verdict. "She's appealing. I hope she has a good lawyer. What's the point? She didn't kill anybody. Take her money away. Send her here. There's an apartment on the first floor available. Let her live out her days as one of the little people. It's wrong to send old ladies to prison."

"I can't argue with that." Faith got up and began clearing their plates and cups. Sadie watched approvingly.

"I'm sorry. I have to be going," Faith told her, slipping her coat from the back of the chair. Sadie got up, too, and put her hand on Faith's arm. She lowered her voice and, in a conspiratorial tone, asked, "You want to have a look at his place?"

"How? It's all locked up." Faith couldn't believe this was happening. How was Sadie going to get her into Fox's apartment? A hidden door in the closet? Morph her through the wall?

"You can get onto the fire escape from Stella's, and it goes right past his window."

The image of Stella, and maybe Sadie, too, as a Peeping Thomasina was almost too much for Faith. In days that weren't filled with any laughter, this one was rapidly becoming high comedy.

"Is Stella home?"

"Stella's always home on Mondays. We'll go up."

Which was how Faith shortly found herself crouched on a cold metal grid, peering through the grimy locked window of Nathan Fox's apartment, the apartment where he had met his death.

The police must have taken various articles away, but Faith didn't have a clue as to what they were. The small room was a shambles. The card table where he wrote was overturned, the typewriter lying on its side. Clippings and papers from the file cabinet covered the floor. There was a cabinet over the sink. The door was open and it was empty, except for a saucepan. There was a plate and a glass in the dish drainer. The refrigerator door was closed. There were no postcards on it and nothing lay on the floor beneath. The grill at the bottom had been pried off. The oven door was open. It needed cleaning—since sometime in the forties. Directly opposite the window was a closet. That door was open, too. The hangers were empty and there was a pile of clothes on the floor. A flat pile. No picture of Emma and Michael. She couldn't see into the bathroom, but she'd seen enough to know how thorough the search had been. She'd also seen enough to know what the person—or persons—unknown had been looking for. The books that filled an entire wall in floor-to-ceiling shelves were virtually undisturbed. And they looked carefully arranged, separated by metal bookends into groups. If the police had picked them up from the floor, Faith doubted they would have replaced them so carefully. The only volumes that had been disturbed were the oversized ones. True, somebody looking for goods to fence wouldn't walk out with a stack of books, but they wouldn't search under the refrigerator, either, or go through the file drawers. Somebody had been looking for something specific— something the size of a finished manuscript.

If there was an outline where Fox had fallen, she couldn't make it out from this angle, but there was a clear space by the door. He'd answered it—expecting whom? Emma—back for a pair of forgotten gloves? No, he'd have noticed them. Emma back with another treat? Who? Who was it who'd knocked—and entered?

"Are you all right, Karen?" Sadie was leaning out the window. "Don't get chilled."

But it was too late for that. Faith was already chilled. Chilled to the bone.

Seven

Lorraine Fuchs lived in Bay Ridge, not far from the
Verrazano Narrows Bridge. The first thing she told
Faith when she opened the door to her tidy brick house
was "I watched them build the bridge when I was a little girl—the Verrazano, not the Brooklyn Bridge." She
gave a halfhearted laugh, yet what struck Faith was not
the woman's attempt at a joke, but the enormous
change in her appearance. She was positively unkempt.
Both her turtleneck and slacks were wrinkled—as if
she'd slept in them. But her red-rimmed bloodshot
eyes weren't indications of a good night's sleep. Her
hair hadn't been braided, and the result was truly scary.
Faith was tempted to march her off to a decent stylist
then and there, subtracting ten years from her age with
the removal of a foot or two of hair.

"I didn't know how to reach you. I was going to tell
you not to bother to come, but since you're here, you
might as well come in."

What had happened to the keeper of the flame? Her
desire to help Faith with the "legacy"?

The house was tidy. Faith was sure Lorraine hadn't moved a thing since her mother died. The living room was papered with dark green leafy fronds. The matched set of sofa, easy chair, and ottoman sported the original nubbly dark brown upholstery. A bookshelf held the classics. A wedding picture, a graduation shot of Lorraine—with significantly less hair—and several sepia prints of a bygone generation stood framed on top of the bookcase. There was a window seat beneath the largest window, overlooking the narrow driveway and detached garage next to the house—its twin to the other side, with the repeat of Lorraine's house next to it. The whole street was the same—house, garage, garage, house—with an occasional low fence or folly such as a wishing well the only distinguishing features. Even the shrubs looked uniform. There was a shelf under the window seat, and Lorraine gestured toward it. It was filled with scrapbooks, folders, and boxes.

"There they are. His whole life. My whole life." She began to cry.

"It must have been such a shock." Faith tried to comfort the woman. She was glad she had her son left at least. "You must miss him terribly."

Lorraine yanked her head up. "Miss him! That bastard! You want to write about him? You want to see scrapbooks? You want to see a book? I'll show you a book!" The woman was screeching. She ran to the shelf below the window seat and grabbed a thick manila envelope from the top of a stack of other items. These teetered, spilling out on to the floor. She kicked at them, waving the other parcel about. There was no address on the front of it, just her first name. 'Be sure I'm really gone, Lorraine,' he said. 'Wait till the funeral, Lorraine—if there's a funeral. Then wait some more.' Well, I waited. Yes, I waited! For what? To find out just who he thought 'Lorraine' was. That's what!"

With her tangled hair draped about her shoulders, she looked like a crazed twentieth-century version of Miss Havisham. The cause for the change between last night and this afternoon? It was obvious. Lorraine Fuchs had read Nathan Fox's magnum opus and blown her lid.

"Who the hell is this?" A young man forcefully pushed open the front door, sending it slamming against the wall, where the torn wallpaper and exposed plaster revealed that this was an habitual form of entry.

Everything about him was large. Tall, verging on obesity, but broad-shouldered, he had a mane of tangled, dirty hair that reached to his shoulders, mingling unpleasantly with his beard on the way. Something about the Fuchses and long hair, Faith said to herself. His jeans were fashionably ripped at the knee, and when he took off his leather jacket, he revealed a Kurt Cobain T-shirt and several tattoos—a large one of Woody Woodpecker in full Klan regalia on his forearm. None of them said MOTHER.

It had to be Harvey.

It was Harvey. "Harvey," Lorraine mumbled in a voice that was both placating and awestruck, "this is Karen. I met her at . . . at the . . . last job I had. She's a friend." The last sentence struck a pleading note. Faith was willing to bet Harvey wouldn't let his mother have a pet, either. Lorraine's luck with menfolk was on a par with Desdemona's.

Harvey walked past them, leaving his jacket on the

floor, and pushed open the swinging door into the next room. He appeared to take no notice of his mother's dishevelment or the mess on the carpet. He was back right away with a can of beer, his attention still elsewhere, his eyes blank, his face devoid of expression.

"Tell your friend to get out. Now."

He hadn't raised his voice once since entering the house, but his flat monotone was terrifying. It was completely devoid of affect and Faith realized that this was true of the rest of Harvey, as well. He hadn't even glanced at her once. Never addressed her directly. The two women were objects, like the furniture in the room. He picked up the remote, put his feet, clad in heavy motorcycle boots, on the coffee table, and switched the television on, flicking through the channels until he came to MTV.

Faith had no problem with leaving. Lorraine looked as if she would have liked to go, too—at least for a cup of coffee. As Faith went out the door, Lorraine said good-bye, added something about Harvey being tired, then leaned forward and whispered, "Come back during the morning. Early. He never comes then. Come Wednesday."

Faith nodded and thankfully made her way back to Manhattan. If every foray out of the city was going to be like the last two, she'd just as soon stay within the confines of the borough for the rest of her life. Maybe a trip or two to someplace like Provence, but definitely she was never going to live anywhere except the Big Apple.

Back at work during the rest of the afternoon, Faith struggled to shake off the sense of deep fear Harvey had provoked. Suddenly, all her other theories were tumbling houses of cards. Whatever Lorraine knew, Harvey knew—and Lorraine knew where Fox had been living, probably knew about Emma. Most certainly after Emma's upstate visit. Emma's visit with Todd. Had it been Harvey on the other end of the phone? Faith hadn't heard enough to be sure. Had they pooled their knowledge and come up with the plot to extort money, a great deal of money, from Emma? It was hard to gauge Harvey's intelligence, but it didn't take much to be a blackmailer—and none at all to kill.

Josie and Jessica had had things under control, but Faith still worked at a fever pitch to get all the party platters and several buche de Noël done and delivered. Howard, who served as van driver when necessary, returned from the last load at six.

"Any changes in the schedule this week? Tomorrow night, we're on, Thursday night's your relative's party, right? Then there's the weekend. That's filled, yes?"

"No changes, but with more platters to do and several takeouts, it's about all we can handle until we move to the new place," Faith answered, adding silently, Until I take care of this Emma business. Until my life veers from the schizophrenic course it's on.

The phone rang, and it was the lady herself.

"Don't be mad, but I had to give them their money again. Yesterday." Uncharacteristically, she came straight to the point.

Faith's heart sank. It wasn't the money—though watching Emma bleed tens of thousands of dollars was gut-wrenching. It was another opportunity lost. If Emma had told her she was going to pay up, Faith could have lurked in the doorway of a nearby building

166

and watched the pickup. Watched Harvey—or Todd—search the Dumpster? She had to find out what time Emma had made the drop. She had to explain this all, but with her staff in full earshot, it was impossible now.

"Can you meet me for a drink? Or I could come by the apartment?"

"You can't talk now. You're working, of course! How stupid of me. I shouldn't have interrupted you!" Emma was contrite.

"No, interrupt me anytime, please. We're *all*"—Faith emphasized the word *all,* hoping Emma would pick up on it—"done here and just about to leave."

"I have to meet Michael at the opening of Geoffrey Beene's new boutique. It's not that Michael's so interested in fashion, but they go way back. Mother Stanstead won't wear any other designer, and Lincoln told Michael he'll be there. Michael wants to talk to him about some fund-raiser."

Making a swift and firm resolve never to call anybody "Mother" anything, except possibly when referring to the nursery rhyme, Faith tried to think when she could sit Emma down and find out what had happened. Both of their schedules were typical New York nightmares. Lincoln was Lincoln Kirstein, the cofounder of the New York City Ballet, and it sounded as if the Beene opening was going to be as luminous as the Milky Way. She wished she was catering it.

"How about tomorrow—lunch?" Emma asked. "It's my Doubles holiday lunch at the Sherry-Netherland and someone canceled at my table."

Faith thought it was extremely unlikely that they would be able to chat about blackmail and murder at the private club's well-known and much-sought-after festivity.

167

"It's always very noisy and gay. Nobody will pay any attention to what we're talking about."

Emma could be right. Faith had certainly been to enough gatherings of this sort to know that people barely listened to one another, let alone a conversation on the other side of a table. The important thing was to see and be seen.

"All right. I can take off for lunch, but I may have to leave early. Meet you there."

"You're an angel, Faith. See you."

Faith wasn't sure what was particularly angelic about going to lunch, but then every encounter with Emma from the very beginning had had unintended and often incomprehensible results, so lunch with the members of the Doubles Club and their guests should be no different.

She decided to call Richard. The idea of going back to her apartment alone was unsettling. Here, with her staff bustling about her, she'd had a hard time keeping Harvey's face from her mind. Home alone, the image of this poster boy for sociopaths would be a waking nightmare. Besides, tonight would be her last free evening for a while, and she might as well make the most of it.

"Got anything special on for tonight? Sweet Richard?" Josie asked as she was putting on her coat. Josie herself was determined to remain unencumbered until she got her restaurant going, but she'd explained to Faith that that didn't mean she had to take any vows. She'd changed from her work clothes and looked terrific in a deep claret-colored velvet sheath that brought out the rosy glow in her warm brown skin. She wore her hair very short—"Don't want to fuss with it," she'd said. It fit her head like a cap, emphasizing her high cheekbones. When she did have her restaurant, she was going to be as much of a draw as her food, Faith predicted.

"If Richard's busy, I may go to a party." People, noise, safety in numbers.

"Go to the party," Josie advised. "Things are getting entirely too intense lately." She raised her eyebrows in an unspoken question—a question she knew Faith couldn't answer.

"You may be right." She'd get dressed up and lose herself in a merry holiday party. It was decided. She could even drop in on the Beene opening. Mother Stanstead wasn't the only one who favored the designer.

But first she tried Richard. Richard *and* the party would be perfect. He was home.

"I left a message for you at your apartment," he said. "Didn't want to bother you at work."

"Bother me. Really. If I can't talk, I'll tell you."

"Okay. Anyway, can I see you tonight? I have to leave town for a few days and won't be back until the weekend."

"I was about to call you." Why was she relieved that he was leaving town? One less thing to think about? Or was it getting harder and harder not to confide in him? Or, she admitted reluctantly, was it that she had no idea how she felt about him and wanted some time apart?

"Nice words. What had you planned to say?"

"The same thing. Except I'm not leaving town."

"Excellent—on both counts."

They arranged to meet at the party and then think of what to do afterward once they were together.

Faith went home and tried on several different outfits before settling on a black velvet coat dress that flared slightly at midcalf. It had a small black lace insert at the bodice. It looked festive and elegant. She pulled her hair back. Richard liked the nape of her neck. He was going out of town for a while. Damn. She was going to miss him, wasn't she? She sprayed on Guerlain's Mitsouko, put on her coat, and went off to the party.

At eleven o'clock, Richard and Faith were walking down Fifth Avenue, which was by no means deserted. There had been a break in the cold spell and the warmth from the day's sunshine seemed to linger in the air. Strolling down Fifth, or any number of other avenues, was one of Faith's favorite things to do. Especially at this time of year, when every window was filled with glittering enticements.

Richard, like Faith, had grown up in the city. It was one of the things they had in common—an unabashed love of New York.

"Where did you go to see Santa?"

"Macy's, of course."

"Of course, but then here at Schwarz's with my grandparents for good measure." Faith didn't think her grandmother had ever been in Macy's—or any other large department store other than Altman's.

At the giant toy store, every day was Christmas, Hanukkah, and your birthday all rolled into one—the one in your dreams. As usual, the windows were filled with outrageous toys—huge stuffed animals, dolls with designer wardrobes, and kid-size working models of their parents' luxury cars.

"I had a car you could really drive." Richard's face was almost against the glass. "Foot power. If you pedaled like hell and were on an incline, you could pretend you were doing five miles an hour."

"Maybe Santa will bring you one of these—except bigger."

"He'd have to bring me a parking place, too," Richard said ruefully.

They walked on, past Tiffany's, the windows bright but empty, the contents resting securely in the vault. A stage set waiting for the principals to arrive. Next was Trump Tower. It looked like a giant Godiva chocolate box. They stopped to gaze past the revolving door into the pink marble atrium. Faith had never seen so many poinsettias—and such enormous ones. But, like those at Saint Patrick's, they went with the place. Excessive, overblown, exorbitantly expensive, it was still a great spot to hang out, gliding up the escalators past the five-story waterfall walls. You could almost convince yourself the brass everywhere was fourteen-carat gold.

Then Steuben. Its curved crystal-clear glass window appeared not to exist at all—fooled you into thinking you could reach in and pluck one of the vases from the display or grab the Excaliber paperweight, complete with sword awaiting Arthur.

"I love New York," Faith said. The city's ineffable magic had momentarily erased all the hideous pictures from her thoughts.

"Did you ever consider public relations? I'll bet someone in the mayor's office would be interested in a catchy phrase like that," Richard teased.

She punched him lightly on the arm she was holding. "You know what I mean."

They walked all the way to the New York Public Library at Forty-second Street, passing the tree at Rockefeller Center.

"Do you skate?" Richard asked.

"I skate," Faith replied.

"Then we'll go skating when I get back." He was, Faith noted, making the tacit assumption that they would keep on seeing each other. They were climbing the library steps. Faith patted one of the stone lions guarding the portals. They had such great Bert Lahr faces. Each had a festive wreath around its neck. Richard was smiling at her. He had a great smile—and the rest of him wasn't bad, either. They had talked about everything and anything, except themselves, and she had no idea if he was getting over a relationship, seeing a lot of other people—although he seemed to be free most nights—or had even been seriously involved before. He was thirty. It wasn't much older than she was if you simply counted the years, yet it *seemed* much older. Thirty. Don't trust anyone over it. That TV show—*thirtysomething*—she'd watched an episode and found it too self-conscious and boring. Too many whiners. But what would she be doing in six years? What would Emma be doing? Going to Washington lunches she didn't want to attend while hubby wheeled and dealed in Congress? Faith devoutly hoped so.

"A penny for your thoughts. Make that a quarter—inflation," Richard put his arms around her. He smelled good—soap, Brooks Brothers spice cologne. It was what her first boyfriend had worn and she was still a sucker for it—and all the heady firsts it conjured up.

"Oh, I was trying to remember which lion's name is Patience and which Fortitude." This had crossed her mind when they'd arrived at the library.

"Can't help you. It's one of those things I've forgotten, if I ever knew—like the words to certain Christmas carols. But I have both—patience and fortitude, that is."

"Where did you get the rest of the Wenceslas verses? Here at the library?"

"I bought a book. It's in my apartment. Want to stop by and sing?"

As a variation on etchings, it was certainly original, and Faith realized she wanted to sing. Wanted to sing very much.

"Baked butternut squash soup with toasted pignolis, butterflied game hens with asparagus risotto, Bibb lettuce and radicchio with pomegranate seeds in a raspberry vinaigrette, cheese plateau, and individual chocolate mousse cakes." Faith had arrived at work early the next morning. The soup was done and she was starting the cakes. The recitation of the menu for tonight's dinner was for Josie's benefit. She'd just come in and they were alone.

"Two questions. Anything else with the hens? Like a chutney? And, more important, where'd you get that glow? 'Cause if it comes in lotion, I want a truckload." Josie laughed. "Never mind. Don't tell, but if it *were* a cosmetic—like those tubes of instant tan—someone would be a billionaire."

Faith tried to look stern and professional. "Chutney's a good idea. We can offer two—one for the firebreathers."

As the morning wore on, she let her thoughts wander. Last night had left her more confused about her feelings for Richard than ever. He wasn't seeing anyone else. Had never been married, but he'd had a five-year relationship that had broken up last summer. It wasn't a tell-all session, to Faith's relief. She'd run as fast as she could from men who insisted on detailing their every conquest—and every heartbreak. For her part, she simply told him she had several good male friends—guys she'd gone to school with, some she'd met since—but she'd never been seriously involved with anyone for too long. As Josie was wont to put it, "I don't hear chimes."

As the morning passed, thoughts of Richard receded and the cast of characters occupying her life, the cast she couldn't mention, resumed their prominent roles. She'd see Lorraine tomorrow morning and ask if she could borrow the manuscript. The earth-shattering tell-all book. It had to be what Lorraine was talking about. It had to be in one of those precious stacks of memorabilia under her window seat. Obviously, there were things in it that freaked out Lorraine. Who and what had been mentioned? There was something sickening about Fuchs sitting at his shaky card table, hammering away at his old Underwood, filling sheet after sheet with his own particular venom. Faith thought of the recent craze for *Mommie Dearest* books. Fox would skewer those hostesses, Poppy for sure, as well as his comrades in the struggle. Politicians, of course, perhaps even his family. Those two cousins at his service—Irwin and Marsha. Maybe they'd taken his sand pail away on an outing to the Jersey shore. Faith had a feeling it was that kind of book. The kind of book a lonely, embittered, disappointed older man writes to get back, to point blame—anywhere but at himself— for his life. Did it mention Emma? Would he do that to his own daughter?

Faith had become convinced that Fox's Marxism consisted mainly of "To *me* according to *my* needs."

He wouldn't have cared what kind of havoc he'd be wreaking after his death—would have positively enjoyed the prospect. If he thought about Emma at all, and possibly he did care for her, he'd have convinced himself that he was doing her a good turn—extricating her from her marriage to a major capitalist pig. Bringing Stanstead down—and who knew how many others in the pages of his book?—was what Nate Fox would have considered a magnificent legacy.

She wondered about his other literary efforts. There had been best-sellers, but in recent years his efforts had barely raised a ripple—a mention in the "Books in Brief" column of the *Times Book Review* at best. It was quite a comedown. Fox had genuinely seemed not to care about money—look at how he'd lived—but he'd cared about fame. And fifteen minutes didn't begin to be enough. He'd had it and wanted it again—even if he wouldn't be around to enjoy it. Envisioning the effect his book would have was enough—mental masturbation.

But what about his agent? Surely he cared about fortune—and fame as a result. The big advance, the multiple printings, the translations, the movie. Faith didn't have a moment to spare to see Quinn, but it was time. Past time. A blockbuster posthumous book—that was money in the bank. Joining some sizable deposits from blackmailing Fox's daughter? But would he be capable of helping his client—a client with steadily dropping sales figures—on his way to push the publication date up? "Agent from hell" was usually an appellation from the publisher's perspective. This might be a new variation. Faith resolved to call Arthur Quinn after lunch and set up an appointment as soon as possible.

Emma had mentioned finding out about Todd Hartley from a bookstore in the Village. Faith took down the Yellow Pages. It was a name you didn't forget. Sure enough, Better Read Than Dead was still alive and kicking. She looked at her watch. She had an hour before she had to meet Emma, and tonight's dinner was under control. She'd be back in time to finish up the rest of their jobs after the luncheon.

"Do you mind if I duck out again?" she asked Josie.

"It's so hard to get good help these days," she quipped, then added, "look, Faith, I know your friend's in trouble, serious trouble, and you can't tell me about it, but whatever you need to do, just do it. I can look after things here."

Faith threw her arms around her assistant.

"When you open that restaurant of yours, I'm going to be there every night with everyone I can think of."

"Once, twice a week will be fine. Now, you go take care of business."

Better Read Than Dead was the type of bookstore Faith loved. It was small, yet the owner had managed to wedge in several comfortable easy chairs and a couch. There were books everywhere and many had little tags on them—"Recommended by Natasha," or "Recommended by George"—which gave a familial feel to the place, as did the large ginger cat curled up in the window. There was no cappuccino, and used books outnumbered new ones. There were no computer terminals. The cash register was original. The woman behind it was, too. She was by Botero—or Rubens. Large, lush in appearance, with a deep gold paisley scarf wound around the neck of her voluminous dark caftan, she wore several strings of amber beads that had become tangled with the glasses resting on her large bosom. Her hair was gray and short. She was very beautiful.

"Looking for anything in particular or just browsing?" she asked. She had a slightly husky voice. Too many cigarettes? She was lighting up now. The voice reminded Faith of something. She couldn't remember now, though.

"Have you got anything by Nathan Fox?"

The woman smiled quizzically.

"I'm doing my thesis on the sixties," Faith lied.

"Oh, that explains it."

Faith bristled. Was it so obvious that the stack next to her bed consisted of *Gourmet, Vogue, The New Yorker,* an Alice Hoffman novel, and a book of Ellen Gilchrist's short stories?

"I had quite a run on Fox the week after he was killed, but I have plenty of books left. Got a good deal on remainders. Take your pick. Five bucks apiece. I got ten the other week, but the demand is down, so I'll give you the regular price."

Faith felt compelled to buy one of each title. Nagging at her was the thought that the key to this whole ugly mess lay in Fox's personality, but she wondered if she'd glean much wading through his rhetoric.

"Did you know Nathan Fox?"

"We all knew Nathan Fox. But this *was* his favorite bookstore—until he became famous and started going uptown." Natasha related this matter-of-factly. If she was bitter, she wasn't revealing it to Faith. "He used to hold court over there." She pointed to the largest easy chair. "I can see him now. You've probably seen news videos. He could hold a room—or a stadium or a park—for hours. But I don't know why you'd want to waste your time on him. He never contributed anything meaningful either to contemporary neo-Marxist political theory or to the movement. Nathan Fox cared about Nathan Fox—not anyone in Vietnam, Cambodia, or all the people killing themselves in dead-end jobs in this country."

Faith wasn't surprised. She had another question, and she asked it obliquely.

"He looks very attractive in the old pictures. He was supposed to have a way with women, in particular."

Natasha laughed. It was deep, throaty, and contagious. "He was a cocksman, if that's what you're getting at. In the beginning, he'd screw anything in skirts, except we were seriously into pants, khaki pants, in those days." She looked at Faith. "And to answer your next question, no, he wasn't my lover, although he would have liked to have been. I started this store with a dear friend. We lived together from the day we met until the day he died last year. Nathan Fox was nothing compared to what I had. Drove him crazy. Then he went uptown—and we didn't see him so much anymore."

So much for solidarity, Faith thought.

"I should put the books in the window," Natasha said. "Somebody's bound to write Nate's biography now. Even before all this, somebody was around last summer asking about him."

"A man or a woman?" Faith asked quickly.

"A man," Natasha answered.

Faith picked up the bag of books. An interesting parcel to check at the Sherry-Netherland, her next destination.

"Did you ever meet somebody named Lorraine in those days?" Faith wasn't sure why she asked this. It just popped out.

"I don't want to talk about Lorraine. It's too sad. Now you'd better go and do whatever it is you do," Natasha said pointedly.

Faith left the store, and looking back, she saw that the woman had flipped the sign on the door to CLOSED.

The red-walled private dining room at the Sherry-Netherland Hotel was filled with poinsettias and pine boughs—and women. The women were greeting one another with squeals of delight. Dress ran heavily toward Adolfo suits in red or green, with Faith having opted for a Betsey Johnson quilted peplum jacket and skirt in soft gray. At the last minute, she'd grabbed a felt hat with roses from Charivari. It was festive.

Emma was waving from her table, and Faith hurried over.

Doubles was a private club and an invitation to one of their holiday lunches was a coup. Fun and famil-ial—without the complications that family events often brought. And Emma had been right: With the buzz of conversation and a spirited performance, complete with sleigh bells, by the West Side Madrigalists, they could safely talk about anything without fear of detection—especially since the seat next to Faith was empty.

The first thing Faith noticed was that Emma was beginning to show the strain of the last weeks. She'd pulled her hair back and her face looked pinched and tired. She was wearing makeup, yet she still looked pale. She was picking at her cuticles again.

Faith had missed the first course and the waiter was serving lamb chops. They looked good—rosy, not overdone.

"How did they get in touch with you? What did they say?" she asked Emma.

"By phone again. Late in the afternoon. After I saw you. It was so quick, I barely had time to take it in. Just, 'Same time, same place. If you don't happen to have the cash, bring jewelry.' Then whoever it was hung up. I was terrified. Michael was home, working in his study. Thank God he didn't answer the phone."

Again a Sunday, at a time when the spot would be deserted.

Emma looked anguished. Faith turned, so that anyone glancing their way would see more of Faith's quilted back than Emma's face.

"It's the hang-up calls. I can't stand them, and now maybe they'll stop. I wrote another note saying this is absolutely the end."

"From now on, if you hear anything at all from them, anything, call me. Leave messages at home and work. I check them all the time. Maybe I should get a beeper."

"Delicious. And so much fun to catch up with everybody. Did you see all those yummy desserts?"

Emma answered quickly—now flushed with the effort—when the woman next to her suddenly remembered her manners and turned to say a few words to the guest on her other side. Having satisfied this social obligation, she turned back to the other conversation, having apparently not noticed Emma's untouched plate or total lack of catching up.

"Eat something," Faith ordered. "And try to smile."

Obediently, Emma the good girl cut off a tiny piece of meat and choked it down.

"What jewelry did you give them?"

"I had the money." Emma sipped some of the white wine at her place.

"The odd ten thou just lying around?" Faith was incredulous. The rich really were different.

"After you told me they probably wouldn't stop, I took some more out—just to be on the safe side."

Emma Stanstead wouldn't be on the safe side unless Faith could figure this all out, but if it made her feel more secure to have stacks of Ben Franklins under her camisoles, so be it.

"I was very careful to notice everything so I could tell you, but there wasn't much to notice. It was a different cabdriver, but I wrote his number down anyway. And there wasn't a soul at the construction site. Luckily, I had the garbage bags left over from the last time."

Lucky, lucky, lucky. Faith sighed. She had to get back to work. This was neither the time nor the place to tell Emma about Harvey Fuchs and Faith's new suspicions about a Harvey-Todd Hartley combo. It was much more likely than anything involving Arthur Quinn. Agents didn't murder their clients. It was bad for business.

"I'm going to hit the ladies' room, then be on my way. Tell Michael everything, please. Get some sleep, and call me." She felt like a physician.

Emma didn't address the first part of the prescription. "I am tired. There's so much going on."

Faith gave her a swift hug and walked across the room. The dessert buffet had been set up on a large round table in the middle of the dance floor. Bird-boned women were circling it, taking "just a taste" of the fabulous-looking concoctions on their plates: St.

181

Honoré cakes, almond tarts, pecan tarts, blueberry crisps, crème brûlées, praline soufflés. Everybody loves dessert.

Poppy Morris was in the ladies' room, reapplying her makeup with a practiced hand. She looked striking, as usual; her suit by whomever was apple green and made all the rest at the luncheon look unoriginal.

"Faith, dear, how lovely to see you. I was going to give you a call after the party. It was wonderful, and I'm so impressed. You're a very clever girl." She patted the low seat next to her and Faith sat down. For a moment, Poppy was intent on her lip liner; then she glanced about the room. Apparently, the sole other occupant, a woman of a certain age applying rouge to cheeks resembling crushed tissue paper, was not someone Poppy cared about overhearing their conversation.

"Emma looks terrible. Do you know what's bothering her?"

Faith had dreaded this moment, predicting it when Poppy had fixed her with her gimlet eye the moment she walked through the door.

"I think she's tired. They go out so much, and she has all these other things—her charity work, political events."

Poppy wasn't buying it. "She's always had those. True, it takes a great deal of stamina to be married to someone in politics, but she doesn't entertain much. It's merely a question of showing up and behaving pleasantly." Clearly, Poppy felt her own role as trend-setter much more demanding—and important.

Faith knew she had to give her something else. Poppy wasn't buying fatigue.

"Well," she said drawing the word out, "I know she's

worried about not getting pregnant." Nothing to hurt Emma in this revelation, and she hoped her feigned reluctance would convince Poppy that this was all that Emma was worrying her pretty little head about.

Poppy snapped her Chanel bag shut. "I knew it! And she simply makes it all worse by agonizing! Not that I'm in any hurry to be a grandmother at my age." She managed to make it sound as if forty were still a speck on the distant horizon.

Faith nodded in agreement. "She told me the doctor said she should relax, but I imagine that's hard when you want something as much as this."

"I don't know why she's having all this trouble. With me, all you had to do was lay a pair of men's trousers across the bottom of my bed and there I was. Not literally, of course."

"It's all right, Mrs. Morris. I know where babies come from. My mother explained it all to me when I was in third grade by using Del Monte pear halves— womb, et cetera. Emma knows, too, because I told her myself."

Faith still remembered their joint shocked wonderment and giggles. She'd never been able to eat those pears again—not that she would now, in any case. *Canned* pears!

Poppy stood up and smoothed her skirt. Once more, she glanced around the room and for the moment, they were alone.

"Michael's going places, and he's the perfect husband for Emma." She gave Faith an air kiss and stepped back. "You know there's nothing I wouldn't do for my daughter—*nothing*." Then she was gone, leaving Faith to speculate about what the hell had just happened.

* * *

Faith went over the scene with Poppy all the way back to work. This was a side Faith had never seen before—the mother lion and her cub. Cubs, if you counted Lucy, but Lucy could more than take care of herself, and Poppy knew it. It was Emma she'd had to go rescue from the commune in the Village, Emma she'd dragged to Dr. Bernardo, and Emma she'd safely married off to "the perfect husband." What did this intensity mean? And why now? What did Poppy know? She'd been at Fox's service and had looked bereft. She and Lorraine had been the only two, Faith noted. But what if Poppy knew about the book, knew that Fox planned to name names? There was nothing she wouldn't do for her daughter. Did this include murder?

Before she threw herself into her work—something she was longing to do—Faith pulled the phone book from the shelf and called Arthur Quinn. He answered immediately.

"Arthur Quinn?"

"This is he."

"Hello, my name is Karen Brown and I'm doing some research on the sixties, specifically on Nathan Fox, for my thesis. I was wondering if you'd have any time to talk with me. I'm hoping to use my material for a biography of Fox."

"Sure, I don't mind helping. What's your time frame?"

"I'm working pretty intensively on it"—she should have said "desperately"—"so, the sooner the better."

"How about tonight? You want to meet me for a drink and we can talk? Maybe a little supper after-

184

ward? I know a great little place on the West Side. Very cozy."

Oh no, thought Faith. Just what she didn't need.

"I'm so sorry. Tonight isn't good for me. How about if I stop by your office tomorrow or the next day?"

"Tomorrow's no good for me. Let's say Thursday. Lunch?"

He seemed determined to make it a social affair. But then meals and doing business are one and the same to agents, Faith reflected. She could be wrong. Maybe he wasn't trying to ask her out. With the weather lately, a "cozy" spot could simply mean he wanted to keep warm.

"Great, but why don't I meet you at your office first? I'd like to see where you met with Fox." What she really wanted to see was what kind of setup Quinn had. How large an agency, furniture by Knoll—or Ikea.

"Better meet at the restaurant. You like deli? We'll meet at the Stage at one."

Didn't the man have an office? And he'd totally ignored her bit about wanting to see where he'd met with his client.

She hung up and gave her full attention to her work—for once.

Lorraine Fuchs had said to come early, and Faith took her at her word. She was heading against the crowd, leaving the city at seven o'clock Wednesday morning. With luck, she'd be back at work no later than nine, and she'd have some new reading material. She let her eyes close. The motion of the train and the sound it made on the tracks was soporific, even though she'd gotten enough sleep for once.

She stopped at a bakery and bought some muffins.

At one time, this section of Brooklyn had been completely Scandinavian, she recalled, but the doughnuts and muffins in the case didn't resemble Danish pastries in the slightest. Still, they smelled good, and Faith firmly believed it was always better to talk about touchy subjects while eating.

Lorraine's street was quiet. No dog walkers. No commuters. She climbed the steps to the front door and pushed the bell. And waited. She pushed again. And waited. She'd been warm enough while she was walking, but now the cold crept through her coat. It wasn't her warm one. That was at the cleaner's.

She pressed the bell harder. It was working. She could hear it ring inside. She should have called, but Lorraine had been specific, telling her to return Wednesday morning. It was Wednesday morning. Besides, Faith hadn't wanted to take the chance of getting Harvey. It wasn't just hearing his voice—although that alone was enough to put her off—but also the thought that he could make things difficult for his mother. More difficult.

Faith leaned over and tried to peer through the front window. She walked around to the side and then to the back of the house. She looked in the back door. The kitchen was immaculate. Either Lorraine hadn't had breakfast yet or had cleaned up immediately. Faith knocked. There was no response. Could the woman be an extremely sound sleeper? Maybe she should find a phone and call. She kept walking around the house. She was by the garage now—and in an instant, she was at the door, pushing it up with all her strength. A motor was running inside.

Lorraine was in the driver's seat, slumped over the wheel. The door wasn't locked, and Faith dragged the woman out into the open air. She was in her night-gown; her hair once again in a neat braid. Faith started CPR immediately, then stopped. It was too late. The woman's face was bright pink, but she was definitely dead.

Eight

"I can't say I'm surprised. Not with the life she led." An older woman in a housecoat with a parka thrown over it was standing looking down at the body in disapproval. She zipped her jacket up. Now it matched her lips.

"Made her parents' life a living hell. They did everything for her. Sent her to college. I'm not one to butt into other people's affairs, but I did say something to Irene—that was her mother. 'Why waste the money? She'll get married. She knows how to type. She can get a job until then. Help you out.' But they were set on it, and now look at her."

Tears of outrage—and grief—spilled down Faith's cheeks. Who the hell was this old harpy? Poor Lorraine. She deserved so much better than this. The saddest part was that the woman was right. Where *had* college gotten Lorraine? She was doing typing jobs at the time of her death. Her death! Had what she'd read in Fox's book been so overwhelming that she'd had to end it all? Or was this "suicide" really murder?

The woman narrowed her eyes. "Who are you, anyway? And what are you doing here?"

"I'm a friend of Lorraine's," Faith stammered in real confusion. "We met at a temp job. We were supposed to have coffee this morning."

"You have a name?" She was leaning over the body now, close to Lorraine's mouth. "Don't smell any booze, but they weren't none of them big drinkers."

"My name is Karen Brown."

"Well, Karen, I'll stay out here with the poor girl and you go call nine one one." She fished a ring of keys out of her pocket, pulled one forward, and handed them to Faith. Faith started off in the direction of the house next door, which she presumed belonged to the woman.

"Not *my* house. Use their phone. We exchanged keys when we first moved in. I took mine back when Lorraine inherited the place. She's got this son, you know."

Faith flushed angrily. What did the woman think? That she was going to case her place while she used the phone? Walk off with her Oneida teaspoons?

She walked unsteadily back to the front door. She'd never seen a dead person before. The odd part was how alive Lorraine looked. Just like the cliché said—as if she were merely asleep. Faith shuddered. Death was something she'd planned to think about when she was much, much older, and until then it could stay crammed way in the back of her mind. But it was going to be very hard to keep Lorraine's still face from creeping forward. Still. The corpse was absolutely still. Not the tremor of a breath, the twitch of an eye. Finally, unalterably, irretrievably still. Faith opened the door with a shaking hand.

The phone was in the kitchen, and after taking a few deep breaths, she dialed 911. The bored voice that greeted her report told her that what was a cataclysmic event in her young life was soon to be just another statistic in a file somewhere.

"An officer will be right there. Don't touch anything."

And that was it.

She hated leaving Lorraine alone with the woman next door, but she had to look for the manuscript. Emma was still alive—for the moment. What if the blackmailer thought Emma knew more about his identity than she did? There were two deaths now, and Faith was certain they were connected. Certain this, too, was murder. For one thing, Lorraine had made an appointment with Faith for this morning and Lorraine was a very conscientious type. The ultimate good girl, despite her illegitimate child and belief in overthrowing the United States government. If she was going to kill herself, she'd do it on a day when she hadn't invited a guest to her home. She knew Faith was coming and that she'd be there early. She'd have intended to offer coffee, not a corpse. It wasn't simply a bizarre question of manners; it was the way Lorraine had lived her whole life—for other people.

But more significant, Lorraine would never willingly have left Harvey. Strange as that might seem to Faith, she knew it was true. Lorraine had been devoted to her son. She wouldn't have abandoned him. And wouldn't a suicide have locked the car doors? To make it that much harder to be rescued?

Keeping her warm gloves on, Faith went into the living room to start searching. She didn't have much time. The police would be here soon and the neighbor would start to get suspicious.

When Faith had last seen Lorraine's collection of Nathan Fox memorabilia, it had been spread out on the floor. Lorraine had grabbed a thick envelope from the top of one pile, which tipped over. She'd scattered it more, pulling at the papers to either side, kicking them. It had been a mess. Apparently, she'd put it all back, but the thick envelope—the one she'd waved about, saying, "I'll show you a book!"—was missing. Faith looked again, but it wasn't there. She made a quick search of the room, lifting sofa cushions, opening the coat closet. Nothing. The kitchen and dining room were the same. It had been a thick parcel, and there weren't too many hiding places. She ran to the basement. It was neat as a pin and bare save for the furnace, a washer and dryer, empty clothes basket, and a few tools on a shelf.

Upstairs, there were two bedrooms and a bath. It was hard to go through Lorraine's pitiful wardrobe, feeling under a stack of well-worn turtlenecks, tights that had been darned, and flannel nightgowns soft with wear. On the bureau, there was a large photograph of Fox and Lorraine, taken many years ago. They both had their fists raised and they were smiling. There was a baby picture next to it, a truly repellent-looking infant, who could only be Harvey. A wedding picture, presumably of Lorraine's parents, was the sole additional object.

Faith felt under the mattress. The bed had been slept in—there was a deep impression in the pillow—but by now the sheets were ice-cold. She glanced involuntarily toward the window. Like Lorraine.

The bathroom yielded nothing save a confirmation of Faith's suspicion that Lorraine had not been aiding in any way what God had given her. Not even lipstick.

The second bedroom in the rear was tiny—room for a single bed and bureau, as well as a small desk and book-case. The drawers were filled with young Lorraine's schoolwork. Papers on the life cycle of the fern and the use of metaphor in *Moby-Dick.* She'd gotten *A*'s. The bookshelf was filled with treasured childhood volumes: *Little House on the Prairie, Misty of Chincoteague, Anne of Green Gables,* and the like. Incongruously, pristine first editions of the works of Nathan Fox were set along-side them. But no unpublished book. The window had eyelet curtains, and Faith felt a stab of pity thinking of the little girl who had lain there reading and dreaming. The only sign that Harvey had ever occupied the room was a Metallica poster taped to the rosebud wallpaper.

Faith was getting angry. She wished Lorraine had never met Fox—or Harvey's father. Again the words "She deserved better" returned—as they would every time she thought of Lorraine Fuchs, Faith realized. Natasha, the owner of the bookstore, had refused to talk about the woman. "It's too sad," she'd said. And she was right.

Nothing under the bed or mattress here, either. A hall closet held linens, a shabby suitcase—empty— and a vacuum cleaner. There was no attic. Faith raced down the stairs, convinced that the manuscript wasn't in the house. She had to get back outside. She'd al-ready been gone too long.

"You took your time." The woman from next door looked at Faith accusingly. She'd dragged a lawn chair from the garage and was sitting next to the body in a crude parody of a summer's day. Lorraine might as well be a sunbather.

"I was looking for an address book, so we could call her son and other relatives, but I couldn't find one."

This was true, and the oddness of it struck Faith even more forcibly out here in the clear light of day. Comrades didn't send Christmas cards, but Lorraine must have had some phone numbers, some addresses.

"He lives in Jersey. Hoboken. But don't expect the brokenhearted son. He's the scum of the earth, that kid. Always has been, but Lorraine would never admit it. 'Too sensitive,' she'd say. 'Misunderstood.' They'd come to visit now and then. We'd all be sure to lock our doors and keep our own kids away from him. Harvey Fuchs never cared about anybody or anything except himself and getting high."

From what she'd seen, Faith was sure the woman was right. A voice nagged at her. What Lorraine knew, Harvey would have gotten out of her eventually, if not immediately. Which included knowing about the manuscript. It was worth a lot of money—possibly in blackmail alone. But he would have had to get his mother out of the way. She would never have let it be used like that. Harvey might have tattoos, but *integrity* had been indelibly stamped across Lorraine's face. Harvey would inherit the house, too, Faith realized. Unless Lorraine had willed it to some politically acceptable group, it would go to her son. Knowing Lorraine, it was probably going to her boy. Were all women this crazy about their sons? Faith hadn't had a whole lot of experience with mothers, and the mothers she knew best all had girls.

The woman continued: "And she doesn't have any relatives. An only of only." She sounded scornful, as if there was something genetically wanting in their bloodlines. "Never saw any friends come to the house, neither. Probably has some Commie friends, but they wouldn't be in the book." She laughed at her joke.

"Communist." She spat out the word. "That's what she was—a Communist." In case Faith hadn't picked up on the allusion.

There wasn't much Faith could think of to say to this.

"Oh?"

"Yeah. Got in with the wrong crowd in college." She made it sound like binge drinking. "Broke her parents' hearts. Bunch of bullshit, if you ask me. There was a man, of course. If he'd a been a Teamster, she'd a learned to drive a rig; a bookie, she'd a run numbers. That was Lorraine."

Faith knew she was right.

"The cops are taking their sweet time, as usual. I'm going in if they don't come soon. It's freezing out here," the woman complained.

"I hear it's bad all over the country," Faith commented. Weather. A nice safe topic, and the nation *was* gripped by the most intense cold in decades. She knew it would take wild horses to drag the neighbor away from the scene, no matter how low the temperature dropped. She was the ghoulish type, someone who not only slowed down to look at an accident but pulled over and stopped.

Faith began to walk up and down to keep warm. She wanted to leave, yet she knew she couldn't. She didn't want to draw any attention to Karen Brown at all, and this woman was sure to point out who had found the body.

"Haven't seen too many, have you? You look kinda sick."

"Not really."

"This is nothing. Harry was so eaten up by cancer at the end that even the undertaker had to look away, but they can do wonders. He was a beautiful corpse. Everybody said so. Of course, my father was the best-looking one. People still mention it to me. So natural, you'd think he would sit up and climb right out of the coffin. People were pinching him to make sure he wasn't being nailed in by mistake."

Thankfully, the police arrived before she could go into further detail—and Faith knew she would have. They got right to work. Another car pulled up. It was the medical examiner. "Bumper crop today," he said cheerfully, buttoning up his heavy black wool coat to his neck.

He waved the neighbor away. She had risen from her chair and had been crouching by his side, next to the body.

She joined Faith, who was standing at the end of the driveway. "Any note?" one of the officers asked.

Faith shook her head. While they had been waiting, she'd ignored the 911 directive and looked in the car, thinking the manuscript might be there, opening the trunk, even the glove compartment. She had, in fact, told the neighbor she was looking for a note.

"She seem troubled lately? Know of any previous attempt?"

Before Faith could say anything, the neighbor took over.

"She's been real depressed since her mother passed—moved in to take care of her—and lately she's seemed worse. I saw her yesterday, and she couldn't keep from crying. Out here on the sidewalk. She's got a bum for a son, and I'm not surprised she took this way out. She didn't have a thing to live for."

The police took it all down and appeared satisfied. They were zipping Lorraine's mortal remains into a body bag, and Faith looked away. Another image that would haunt her for the rest of her life.

The officer turned toward her. "Anything to add?"

"I didn't really know her that well. I think she was a bit depressed, but I wouldn't have said she'd take her own life."

"Well, you really *didn't* know Lorraine, then, did you?" The neighbor snapped. "She's always gone to one extreme or another, and she's done it this time. Maybe she just meant to get Harvey's attention. It would take something like this to get him to even look her way."

Once more, the woman had the Fuchs family to a tee. She told them where Harvey lived and that the last time she'd seen him in the neighborhood had been on Monday. "Rides a Harley. He's hard to miss."

"Where's the key to the house? You called from there, right?" an officer asked.

Faith had given the keys back as soon as she had returned. It was hard not to. The woman had had her hand stretched out. Now she slipped it off the ring and gave it to the police. One of the officers went inside.

"I got to get to an autopsy," the medical examiner said, walking past them on his way to his car. He stopped. "Bring her in, but I don't think there's any doubt here. Carbon monoxide poisoning. Classic suicide." He looked over at Faith with sympathy. "She didn't suffer at all. She got drowsy and slipped away. One of the ones I brought back described it as feeling like all his cares were floating away from him and then he fell asleep."

"If I'd gotten to her earlier, could I have saved her?" She gave voice to the fear that had been plaguing her since she'd dragged Lorraine's body from the car, a shiny 1975 Ford Galaxy that must have belonged to her parents.

The man shook his head. "You would have to have been out and about in the middle of the night. I think she must have gone to bed, felt overwhelmed, and waited until no one was likely to be stirring. Say two, three this morning. Then she went out to the garage. She would have been beyond help of any kind in an hour, hour and a half."

They were taking Lorraine away, and there was no need for Faith to stick around. She was seized by an overwhelming desire to get back home, to get back to Manhattan.

"Is it all right to go now?" she asked. The officer looked weary.

"Yeah, we know how to reach you, right?"

Faith nodded. She had given the false name and an address, and a phone number two digits off from her own. She was certain they would never be in touch. The lies had come easily—at this point, she was even beginning to feel she *was* Karen Brown.

The ride back to the city was interminable. The train lost power several times, with subsequent starts and stops, flickering lights and darkness. It suited the day.

Faith wanted her aunt Chat's party to be perfect. It was a swan song for the fabulous apartment in the San Remo, a swan song for the Manhattan chapter in Chat's life—a lengthy and good read. It was also a swan song for the eighties—this hectic decade where fortunes had been made, lost, and made again. Chat had been a player, a rueful one, but still a player, and she'd sold her advertising agency for a very tidy sum. She'd told Faith she didn't want anything trendy—no kiwi, no sushi, and definitely no quiche. Faith and Josie had decided to do a dinner buffet on a Merrie Olde England theme—except, Faith said, with edible food. There'd be roast beef—it had proved popular at the Stansteads' and other parties Faith had catered—but not overcooked in the traditional English manner. She'd serve it with horseradish sauce or gravy and individual Yorkshire puddings. Chat, a devout Anglophile, was thrilled with the notion and insisted on her two favorites: angels-on-horseback and potted shrimp. She also ordered brussels sprouts. Faith was happy to comply, but for those who wanted their angels (oysters) cold and not wrapped in crisp bacon, she planned a large *fruits de mer* station. Potted shrimp and a large assortment of pâtés were fine, yet brussels sprouts were not what people wanted to see at a dinner party, even sophisticated New Yorkers. She wasn't worried, though. She had a wonderful recipe that never produced leftovers. It was a simple one. The sprouts were steamed until just tender, then quickly sautéed over high heat in hazelnut oil with a dash of balsamic vinegar before mixing them with finely ground hazelnuts. It worked well with walnut oil and walnuts, too.

Josie was all for a suckling pig with an apple in its mouth, but Faith felt that was a bit too Henry VIII and decided to serve Scottish salmon with a light hollandaise for the non-meat eaters. The staff would circulate with a variety of hot and cold hors d'oeuvres. Chat had decreed that champagne and claret cup would be the only libations offered. "If they want anything else, they can go to another party." Faith doubted anyone would, but she resolved to tuck in some British ale and a few bottles of red and white wine. Champagne gave some people a headache.

For dessert, there would be Stilton and pears, as well as a plateau of other English cheeses—Wensleydale, Cheshire, Cheddar, and biscuits. She added several bottles of Cockburn port to the list. Nobody wanted to be bothered to crack walnuts unless he or she was lingering after dinner at a long table in a stately home. She'd made several batches of sugared ones and a few spiced. A spectacular trifle that had taken Josie hours to concoct was waiting in one of Have Faith's refrigerators. It had to be made the day before, and knowing it was there in all its glory was setting Faith's mind considerably at rest. To fill in the cracks, if anyone could possibly still be hungry, they'd done miniature versions of treacle tart, Maids of Honor, Chelsea buns, and, with a nod across the Channel to the Sceptered Isle's ancient enemy, dark chocolate and Grand Marnier soufflés.

"You think people will like it? It's not too theme park? Not too 'Tom Jones takes a bite of the Big Apple'?" Faith asked anxiously.

Josie was quick to reassure her. "They'll love it. People are tired to death of all that Yuppie food—you know, mixed field greens and caramelized rutabagas. After this party, they won't have to gorge themselves on Ring Dings when they get home. And you know how nuts New Yorkers are for anything with the slightest trace of an English accent. Why do you think Ralph Lauren has made it so big with all his *Brideshead* rip-offs? Like his cowboy stuff. Live the fantasy."

Josie's right, Faith thought happily. New Yorkers love anything British. Look at what happens when any of the royals come to town. And she'd grown up hearing her grandmother's friends casually insert little references to "dear Wallis and the duke" into their conversations. The whole country is a sucker for the accent. What was it Hope had said about Adrian Sutherland? That anything he said sounded important because of it?

"Just so long as we don't have to dress up as wenches or wear those tall pointy hats with the scarves drooping out the back," Josie said.

Faith laughed. They'd been working since seven o'clock and it was almost time for her to meet Arthur Quinn for lunch. Josie had tuned the radio to WQXR and they'd been playing Christmas music all morning. The thought of adopting her false identity and plunging back into the dark morass that had opened up when she'd met Emma at the first party was profoundly depressing. She felt truculent. This is Christmas. We're doing a great party tonight. I'm not supposed to be running around trying to solve a murder. Two murders. And blackmail.

She got up and went into the bathroom to change. She didn't have a choice.

"You okay?" Josie asked when she came out.

"Possibly," Faith answered.

It wasn't a day for walking. A light snow was starting to fall and the sky was a dense gray, but Faith got off the bus at Times Square to finish the trip to the Stage Deli on foot. She wasn't claustrophobic, but suddenly she needed to breathe some fresh air—a term used lightly to describe the atmosphere hovering over the city.

She'd come down to the Square a few New Year's Eves when she'd been a teenager, been to innumerable Broadway shows, but had never developed any sort of fondness for the neon sleaze that others were bemoaning now that the redevelopment plan spoken of for years was finally going to happen. Replacing porno flicks and arcades where strung out runaway teens sold drugs or themselves with a visitor's center, new theaters, and hotels didn't upset her in the slightest.

She looked up into the sky. The flakes were getting thicker, falling in a dizzy, random pattern. Who would arrange for Lorraine's burial? She couldn't imagine Harvey taking charge, speaking to a funeral home, selecting a casket, planning a service. The neighbor might. She seemed to have a real feel for death—a mortuary groupie. It upset Faith to think that Lorraine would go out of this world in much the same fashion that she'd lived in it. There was only one way to express it—the woman had been totally screwed.

Yesterday and today, Faith had said several prayers for the dead woman, but she found no ease. She'd called her father and asked that at the next church service he add the name Lorraine to those "newly gathered." "A friend of yours?" he'd asked. She'd answered, "Yes." He'd waited for her to say more and when she hadn't, he'd said, "You know I'm here." Faith had replied gratefully, "I know, thank God." He'd given a low laugh and said, "I do."

Who killed Lorraine Fuchs? As she made her way uptown, her steps fell into rhythm with the words. Who killed Lorraine Fuchs? Who killed Cock Robin? Not I, they all said. She pulled her hat down farther over her ears. Was this matricide? Harvey? Or someone else? Someone so eager to get his hands on Fox's manuscript that he'd kill for it? Someone named in it—or someone who wanted to publish it? Lorraine had been the type who would have blocked publication if there was anything in it that she'd thought would hurt someone—especially herself. Except, Arthur Quinn wouldn't be worried about that, especially since Fox couldn't be sued for libel. But a publisher could. It was all so complicated. And how had the murderer gotten Lorraine into the car? There were no signs of any struggle. The neighbor hadn't smelled alcohol. Maybe an autopsy would show signs of some drug, some narcotic. Or maybe someone had roused her from her sleep with some story to lure her out to her car—a need for help. Harvey could have done that. Except she hadn't been wearing a coat. Yet, if she'd thought Harvey was in trouble, she might not have even bothered with that. Or it could have been removed—with her purse—after she was unconscious. But wouldn't she have tried to get out of the garage, even with the door shut tight? It didn't have any windows. Faith wished she could tell the medical examiner to look at her hands. See whether she'd tried to lift the door. Again, she would have put her gloves on with her coat. Faith sighed. It just might have happened this way. Or some other way that hadn't occurred to her yet. Who killed Lorraine?

She was so preoccupied that she almost walked past the deli. The Stage was on Seventh Avenue at Fifty-fourth Street. It was opposite a cluster of hotels, and when she looked in the windows at the crowd, she wondered how they would be able to get a table—let alone conduct any sort of conversation. She'd told Arthur Quinn that she'd been at the service, so she knew what he looked like. She'd said she would wait for him by the cash register. He came in just after she did.

"Mr. Quinn, hello. I'm Karen Brown." She put out her hand.

Arthur Quinn was short but well proportioned. He had a gray crew cut and those large black glasses frames that were Carrie Donovan, the *Times'* fashion editor's trademark. He looked owlish and very literary, which was probably the effect he was cultivating.

"Mr. Quinn! Come on—good to see you. We have your regular table," said one of the waiters, hailing him. Quinn gave Faith a big grin.

"I come here a lot. They like me."

Quinn's table was for two, a rarity, and wedged in the back, away from the total craziness of the counter. He didn't look at the menu.

"You know what I want," he said to the hovering waiter.

"Yes, and your coffee right away."

Faith had been surrounded by food all morning, yet until now, yesterday's visit to Brooklyn had destroyed her appetite. Maybe it was the smell of all the artery-blocking food coming from the Stage's kitchen or maybe it was adrenaline, but she was ravenous.

"Matzo ball soup and a whitefish-salad sandwich on dark rye—and coffee now also," she ordered, handing the oversize menu back. "And plenty of pickles."

"My kind of girl." The agent beamed. Faith was beginning to like him, too, but it was important to keep her guard up. What did she know about the man anyway, other than the fact that he gave a helluva funeral oration? Faith had friends who'd gone into both sides of publishing. Springing for lunch, albeit not at the Four Seasons, for an unknown with merely the sketchiest idea for a book would have been out of character for the agents Faith knew. They'd have told a neophyte to send a query letter.

"So, you're writing your thesis about Nate—and

maybe a book?" He drank some coffee and his cup was immediately refilled.

"I came across him in some research I was doing on the radical movement and thought he'd be a compelling subject," she lied.

Quinn nodded. "I've always thought he would be, and now more than ever, but if you're seriously thinking of getting something published, you have to work quickly. He won't be hot for long. The public has a very short memory."

Faith nodded and asked, "At the service, you spoke about how long you'd known Nathan Fox and how you met. What was he like at that age?"

Their food arrived. Quinn's regular order turned out to be an overstuffed corned beef on rye with a side of latkes, each the size of home plate. Another waiter brought dishes of applesauce and sour cream for the potato pancakes. "Hold the coleslaw for a while," he instructed. Faith inhaled the strong chicken flavor of her soup and cut into a matzo ball with her spoon. Baseball metaphors abounded at places like the Stage and the dumpling was as large as what Mattingly hit out of the park, but as light as air.

After chewing contemplatively, Arthur Quinn answered her question. "Nate came to see me. No appointment. Just walked in off the street. Got my name from the phone book. As I said, he was a skinny kid, still in college—he stayed there a long time, the draft, you know—yet there was something about him. Something that made you look twice. Intense, sure. But funny, too. He had the first book right there with him— *Blow Up Along with Me, the Best Is Yet to Come*— wordy, but a catchy title, I told him. After he told me what a parasite I was, we shook hands and had a deal."

"It was a best-seller, right?"

"Mega. There wasn't a student in the country who didn't sleep with it under his or her pillow, and the parents all bought it to see what their kids were up to. We made a fortune."

Faith was curious. "What did Nate do with his money? He wasn't underground then."

"No, that came later. Nate was a good Jewish boy, and good Jewish boys take care of their parents. He paid off the mortgage on their house and put most of the rest in mutual funds for them, that sort of thing— bitching and moaning about investing in a decadent system, but they couldn't keep it all in a sock. He rationalized that he was getting back what was owed them. Both his parents sweated at low-level jobs to educate him. He was an only child and he was pretty cut up when they died not too long after he'd done all this. Then he gave everything to an aunt, Marsha and Irwin's mother. The Fox family was very religious. Orthodox, kept kosher. The whole bit. But Nate was a rebel from the start. Wouldn't be bar-mitzvahed. Told them he couldn't do something he didn't believe in, and they respected that, although I know they were upset. His grandfather had written some kind of pamphlet protesting the pogroms and got out of Russia just as the Cossacks were about to bash in his door—and head. Nate grew up on this stuff and identified with him, even though he died before Nate was born. Nate was named for him."

Faith had brought along a little notebook and was scribbling away. Her sandwich arrived. It could have fed an entire Russian village.

"He sounds like a romantic," she said.

"He *was* a romantic—at least when he was young.

In the beginning. And"—Quinn actually winked—"he certainly was one as far as women were concerned."

"I've heard that," Faith said, taking a bite of the whitefish salad. It was smoky, but not too smoky. Delicious.

"You have no idea. The guy was golden. He'd leave one of those demonstrations with his pockets stuffed with women's phone numbers. He was like a rock star. Then the asshole had to go and shoot himself in the foot."

And you, Faith surmised. Out loud, she said, "The holdup?"

"It wasn't much of a holdup. You understand this was the thing to do in those days—redistribution of the wealth, money to fund the revolution, that kind of thing. Maybe Nate was getting bored with his uptown dinner parties. Maybe he wanted to make a big splash."

"Or maybe he really believed in what he was doing?" Faith suggested. She was supposed to be a student, after all. An idealistic one.

The agent laughed. "There's always that possibility. In a weird way, I think he thought he could pull the whole thing off. That he was above the law. He'd still be able to live the way he had been living. He would simply add 'knocking off a bank' to his list of accomplishments."

He turned to his pancakes. The sandwich had vanished. How did he stay so trim? Hours at the gym? Tapeworm?

"Anyway, he botched it. The other two guys surrendered to the authorities, did some time, and live in Jersey now with mortgages and lawns like the rest of the world there. Fox had to be dramatic and disappear. Not that it didn't help sales, at least for a while. He wrote his biggest book—you know, *Use This*—when he was on the run."

Faith had forgotten that Fox had had accomplices. Lorraine had mentioned the driver of the getaway car, too. Were they somehow involved in all this, bearing a grudge against him, perhaps knowing about the tell-all book? But from the sound of it, at least these two were grandfathers growing tomatoes. She filed them away for future thought. She wanted to get Quinn to talk about Lorraine.

"Mr. Quinn—"

"Please, call me Arthur. I'm not that ancient."

"Arthur," so be it, "was Nathan Fox ever married?"

"Not that I know of—and I'd know. For one thing, a wife would have wanted to get her hands on the royalties, and no one ever did. There's poor Lorraine, but they were never married. Too bourgeois."

"Who was she? It could be an interesting chapter." Faith prodded.

"Let's say interesting, but not favorable to Nate. I saw Lorraine at his service, which reminds me that I was supposed to call her. She was a cute thing years ago. Great smile, lots of energy. Didn't age well. Fox used her like a box of Kleenex."

Faith hoped she could come up with less tired similes, then remembered she wasn't actually writing a book.

"Why do you say that?"

He sighed. "Lorraine was the eternal coffee maker. She'd do anything for Nate. Went into hiding with him and must have supported him. I always suspected she arranged for the manuscripts and occasional letters to get mailed to South America somehow. I mean, Fox couldn't exactly walk into the post office when his picture was on the wall. She gave up her whole life for him and he didn't give a shit about her. Thought of her as something he was due, the handmaiden to the great man. She had a kid, not Fox's, though. I remember going to his place once, and she was living there with the baby. First thing Nate said when I came in was that the brat—I think his name was Harold, something like that—wasn't his. Lorraine was all teary and thankful that Fox was letting them be with him. She didn't realize that if he could buy a machine to cook, clean, wash, and occasionally fuck him, she'd be out the door."

Faith concentrated on chewing. It was all she could do to keep from screaming that the woman was dead and shut up. But she had to hear—she had to hear more.

"Kid got in some kind of trouble when he was a teenager. Lorraine called me from a pay phone somewhere and told me she had to have money for a lawyer. Told me to give it to her parents in cash. They lived over in Brooklyn. This explains why the kid never turned Fox in for the reward. Fox must have had something on him. Lorraine, of course, would have died for Fox."

Did die for Fox, Faith thought dully.

Quinn signaled for his coleslaw and more coffee. "Nate used to joke about Lorraine, compare her to all the women he was screwing—and believe me, there was a long list. In her head, they were Lenin and Krupskaya. In his, they were Lenin and, say, that lamppost over there." He pointed out the window.

"Weren't you worried that the authorities would find out about giving her the money?"

"Not by that time. At first, everybody who'd ever had any contact with Fox was under surveillance—

phones tapped. All that stuff the feds like to do. It didn't make much sense. Nobody had gotten hurt. It wasn't like he'd killed a cop or something. He didn't even get any money, but they thought he was involved in some of the other nuttiness of the time—the bomb factories, the whole bit. He wasn't, and after a while they must have figured that out."

"So, it was pretty safe for Fox to start living here?"

"Not as it turned out."

Faith blushed. It had been a stupid question.

Arthur patted her hand in an avuncular way. "I know what you mean. Yeah, if he hadn't gotten himself murdered, it would have been safe. He used to say he'd been underground all his life, but that was before he really was, and I think he regretted losing his freedom."

Faith thought about Emma's wistful remark: "Besides, he did so miss leaving the country."

"At the service, you spoke about a book—one that he said wasn't to be published until after his death."

"Yeah, he'd been writing to me about this one for years now. I haven't gotten it yet. I really have to get ahold of Lorraine. If Fox was in the city, then she was, too. Probably moved back home. If not, her mother will know where she is. She doesn't have to ship overseas anymore. She can just drop it off."

Either Quinn was a consummate actor or he had no idea Lorraine wouldn't be mailing parcels of any kind in the future. Or that her mother had died.

"Why do you think Lorraine has the book?"

"It wasn't in his apartment, and crackheads usually don't take reading material. I'm his executor, and the police have given me a list of everything they took out of the apartment. It wasn't on it. They let me look around, and it wasn't there. Ergo, Lorraine has it—not that any number of people wouldn't love to get their hands on it, from what I understand. Let's simply say he names names." The agent rubbed his hands together in gleeful anticipation of publishers vying for this last, great book.

Faith pressed further. This remark confirmed her suspicion that Quinn knew exactly what kind of blasting powder Fox had used. "Names? What kinds of names? People in the radical movement?" She was fishing.

Quinn tipped his chair back and grinned. An audience—an attractive one.

"Karen, honey. People don't shell out fifteen dollars to read about hippies and pinkos. In his heyday, Nate traveled high, wide, and handsome in this city—and he was always a boy who kept his eyes and ears open. Plus, pardon my crudeness, his pants. I know for sure that one major figure will be heading for a fall when the book comes out."

"Who is it?" If you don't ask, you don't get.

Quinn shook his finger playfully and laughed. "How do I know you don't work for the *Post*? Besides, I don't know myself. I have a couple of guesses from what he'd write to me, but nothing for sure. Honest— on my mother's head."

Faith abandoned this line of questioning. Mother or no mother, he wasn't going to tell her. But at least she had a better idea of what was in the manuscript.

"You said you were his executor, so he left a will?"

"Oh, yes."

Faith was getting more information than she had dared to hope.

Quinn continued. "Nate was very worried that his

name would be erased by the sands of time, and he left a will setting up the Nathan Fox Foundation to edit his unpublished writings, set up an archive at some institute of higher learning. He was savvy enough to know that he'd have to pay to be remembered."

"Dessert?" Quinn asked as a wedge of cheesecake dripping with gory cherries was placed in front of him.

"Just some more coffee, please," Faith answered. Delicious as it was, her meal was beginning to sit heavily—or maybe it was some of what Quinn had revealed that was turning her stomach.

The check arrived, and after a token protest, Faith allowed the agent to pay. Belatedly, she asked him if he'd be interested in her book. That had ostensibly been the whole point of the meeting, hadn't it?

"It's pretty sketchy at the moment—an outline," she said.

"Sure, sure. I'd like first crack at it. Make it a nostalgia piece. That always goes over big. Don't waste time, though. His current fifteen minutes are going fast. Still, could be a Movie of the Week docudrama in it or one of those biographies on cable."

Warhol's fifteen minutes of fame. Fox had had considerably more, but the agent was right. A year from now, few would remember and even fewer care.

On the way back to work, Faith's mind was filled with all the questions she should have asked. Quinn had been voluble, but was it to keep her from asking other questions? Questions about Arthur Quinn? She'd never even gotten him to speculate on who had killed Fox, although his remark about "crackheads" suggested he had bought into the robbery theory—or wanted people to think he had. To preserve her credibility as a possible client, she should have asked him who else he represented, where his office was, what his percentage was. She'd call and suggest another meeting, insistent this time that it be at his office—if he had one.

There was no question that this posthumous book, incendiary or not, would sell better than recent books by Fox. Natasha's bookstore was crammed with remainders, and Faith was sure his titles weren't on the shelves at Barnes & Noble. Quinn seemed so familiar with the manuscript, maybe he already had it and was biding his time, waiting until the investigation into Fox's murder was on a back burner. Maybe Fox *had* been killed in a robbery attempt and then his agent found the manuscript in the apartment. Or maybe Quinn had gotten it from Lorraine—gotten it after turning the key in her car's ignition and closing the garage door. Faith shuddered. How did it all connect to Emma? To the blackmail? How much did Quinn really know about the life of Nathan Fox?

One thing was clear after this lunch—and it wasn't the half-sour pickles faintly starting to repeat on her. What Lorraine Fuchs had learned from Fox's book was that her idol didn't merely have feet of clay, but an entire body—with a heart of stone.

Chat had hired a jazz combo. "I know it's not in keeping with the theme, darling," she told Faith, "but if I hear one more 'Hey, nonny, nonny' madrigal, I'm going to toss my crumpets."

The combo was setting up and Faith took one last look at the room. She'd done pyramids of red pomegranates and dried hydrangea sprayed a glittering gold, trailing heavy satin ribbons from top to bottom—all set in verdigris urns. She'd used yards more of the ribbon on the pine swags and cones dusted with artificial snow that decorated the mantel and doorways. A table in the hall held a simple flat containing dozens of deep crimson tulips—new, pale green grass carpeting the surface of the soil. Chat had a standing order at Mädderlake, and they had outdone themselves for the party with this hint of spring, plus the wonderful overflowing vases of Christmas blooms—from large, lush amaryllis trumpets to tiny, tight snow-white ranuncules—throughout the apartment.

The buffet was Lucullan enough for any Falstaff—its centerpiece a cornucopia of clementines, lady apples, Seckel pears, and holly entwined with garlands of small gold beads. To complete the decor, Faith had filled the large room, which stretched the full width of the spacious apartment, with candles—votives, candles in candelabras, tall, thick altar-type tapers.

Up this high, there was no need for privacy, so Chat's windows were bare, framing views of the city that changed with each passing season, each passing hour. Now the night sparkled—a gleaming white crust of snow covering the park, tiny lights in the bare branches of the trees surrounding Tavern on the Green. Then there were the lights of the avenues, buildings, bridges, stretching as far as the eye could see. The Chrysler Building with its Art Deco curves and the Empire State Building still pierced the heavens, despite the manic building boom on all sides. The Empire State Building sported seasonal red and green lights—gaudy, like the trappings of the city below, always too dressed up to sleep.

The doorbell rang. The combo started playing Coltrane. The party had begun.

Chat was ecstatic. "You're a genius, my sweet. Only

213

twenty or so people have raised what they call my 'defection' or, alternatively, 'the flight to Jersey.' You've turned what could so easily have descended to bathos into a madcap celebration instead! I'm booked until next fall with weekend guests!" Faith knew her aunt had been anxious about the party and the aftermath. The apartment had been sold. There was no turning back. She loved her friends—and New York. She simply wanted to try something different.

Faith thought things were going pretty well herself. No need to mention the pâté that crumbled to pieces when they started to slice it—she had extras. No need to mention the comments made to Faith about Chat's move to New Jersey: "Surely London would be more simpatico—and convenient."

At eleven o'clock, someone suggested they head across town to the Carlyle and catch Bobby Short's show. People started drifting out.

Faith was collecting dirty plates and glasses from Chat's den when her mother walked in. The Reverend Lawrence Sibley had been unable to attend his sister's party. It was, like Easter, his busy time. Faith was sorry. This was the first time her parents would have been at anything she'd catered. Her mother sat down on a large leather couch and patted the cushion next to her.

"Take a few minutes to rest. You've earned it. The food was delicious and everything looked perfectly wonderful. I'm going to recommend you to all my friends and clients." Her mother smiled mischievously. "Nothing like nepotism."

"I wanted it to be very special for Chat." She sat down and looked around the book-filled room, dominated by a large Biedermeier desk. "I'm going to miss this apartment," she said.

"Me, too," replied her mother. She spied a pack of Gauloises someone had left and took one out, looked guilty, and put it back. "I only smoke at parties. You know that."

"Sure, sure," Faith said. "But don't let me stop you. I'm not your mother."

"But *my* mother would." Jane Sibley sighed.

"Granny looked her usual gorgeous self tonight. We're having lunch at Altman's tomorrow. She's got this thing about saying good-bye to Charleston Gardens."

"I'm sure they haven't done this much business in years. It's nice of you to go." Jane lit up, keeping an eye on the door in case her mother suddenly appeared.

"I want to go. Hope is coming, too. What do you think of Phelps?"

Hope and beau had made a brief appearance early in the evening, then dashed off to something Adrian Sutherland had asked Phelps to attend.

"I make it a practice not to think anything of the young men my daughters date."

"Come on, Mom," Faith wheedled.

"Well, he seems a little like people I know who are always holding out for something better—an invitation, job, what have you."

"And in the end they get stuck—like those girls in the dorm who turned down dates early in the week, hoping their Prince Charmings would call on Thursday—of course no one would ever admit to being free if the call came on Friday."

"I remember." Her mother laughed. "And nine times out of ten, they'd end up washing their hair on Saturday night!"

Faith was tempted to tell her mother about Phelps's

request to borrow money from Hope, but it was a moot point now. Hope had come into the kitchen and told her sister that he didn't need the money after all. That he'd had a "windfall."

"I hope she knows what's she's doing, that's all," Faith said.

"Do you?" her mother countered, stubbing the cigarette out in an ashtray.

"Okay, fair enough. Now, I have to get back to work. I don't want to keep the staff."

Her mother put an arm around her daughter's shoulders. "Daddy said you'd lost a friend recently. Who was it?"

This wasn't like telling your mother about getting a bad grade in geometry, or the fight you'd had with your supposed best friend, yet Faith wished she could pour her heart out, as she had on those long-ago occasions.

"You never met her. She was older. Someone I just got to know recently."

Her mother frowned in sympathy. "Heart attack?"

"Something like that."

Jane gave Faith a kiss. "Take care of yourself, darling. I'm going to take Granny home now—if she'll leave the party."

At the doorway, her mother stopped. "I had expected to see Poppy here tonight. She's such a friend of Chat's, but then the life she leads means her time is not her own. I always felt sorry for Emma. You were great friends once."

Why was her mother bringing this up?

"Yes, were—and are. Why did you feel sorry for Emma?"

"Oh, the 'poor little rich girl' thing. She had everything materially, but not much emotionally. It was how

Poppy had been raised, so I suppose she never noticed that the child was starved for affection. Arrests development, you know. I wonder if Emma will ever grow up—even if she is a happily married lady, from all reports." Her mother's intonation gave Faith pause and she set the tray down.

"Have you heard otherwise?"

"Madeline Green was talking to me about an hour ago and asked if I had seen Emma lately. I haven't. She wondered if you had mentioned anything to me, and again I was ignorant. You know Madeline is Emma's godmother and has always looked after her."

"What do you think she was getting at?"

"I asked her, of course." Jane was a lawyer and interrogation of all sorts came naturally.

"What did she say?"

"That Emma had had bouts of illness and was behaving in a rather disoriented manner. She mentioned that Michael is quite worried about her. Madeline wants to take her to some sort of clinic. Part of it is that she's consumed with not being able to have a child. Madeline is convinced that she's worked herself up to the point where she can't, simply from stress. And Emma is getting very thin. Madeline thinks she may be taking some sort of diet pills."

"What she's saying is that she thinks Emma is on drugs and/or anorexic," Faith fumed, any kind thoughts she'd cherished in the past about Emma's godmother vanishing like Cinderella's coach. "I've seen quite a bit of Emma lately. You know I catered a party for her, and she and Michael have been at other events I've done. She invited me to one of the Doubles lunches."

"Oh, what fun. I went on Monday. Don't get angry, Faith. I wanted you to know what people are saying.

Perhaps Emma is depressed. Infertility is very, very hard on a woman."

"Please do me a favor. When you hear things like this, especially anything to do with drugs or an eating disorder, deny it on good authority."

"The good authority being . . ."

"Me. I can tell you with absolute certainty that Emma is not on drugs, purging, or more than normally depressed about their inability"—Faith stressed the word *their*—"to get pregnant."

"Thank you. I was sure you'd know." Her mother left, leaving a Gallic mélange of Arpege and Gauloises hanging in the air.

Emma disoriented—clinically depressed. Emma on drugs. Faith piled dishes noisily and crumpled napkins that had been tossed carelessly about. It was totally un- thinkable—wasn't it?

Nine

This was a new thought. An insidious thought. Could Emma have made the whole thing up? Faith's head ached. She had sent her staff home, then stayed at Chat's, drinking champagne with her aunt and a few of her closest friends. Now she was trying to find a cool spot on her pillow, turning it over and over. Images from these last weeks were tumbling, too—spinning about in her mind like numbered lottery balls before the drawing. Yes, she'd seen the blackmail threats, but there was a computer and printer in the apartment, tastefully enclosed in an antique secretary in Michael's study, his home office. Easy access for Emma. And the telephone calls. Emma had deleted one phone message and taken the next call herself Faith had only Emma's own reports of all the hang-ups. She'd dropped off the cash herself—alone. Feeling slightly feverish, Faith turned on the light and got up. The inside of her mouth was all fuzzy. She panicked. What if she was coming down with something! She couldn't be sick now! Advil and Pellegrino—that's what she needed. She hadn't had that much to drink. Maybe her body was trying to tell her something. Something like slow down. Well, she could do that in 1990. Not now.

She was hungry, too. That was what this was—a hunger headache. She hadn't had the time, nor inclination after that big deli lunch, to eat much. She opened her refrigerator, which, unlike those of her peers, who either ate out or dialed in, contained real food. She grabbed some Gruyère, Westphalian ham, butter, and mustard—moutarde d'ancienne from Fallot. Grainy, spicy, the essence of Dijon. Soon a croque monsieur, the French version of a grilled cheese sandwich, was in the frying pan. Either the Advil had kicked in or simply the smell of food was enough. Her headache was almost gone.

But why would Emma concoct this whole thing? Faith put the sandwich on a plate and poured some more mineral water. The cheese had melted and the outside of the sandwich was crisp and golden. No, Emma hadn't made this all up. Faith thought of Lorraine's body being zipped into the bag by the police. She pictured Emma's fearful face. This whole thing was not the product of an overactive imagination or a disturbed psyche. It was, unfortunately, only too real.

Christmas was only three days away. It fell on a Monday this year, which meant all the parties, especially office parties, were over. Have Faith had a large luncheon on Saturday, a smaller dinner that night, a number of take-out orders and platters, but no more big events. Faith was making supper for her own family on Christmas Eve, before the eleven o'clock service. Chat and her grandmother would be there. Hope said she might be bringing Phelps. Christmas dinner the following day would be bigger. Besides relatives, there were always extras—people in the parish who had nowhere else to go. Over the years, they had become family, too.

There was always this lull in the city before New Year's. The streets belonged to the tourists who poured in from all over the globe to gaze up at the tree, see the Rockettes at Radio City, and stand in line to get into Mama Leone's or the one remaining coin-in-the-slot Horn and Hardart Automat on East Forty-second Street. Poppy Morris's crowd headed for balmier places with white sand or colder ones with fresh powder—making sure they were back in time for the right New Year's Eve celebrations. Faith had three parties that night, fortunately all on the West Side. She planned to dash between two of them, leaving Josie in charge of the third. Then she was closing to give everyone a break. She'd be busy overseeing the move.

At work, they had already started to pack up some of their equipment. When Faith arrived after an early lunch with her grandmother and Hope, Josie was busy dividing utensils—those they'd need over the next week and those they wouldn't.

"Are you sure you don't want to go home for Christmas?" Faith asked. They'd been through this before. "You could leave tomorrow morning—or tonight even."

"I know I'm expendable, but I want to go the week after and stay. My family is all excited because they're going to get two Christmases this way. Besides, I want to have a good long talk with your mother. Does she know the hours you keep?" Josie was coming for Christmas dinner.

"Just what I need, an industrial spy," Faith commented wryly.

They spent the rest of the day packing and preparing the luncheon and dinner for the next day. The menus were simple. For the lunch, they'd start with fennel soup garnished with pomegranate seeds, then a Scandinavian recipe Faith had picked up for a fish mousse with shrimp sauce, followed by a variation on that old New York favorite, Waldorf salad [see the recipe on page 281], or a simple mixed green salad, and for dessert, mocha buche de Noël. For the dinner, she was preparing a reprise of the roast beef that had been so popular at the Stansteads' and Aunt Chat's.

"I don't know if I can make another meringue mushroom. These French logs are getting on my nerves," Josie complained. "Why don't we give them some sweet potato pie instead? I have a great recipe—laced with a little bourbon. Give the guests a kick."

"I know what you mean," Faith agreed. She had no idea the rich French pastry would prove so popular, but when New Yorkers adopt something, they adopt it wholeheartedly, and this year it was buche de Noël. "Write down the pie recipe. I'll make some for Christmas Day."

"*I'll* make some—and the oyster stuffing for the turkey, " Josie said. "But not now. Got a date. What are you doing tonight?"

"I'm not sure," Faith said. She'd been feeling edgy all day. Her headache last night had not been a precursor to any illness, but it did presage a kind of malady of the soul. She couldn't get Lorraine Fuchs out of her mind, couldn't get away from the feeling that she had failed—and was failing—the woman. And all day, she'd been worried about Emma. Obsessively wondering what was going on. She couldn't call when Josie was there. She was also missing Richard. Or someone like Richard. She should be going out tonight, but when she thought of possible substitutions, she lost her enthusiasm.

"Your honey not back yet?"

"No." Faith managed a smile. This was ridiculous. She'd call a friend, take a pin, and stab at the huge list of holiday concerts and plays in the *Times*. A few days ago, she'd been bemoaning her lack of time to indulge in holiday gaiety, and here at last was an opportunity to revel in the season. Revels. Maybe she'd go to the Christmas Revels.

"You can come hang with us," Josie offered.

"You're a sweetheart, but I have some more things I want to do here. Then I'm going to make some calls and go out. Don't worry."

"I'm not, but . . ." Josie frowned.

"But what?" Faith asked.

"Take care of yourself. That's all."

The first call Faith made when her assistant left was to Emma. She wasn't home, but Faith left a message, telling her she was still at work and to call back there or try at home. Next she tried Richard on the off chance that he was back. She didn't leave a message.

The sheets of packing paper they'd been using were piled up on the stainless-steel work area and Faith took a pencil from next to the phone, sat down, and started idly listing names: Emma Morris Stanstead, Michael Stanstead, Poppy Morris, Jason Morris, Lucy Morris, Nathan Fox, Arthur Quinn, Lorraine Fuchs, Harvey Fuchs. She paused. Todd. Todd Hartley. Natasha from the bookstore in the Village. Husky-voiced, exotic Natasha. Husky-voiced. One of Emma's messages had been high-pitched, one deep. Who else? Fox's cousins—Irwin and Marsha. Adrian Sutherland. Phelps Grants. She wrote "Emma" in the middle of the big sheet of paper and began rewriting the names, grouping people around her in constellations. Michael, Adrian, and Phelps. Poppy, Jason, and Lucy. Faith drew a line from Lucy to Adrian. Nathan, his cousins, Quinn, Lorraine, and Harvey. She drew a line from Nathan to Poppy. She put Todd alone. Natasha alone. Emma in the center, Emma the common denominator. Faith stared at her work, trying to think of more lines to draw. Everyone connected to Emma, but what were their links to one another?

The phone pulled her from her speculations. It was Emma.

"You do work terribly hard, but I suppose cooking all those things takes quite a bit of time," Emma said.

"Yes, it does." Faith knew that neither Emma nor her mother before her had ever so much as made a peanut butter and jelly sandwich. Poppy's onetime s'mores had been an aberration, obviously, and quite amazing.

Faith continued. "Just checking in. You've been on my mind a lot today." She hadn't told Emma about Lorraine Fuchs's death—or her meeting with Arthur Quinn. There was no point.

"I'm sorry we couldn't come to Chat's party. I'd hoped we could get away early and drop by, but things are getting very hectic. Michael's decided to announce his candidacy the first week in January, so when we're not out, he's buried in his office here with Adrian and these other people. That cute guy who was with Hope at our party has been here a lot. He seems nice. At least he smiles a lot. You can't imagine how much the apartment smells like cigar smoke."

224

The new Boss Tweeds. Faith had a sudden irreverent image of the Thomas Nast cartoons updated. Make that Hugo Boss.

"Why don't you come over and have a cup of tea? We always seem to be meeting so frantically. I don't have to go anywhere until after six—and that's just around the corner on the next block. The man came and put the tree up today. It looks lovely."

The idea of sitting in Emma's beautiful living room, tree or no tree—and what man, Saint Nicholas?—was very appealing. I'll decide what I want to do from there, Faith told herself as she accepted the invitation.

Faith decided to take the bus uptown, then walk to Emma's. She had by no means had her fill of window-shopping. Plus, she still had a few more presents to buy. She wasn't sure what to do about Richard. He'd said he would be back before Christmas—and his family lived in the city, so she was sure he would. It would be awkward if he had something for her and she didn't have anything for him. It would be *very* awkward if she had something for him and he didn't have anything for her. On Madison, one of those toy stores that's really for grown-ups had a window filled with snow globes. She went in, attracted by one that had the city in miniature, even a tiny yellow cab. The proprietor took one from the shelf and handed it to her.

"It plays 'New York, New York,' " he said.

Faith wound it up and shook it. The hokey song was perfect. A blizzard of artificial flakes swirled and fell into a heap. She shook it again. Richard would love it.

By the time she got to Emma's, it had started to rain. And she wasn't dressed for it. Her warm waterproof coat was still at the cleaner's. She hadn't had time to

225

pick it up, and now it looked like it might stay there until spring. She looked around for one of the umbrella salesmen who mushroomed forth at the hint of moisture, but there wasn't a single one in sight. She had about five of these collapsible black umbrellas, but they never did her any good when she needed one, shoved to the back of the closet as they were. The rain began to come down harder. Her hat was plastered to her skull, and whatever her plans for the evening turned out to be, home and a hot shower would be first. She sprinted into Emma's building, almost colliding with the doorman, who was hastening to greet her with an open oversize umbrella.

"Too late, Bobby!" she exclaimed.

He shook his head sadly. If only I'd been at her side at the ready when the first drop had fallen, his expression said. "You're wet right through. Now, you go up and I'll let Mrs. Stanstead know you're on the way."

The doormen were all sweethearts in this building—and Faith was sure it wasn't just because the Stansteads tipped well.

Emma was at the door. "Come in and get dry. Tea's ready—or a drink, if you'd rather."

"I'll start with tea," Faith said. She stripped off her sodden coat, and miraculously, her clothes were mostly dry. She followed Emma in. The fire was a welcome sight and she went over to stand in front of it as she admired the tree.

It was real and the room smelled of balsam, not cigar smoke. Yards of gold and silver beads wound around the boughs. Clear glass balls that looked like shimmering soap bubbles reflected the tiny white lights strung from the top of the tree to the bottom. The only other decorations were the Alice in Wonderland figures from the Gazebo, made by Gladys Boalt. Each cloth character was a work of art—small figures with intricately fashioned garments and hand-painted features. The White Knight, pensive and be-whiskered, rode close to the star near the ceiling, his eccentric accoutrements in miniature suspended from his saddle.

"Emma!" Faith cried in admiration. "Your tree is incredible."

Emma was pouring tea. "I began buying the Alice in Wonderland ornaments when I was in college—as treats. Michael gave me all the ones I was missing the first year we were married. I like to think of them as the Met's Neapolitan figures of the future."

"And so they are," Faith agreed, examining the caterpillar's tiny hookah and the dormouse in a teapot carried by the March Hare.

By tacit agreement, the two friends talked of nothing but the season. Emma had bought Michael a new car, a 325 i, the BMW convertible—black. "I know it's kind of boring, but he'll love it—and be surprised. He thinks I'm getting him a smoking jacket from Charvet. I let him find it. Men are such little boys about presents."

Faith showed her the snow globe. Emma liked it so much that Faith resolved to go back and get one for her.

Before they knew it, it was six o'clock.

"I wish everything I did could be as nice as just sitting here like this," Emma said wistfully. "So cozy. So normal."

"I'm assuming if you had anything to tell me, you would have," Faith said, hating to destroy the mood.

Emma nodded. "I really think it's over—at last."

Faith desperately wanted to believe her—and knew she didn't.

"You can't wear this. You'll have to take one of mine," Emma said, hanging Faith's coat back in the closet. "You can get it when you're over this way sometime. Here. This will do." She took out a fur-lined raincoat from Searle. It had a hood and was appropriately scarlet. Emma had worn it to the luncheon the other day.

Faith was about to ask for something simpler, something cheaper, but just as Emma never had to buy an umbrella on the street corner, she wouldn't have a Burlington Coat Factory special, either.

"Thank you. I'll take good care of it and bring it back tomorrow."

"Don't be silly. I've been wearing it so much lately, I'm tired of it. Keep it as long as you want."

"Call me?" Faith asked.

"I promise," Emma replied.

Descending in the elevator, Faith thought about how her hugs with Emma had progressed from swift affection to this last one, a kind of bear hug, each one intent on reassuring the other—reassuring and comforting.

Outside, the rain had let up slightly, but there was enough for Faith to be grateful for the hood on Emma's coat. Damn, she had meant to give Emma back both the key to Fox's apartment and the key to this one, which Emma had given her for the party preparations. She'd do it when she returned the coat.

Halfway down the block, she looked over her shoulder and noticed a dark car pull out from across the street near the intersection, switch on its high beams, and accelerate. Parking on her side was forbidden at this time of day and there weren't any cars.

No one wanted to chance a stiff ticket, or worse—the boot. She walked faster, feeling irrationally nervous at the way the car had now slowed down, slowed down to her speed. Suddenly, it swerved up onto the sidewalk and aimed straight for her. She screamed and tried to run toward the building, but the car cut her off, blinding her with its headlights, chasing her into the street. The surface was slick and shiny from the recent downpour. She ran as fast as she could, but there was no escape. Her heart was pounding and the cold night air stabbed her lungs as she fought for breath. She could feel the heat of the engine. If she reached her arm back, she was sure she'd be able to touch the hood.

I am not going to let this happen, she thought. I am not going to die this way!

She plunged to the right and back up on the sidewalk. The car followed, taking down a small tree girdled with wire mesh. If she could just make it back to the Stansteads', but the car cut off her retreat. All the surrounding buildings were town houses. No doormen. No open doors. It was all happening so fast! She couldn't think. Her heel caught in a crack in the sidewalk. She stumbled and her shoe came off. If she fell, she'd be dead. She kicked the other away and splashed on through the icy puddles.

The car bore down upon her. She had only one chance. With a last burst of speed, she raced directly in front of it, crossed the street, and rolled between two parked cars, inching her way under the first one.

Brakes squealed. The car stopped. For a moment, she thought the driver would bash into the parked cars, or worse—come after her on foot. She shut her eyes tight, waiting for the slam of a car door. Waiting for a hand to reach out and grab her. Waiting for a hand with a gun. Nothing. Then it sped off. The driver. The killer.

She lay in the filthy runoff, eyes still closed, panting. There had been only one person in the car. She'd been able to see that much. It looked like a man, but a man with long hair. A man like Harvey Fuchs.

"I slipped and fell," she spoke before the bewildered doorman could voice his alarm.

The elevator rose slowly. Emma's coat would never be the same. Nor would Faith.

Emma opened the door in surprise. She was in her slip.

"Faith! What—"

"Someone just tried to kill me with a car. Tried to kill me, thinking I was you."

Emma in the distinctive Red Riding Hood coat. Emma the real target.

"Me? Kill me?" Emma looked as if she was about to faint. She sank onto the seat of a Thonet chair set against the wall.

"I had the hood of the coat up, so whoever was driving must have assumed it was you. We're about the same size, and I was coming from your building." The adrenaline that had flooded Faith's body as she had fought for her life still coursed through her body. She was standing in her stocking feet, numb with cold, dripping dirty water onto one of the Stanstead's Oriental rugs, but she felt as if she could take on a tiger or two. She was alive. She had saved herself. Now she had to save Emma, save her from herself, save her from the forces of evil. Faith tossed off the scarlet coat, letting it fall in a heap on the floor.

"Emma." She tried hard not to shout. "Emma! This is very, very serious now. It's not just Christmas cards and Dumpster drops. They tried to *kill* me—that is, you! Maybe the idea was just to scare you, but I don't think so. These are not people we should be dealing with alone anymore. All bets are off. Your father was murdered—and they're trying to get his daughter! Yes, it's going to cause some very unpleasant publicity in the short run. But the point is the long run. The point is being around! You *have* to tell Michael—and the police!"

"Michael. Michael will be waiting at the party and wondering where I am. I have to get ready," Emma jumped up and looked about the hall wildly, as if expecting her husband to emerge from the closet.

"Haven't you heard a word I've said? Emma, I know this isn't something you want to think about, but you *have* to—there are no choices anymore!"

Faith was overwhelmed by depression and fear. The adrenaline began to ebb. She wanted to go home. Get cleaned up and pull her quilt over her head for a long winter's nap. Granted, Emma was crazy in love with her husband, but what use would she be to him dead? She'd told Emma the truth. Faith was positive the driver hadn't meant to inspire fear—though it had succeeded. He meant murder. They must think Emma knew something she didn't—or didn't know she knew.

She followed Emma into the bedroom, leaving little wet marks on the carpet as she padded after her. At the moment, she didn't have the energy to both reason with Emma and think about getting dry.

"Look, if Michael had any idea that you were going through something like this and not telling him, how do you think he'd react? He's your husband, for God's sake! Somebody's not just blackmailing you now! He'd want to protect you, save you! Men are like

231

this—especially about their wives!" Faith knew she was ranting, but her words seemed to have little effect on Emma, who was zipping up her dress and slipping into her shoes, apparently oblivious of her friend—and the fact that she had put on a Versace white linen shift more suitable for Portofino in July than Manhattan in December. She seemed to be in a dream. Drugged, but Faith was sure it wasn't pharmaceutical. It was Emma's own particular drug. She'd simply shut down.

Faith grabbed her shoulders and sat her down on the end of the bed.

"Emma, you've got to listen to me!"

Emma's eyes—so startling blue, deep blue like a sea of scilla in spring—focused on Faith's desperate expression. "I *have* heard you, but I don't want to. I can't think about all this. It can't be happening."

Faith sat down next to her. "But it is," she said softly. "Tell Michael. Start there. Tell him tonight, when you come home. Tell him everything."

There was a long silence and Faith wasn't sure she'd gotten through; then Emma stood up and walked to her dressing table.

"I'll tell him about the blackmail, about getting pregnant when I was a teenager." Emma's voice sounded surprisingly resolute. She stood looking in the mirror. Faith could see her face: Her lips were pursed and she was frowning with the intensity of her resolve. She picked up a silver-backed hairbrush with her monogram. "But"—she smoothed her hair back with several swift strokes—"I won't tell him about Nathan Fox. Not about my father. I can't do that to him. If I get another threat, I'll tell them I've told Michael all about it and let them assume it's everything."

"Are you sure—"

She cut Faith off. "It's a chance I'll have to take." She put the brush down and faced her friend. "The worst part is thinking that you could have been killed. That's what I can't face. It was supposed to be me, and if anything had happened to you, I could never have lived with myself. Every step of the way since this has started, you've been with me, and maybe I've done a lot of things wrong, but you have to believe that I thought I was doing what was right. What was right to protect my husband. I never thought it would end up like this. End up with you almost—" She gave a short sob. "Oh, Faith, weren't we little girls just yesterday? Doesn't it seem that way to you? If I had known what was going to happen, I'm not sure I would have wanted to grow up."

"We were and you did—admirably," Faith said firmly, although she'd been having the same feeling. "But nothing happened. I'm fine. And we'll be fine. We've come this far . . ."

Emma wiped her eyes with the back of her hand. "And we'll see it through." She looked at Faith's feet. "You don't seem to have any shoes on, and I'm afraid to give you anything that might connect you to me, but shoes are shoes. The coat was different. No one knows you've been involved in all this, and I swear that no one ever will, as long as I live." Emma *did* look like a little girl now and Faith had a sudden vision of a long-ago secret club, another oath. Yes, they were all grown up, but the rules were the same.

Emma was rummaging in her closet, pulling out shoe boxes. Faith was waiting for the right moment to tell her that she needed to grab another outfit for herself, as well.

"Tonight. This can't go on. There's no question. It's

just drinks—the thing I'm meeting Michael at—and I'll make dinner reservations for us afterward. Michael's been complaining that we haven't had any time alone together for ages, so I'll surprise him."

Surprise him, yes, Faith thought. Telling Michael part of what was going on was better than nothing—it was a start—and she was sure he wouldn't stand by while his wife was being blackmailed. Maybe Emma was right. Maybe they would assume she'd told him everything, especially after tonight. She'd be frightened enough to do anything.

Emma handed Faith several boxes of shoes. "Try these. We'll go to the Post House. Michael likes it."

Faith had retrieved Emma's coat from the hall and was holding it up, examining the damage. It had kept her warm and dry, but it needed a dry-cleaning wizard now. Emma snatched it from her on her way to the bathroom. "Juanita knows some super dry cleaner. But I don't think I want to wear it again." Nor did Faith.

The Post House. A good choice. Faith believed it was always better to reveal potentially explosive or emotional information in a public setting, where presumably good breeding will prevent too crazed a reaction. She'd broken up a number of times this way. The Post House was one of New York's newer temples to beef and already was very popular. Michael would be surrounded by any number of men he knew, all ordering enormous and expensive slabs of meat. It was a place where guys like Michael Stanstead felt at home. Maybe Emma was a better politician's wife than she appeared.

"All set. I made reservations for nine o'clock." Emma blushed slightly. She was in her slip again and reaching for a simple long-sleeved black jersey dress.

Apparently, the mirrors in the bathroom had reflected dress white, the fairest in the land, but better off in black for now. She was snapping a simple gold cuff bracelet around her slender wrist. "There's a phone in the bathroom. Michael—"

Faith finished for her, "likes it." They both laughed, but it was nervous laughter. Emma glanced out the window. The rain had stopped. But neither woman really wanted to go outside.

The phone was ringing when Faith got out of the shower. She had taken a cab home. Walking into the apartment, she'd shed garments as she made a beeline for the shower, then stood under the hot spray, trying to think of nothing but the warmth seeping into her bones. After a while she began to come to. Had she been in for a half hour, an hour? She'd lost all sense of time. She'd turned the water off, reached for a towel— and the phone rang. For a moment, she considered letting the machine get it, but she flashed on Emma.

In the street, outside Emma's building, Faith had lived the seconds of her attack all over again—and again. She'd seen one of her shoes, but nothing on earth could have made her pick it up. She'd insisted on dropping Emma off at her cocktail party, over Emma's protests that it was only on the next street. Faith had extracted a promise from her that she wouldn't go out alone—anywhere.

She hastily pulled her terry-cloth robe on and lunged for the receiver, hitting her shin on the corner of the bed in the process.

"Hello?"

"Faith, great! I thought you'd be working or out. I just got back, and my agent has sold the book! Please,

please come celebrate tonight. If you have a date, break it!"

It was Richard.

Faith didn't believe in playing games, yet she also didn't believe in appearing too available.

"My plans for tonight aren't definite. I think I might be able to make it." All of which was true. She was elated. Something good happening to somebody. This alone was cause for celebration. She very much wanted to go out—and, she admitted to herself, she very much wanted to go out with him.

"Fantastic! The sky's the limit. You pick."

Faith didn't have any trouble choosing.

"Let's go to the Post House."

"You're a quixotic woman, Faith Sibley. I would never have predicted this as your kind of place. Bouley, yes. The Quilted Giraffe, of course. Le Bernardin, absolutely. But a steak house—albeit a very plush one—no."

Richard was sitting across from Faith, sipping a very dry martini. He was ebullient, and the small amount of alcohol he'd imbibed didn't account for the one-hundred-kilowatt glow suffusing his face.

"Major milestones call for drama, and what could be more ostentatiously dramatic than this place? The steaks are the size of a turkey platter and we're surrounded by power brokers, movers and shakers—fitting for an incipient best-selling author. Here's to you—and the book." Faith held her glass aloft. She was drinking a kir royale and planned to have at least one more. Then maybe she'd be able to concentrate on Richard and not keep seeing headlights bearing down upon her. "What's the title—or can't you tell yet?"

"My agent wants to keep it all very hush-hush. Make a big splash by teasing the public with ads in the weeks before it comes out. Who is so-and-so? What southern town will never be the same again? That sort of thing." He was clearly enjoying himself. "But what I can tell you is it's a story of good and evil. Of being tempted—and yielding to temptation."

"Sounds very Faustian—or biblical. Maybe you can work Eve into the title—or the apple."

"Or the serpent." Richard laughed. "Plenty of snakes down in that neck of the woods. Not too many apples. Not like here. Not like the Big Apple. The biggest, reddest temptation known to man or woman. If you can't fall here, you can't fall anywhere." The martini was loosening his thoughts—and tongue.

"I couldn't wait to get back and tell you, Faith. When I've finished the manuscript, will you read it?"

"Of course. I'd be honored." And she was. She had a sudden vision of herself married to a great author. Shielding him from his adoring public so he could write undisturbed. Making his favorite foods, coaxing him from the black despair of writer's block. She drained her glass and caught the waiter's eye for another.

Wait just a minute! a voice inside her head cried out. Handmaidens to great men! Think of poor Sophia Tolstoy. Dorothy Wordsworth. Lorraine Fuchs.

"Want to order?" Richard asked. "I'm starved."

Faith wasn't very hungry, but she wanted to stretch the meal out. The Stansteads were nowhere in sight, but it was only quarter after nine. Richard and Faith were not in Siberia, but not at an A-list table, either. Still, it commanded a good view.

"Mixed grill—rare; baked potato—butter on the

side; and Caesar salad—do you want to share one?" Faith asked Richard.

"Sure, I love anchovies. Let's see. Think I'll go for the prime rib—make that medium rare—sorry, Faith, I know that's overdone—and baked potato with butter and sour cream—not on the side. How about shrimp cocktails first? We're celebrating, remember. Plus, we might as well go the whole nine yards if we're going to have this kind of meal. I plan to have cheesecake for dessert, if I can manage it."

Faith agreed. She hadn't had a shrimp cocktail in years. It had been Hope's favorite as a child and the only thing she would ever eat when the family went out.

"And the wine list, please," Richard added.

When it arrived, he turned it over to Faith. "You pick. Until recently, springing for a bottle of Blue Nun meant I had a serious date. I tend to stick to beer—sometimes even imported ones."

"Have a beer, then, and I'll have something by the glass."

"No, pick something. Something French. Something red. I know that much."

Faith ordered a Gigondas—it was big and oaky enough to stand up to the food—and sat back. The Stansteads had just walked in and were being shown to their table. It wasn't close enough for Faith to overhear anything, but when they were seated, she could see Emma's back and Michael's face, so long as the people at the tables in between didn't lean the wrong way. The Stansteads didn't see her and Richard was facing away from their table. Would Emma plunge right in, or wait for postprandial complacency?

The shrimp were enormous—and tasty. Richard was

regaling Faith with tales of different assignments. It should have been a great evening.

By the time their main courses arrived, Faith could see that Michael was holding Emma's hand. His arm was stretched across the table, snaking around the bread basket, and he was looking at her with a complicated expression of love and sadness. Obviously, Emma was letting the cat out of the bag—or a few whiskers. Faith couldn't see Emma's plate, but Michael's food was getting cold. A waiter appeared to pour more wine and Michael motioned him away. He was looking at his wife intently. Faith stopped chewing. Michael put his other hand over Emma's. It was hard to tell at this distance, yet Faith was pretty sure there were tears in his eyes.

"So then I asked Prime Minister Kaifu—Faith, are you okay?"

"What? Yes, sorry. I got a little preoccupied there for a moment. Tell me about the Japanese prime minister," she said, resuming normal functions, savoring the really excellent meat, done perfectly. It wasn't going to be hard to prolong the meal. She was taking very small bites.

Faith liked to have her salad after her main course, European style, but in deference to the setting, she hadn't said anything, and it arrived with much aplomb. Like the rest of the city, the restaurant was bedecked for the season and the comfort of yet more pine boughs and lots of red and green was turning Faith's thoughts away from her near-death experience and toward her companion. The wine was helping to quell her feelings of dislocation. After all, 'tis the season to be jolly, she admonished herself. And Richard was fascinating. And damn good-looking. Nothing like the aura of success

239

to enhance a man—or woman. She looked around her. The room was crammed with perfect examples.

"We go up to Westchester to my sister's for Christmas Day. Watch her kids play with the wrapping paper. I keep telling her not to bother with presents, just wrap empty boxes, but she seems to think that puts me in a league with Ebenezer Scrooge. She's got twins, eighteen months old. And believe me, they could care less."

This whole kid thing was more complicated than Faith realized. She thought of the weary mother at the Met whose baby would sleep only when in motion, and now apparently there were little tykes who could be satisfied with crumbling and tearing paper—never mind what the treasure inside might be. She made a mental note to ask her mother about this. Somehow, she couldn't quite picture it. Not care about the present? She knew reasoning developed slowly—echoes of college psych and Piaget reverberated in her head—but what about emotions? What about good taste?

"I don't know anyone with children yet—I mean my friends, people my age. It's probably all going to happen at once. I keep hearing people are 'trying.' " The irony of it all struck her anew. Before marriage, "trying" meant avoiding; after, it meant the opposite.

"I'd like to have a couple of kids someday—but not for a long time. I'm not around enough to be a decent father."

What were they doing talking about kids? Faith decided to change the subject. She still had her eye on the Stansteads. A waiter had taken Emma's almost-untouched plate away. Michael had freed his hands and eaten most of his. Now, the sommelier was bringing a bottle of champagne. Michael's hands were back, locked on Emma's. Faith thought of the fervent pleas from the class secretary for alumnae news. Between the two of them, Emma and she could fill an entire issue simply by recording today's events.

"Have you finished your profile of Michael Stanstead?" The question popped out before Faith had time to think about whether she really wanted to introduce the subject or not. But perhaps Richard had uncovered something—something that would help Faith draw some more lines between all those names, find a connection to explain the nightmare Mrs. Stanstead's life had become. Emma might be telling more than half the story to Michael, if not all, but Faith didn't plan to stop her own investigation. It wasn't just Emma, or Emma's father. It was Lorraine, too.

"No, apparently he's announcing his candidacy for the House sometime in January, and I want to cover that—the beginning of the campaign. The magazine agrees."

Faith started to tell Richard that she knew exactly when Michael Stanstead would be declaring, but she stopped herself in time. Richard knew Emma and Faith were friends, but this was insider information, and she didn't want him asking any follow-up questions.

"Do you think he has a chance?"

"It's a safe district, and while I wouldn't say he's a shoo-in, he's definitely in the slipper category. Yes, yes, I know it's spelled differently." Once more, Faith was struck by the way Richard's good fortune was affecting him tonight. The man wasn't simply over the moon; he was orbiting.

"He's attractive, intelligent, knows the right things to say—tough on crime, soft on pets and babies. Opposed to big government and big taxes. Champion of the little guy. An individualist himself. Came from money but made his own. No, short of some kind of major scandal—like he's secretly been funding Noriega or received tips for bets from Pete Rose—he should win."

"What do you think of him? What's he like?"

"I thought you knew him? Didn't you tell me you went to school with his wife? Stunning lady, by the way, but she doesn't seem to have much to say. Can't hold a candle to you."

"Thank you." Faith wasn't sure whether he was complimenting her powers of speech or appearance, but a compliment was a compliment. "I did go to school with Emma. We're very good friends, but I've never gotten to know Michael." This was true of a lot of her friends' husbands. They were all still back in junior high, when the boys stayed on one side of the dance floor and the girls on the other. Michael was surrounded by men in suits. There was an occasional woman, women like Lucy, like Faith's own sister, Hope, but the sexes hadn't reached that gender melding Faith supposed was the goal—at least when it came to jobs, positions of power, that kind of thing. Faith intended to hold on to her own idiosyncrasies. Yet, at the parties she attended, the parties she catered, everyone mixed at the beginning, but by the end of the evening, those who weren't in matched pairs—or trying to be—had precipitated out into male and female conversational groups. What would it be like in ten years? At the end of the next decade, the end of the century. The great big millennium? She was not given to predictions or pronouncements, but she was sure that the battle of the sexes would still be going its own intriguing, irritating, and irrational way.

242

Richard was cutting a large piece of romaine lettuce. Everything about the meal had been slightly oversized, so far. As he ate, he seemed to be phrasing his reply. "I like Michael. He's very straightforward. Nothing coy about his answers, and he hasn't refused to talk about anything; plus, it's all on the record. I told him that at the start and he had no problem with it, he said. Seems to care a great deal about his wife, the rest of his family. But also cares a great deal about Michael Stanstead. He's very ambitious. But it goes with the territory. You wouldn't be running the way he is if you didn't have that drive. He's ruthless, but so far I haven't picked up on any cruelty. If he's stepped on any fingers on the lower rungs of the ladder, I haven't found them yet, but I'm looking. Works like crazy. What else? Smokes god-awful cigars, very expensive, and drinks, but not to excess. Frankly, I thought he'd be a more interesting subject."

This was a surprise. The one thing Faith hadn't thought was that Emma might be married to someone dull.

"Any hobbies, any passions?"

"Plays tennis and squash. Keeps a sailboat at their summer place in the Hamptons. There is one thing, though."

"What's that?" Faith sat up straighter.

"He's not like a lot of politicians I know who get off on adoration. They need to have the crowd cheering, and if one person isn't clapping, they take it personally. Stanstead projects an image of someone who is totally sure of himself. Not conceited, but removed. He doesn't need everyone to love him, just vote for him. It's remarkably effective and makes people want to get close to him all the more. It also gives him a slight air of mystery—and he needs that, because charisma is the name of the game these days."

Emma and Michael, across the crowded room, which was filled with the noise of holiday cheer, were drinking their champagne. They were both leaning back in their chairs. Faith couldn't see her friend's face, but at some point in the conversation, she'd pulled the clasp from her hair and it hung loose, Titian red, the reflected light turning strands to gold. Every once in a while, someone would stop to speak to them. Earlier, the way they had been sitting signaled, Do not disturb. Now, they were holding court. At least Michael was. He may have manufactured whatever charisma he has, Faith thought, or may not have much to say except about politics or business, but the elixir is working tonight. He looked like a leader.

"They're here, behind you. Michael and Emma," Faith said, discreetly pointing her finger.

Richard turned around and stared for a moment, then nodded his head, acknowledging Michael's slight wave. Apparently, he couldn't see Faith, or didn't recognize her.

"Yes," Richard said. "White House material for sure. I might even vote for him myself. And the people joining them now are his wily factotum, Adrian Sutherland, and Lucy Morris, Stanstead's sister-in-law, whom you must know. Every great man needs an Adrian Sutherland. Brainy, part British, not a bit dull, and not quite as scrupulous as his boss, from what I've been able to pick up."

Faith craned her neck to peer around the very large woman who was still clinging to her sable coat as she lowered herself into a chair between the two parties. Adrian and Lucy again. Coincidence? New York is a big city, with more restaurants per capita than any other place in the country. And Adrian and Lucy just happen to walk into this joint? Adrian and Lucy. A waiter was bringing more champagne and menus to the Stanstead table. She gave a sudden start as she felt a warm hand cover her own.

"Eventually," Richard said, "you can tell me what this has all been about. Now brandy here or someplace else? Yours or mine, for instance?"

Ten

"Stanstead, the guy whose party we did a week ago, is up on the dais, but your friend, his wife, isn't with him," Josie said as she came through the door to the kitchen of the community center where the luncheon was being held. "There's an empty place setting next to him. He must be one of the honorees or he's going to give out the awards. Isn't he in politics?"

Faith's heart sank, then began to beat rapidly. She had tried calling Emma this morning, but the line had been busy, and Faith hadn't had a moment to spare herself—jumping out of bed, throwing on her clothes, and rushing straight to work. Josie had grinned and said, "My, my, my, we don't often see the boss so disheveled."

Now the rest of the staff was back in the room after serving the first course, awaiting instructions. "Clear the soup, but remember—not until everyone at the table appears to be finished." Faith hated it when plates were cleared while some of the people, usually including her, were still eating. In some restaurants and at many parties and events, it seemed there was someone in the kitchen with a stopwatch and the wait staff was all competing for the blue ribbon. On more than one occasion, she'd literally had to hold on to her plate.

"Meanwhile, be sure water and wineglasses are full and that there's plenty of bread. We're running low on the buckwheat walnut rolls, but there are plenty of the sourdough ones and Parmesan bread sticks. Josie, when you clean the guest of honor's table, remove the extra place setting." It would look a little tacky, and very obvious, to do it now. Maybe it wasn't for Emma. Maybe there was another no-show.

The staff scattered and Faith looked around the kitchen. Jessica was doing the salads. Almost everyone had ordered the Waldorf ones. The desserts were ready as well, and the fish mousse, the main course, was keeping warm, awaiting the shrimp sauce. She had a few minutes. Coming in, she'd noticed a pay phone by the rest rooms. And now, grabbing some change from her purse, she went to call Emma.

Just as she was punching in the number, Michael Stanstead emerged from the men's room. His hair was glistening ever so slightly with water from his comb. He really was extremely attractive. Photogenic. Telegenic.

"Faith! I might have known. That soup was superb! *Finocchio?*" He kissed her on the cheek. Apparently, they had reached that stage.

She nodded. It was nice to be appreciated. "It's not an Italian recipe, so I simply call it fennel soup."

"I'm sure there's nothing simple about the stock—or the rest of it. Emma and I spent a week in Tuscany taking cooking lessons last fall. I didn't even know what *finocchio,* or fennel, was. Now I've become fa-

247

mous for my *tagliatelle alla bolognese*. Actually, I've only made it once since, but I do know how. And I've enlarged my food vocabulary enormously."

Faith was having trouble picturing Emma in a *cucina* of any kind, even one in the luxurious *castello* where this was sure to have been located—a program complete with side trips to vineyards, more extraordinary houses, and the odd Giotto or Piero della Francesca that happened to be tucked away nearby at the dear contessa's little house—one with a moat.

As if reading her mind, Michael said, "Emma spent most of the week sunbathing in the courtyard." A frown crossed his face. "She hasn't been all that well, you know. She was supposed to be here today, but I insisted she stay in bed."

"What do you think is wrong?" Faith wanted to hear his version, especially after watching from afar last night. It wasn't likely that he would mention his wife was being blackmailed—even to her old school chum—but he might say something about trying to get pregnant.

He did. "She's been getting despondent over the whole baby thing. I've told her, the doctor's told her, not to worry so much. It'll happen. But she's going back for a full work-up of all systems after Christmas. Could be merely not enough iron or whatever. Could be something else."

It was something else.

"Duty calls. For both of us, I imagine. Can't wait to see what's for dessert? Zabaglione? Biscotti? What are you going to give us?"

"Think a little farther to the west. Be surprised," Faith said in a slightly teasing voice. "I'll give you a hint. It's seasonal."

Michael laughed. "Just so long as it's not fruitcake."

Faith shuddered. The mere thought.

The moment he was gone, she dialed again. She'd been reassured, but she still wanted to talk to Emma.

"Oh, Faith, I just left a message on both your machines. I should have listened to you ages ago! I have the best husband in the world!"

"I just talked to him. I'm catering the luncheon he's attending. He said he told you to stay in bed." Emma hadn't seen her the night before, and Faith decided to let her friend have the pleasure of telling all—or all that was applicable.

"I didn't even wait until after dinner to tell him, just blurted it all out right away. Michael couldn't have been more understanding, and he was upset that I hadn't told him sooner. Hadn't told him about the miscarriage especially. I know I'm going to get pregnant now. He said that psychologically this had probably been what's kept me from it so far. That somehow I didn't want to go through it all again—I mean that deep inside I was afraid something would happen again and I'd lose the baby."

There was something to that, Faith thought. "I'm glad it worked out. I felt sure it would. What did he say about"—a woman teetering unsteadily on her high-heeled Charles Jourdans, even though it was only noon, was making her way to the ladies' room--"about the rest of it, you know." No matter how tipsy the woman might be, the word *blackmail* would be a splash of cold water, and in New York, the six degrees of separation were reduced to about one in this circle.

"He was a lamb about that, too. He couldn't believe what I've been going through. He was teary when I told him about the baby—right there at the Post

House—but he was really angry about the blackmail. He's going to put a stop to it immediately. I should have realized it would all be fine. Michael knows the police commissioner very well and he's going to get in touch with him. He's having something done to the phone right away so the calls can be traced. And he wanted the blackmail notes to take to the police, but of course I'd thrown them all away, since I didn't want him to find them."

Faith felt an enormous sense of relief. Somebody else could be in charge now. She didn't have to shoulder the responsibility for Emma's well-being single-handedly anymore. At the same time, she felt a bit let down. She had convinced her friend to do the sensible thing. But she hadn't figured anything out. Of course, the most important thing was that Emma was safe and sound—and would continue to be.

"Since he knows the commissioner, don't you think you can tell him everything?"

Emma had sounded giddy before; she sobered up immediately. "Maybe in a little while. Not right now. Things are too perfect. Maybe when we're away. And Faith?"

"Yes?" What was coming next? With Emma, it could be anything from another revelation, like she'd set up a trust fund for the blackmailers so they absolutely wouldn't bother her again, to a surefire tip to prevent cap hair in the wintertime.

"I told Michael I hadn't told anyone else, because I thought he might be hurt that I'd confided in a friend first and not in him. I'm sure he would understand I was trying to protect him, but it just seemed better to make him feel that he was the only one. Kind of an ego thing."

Faith understood completely. She pictured the scene last night—champagne and roses, figuratively, although she wouldn't be surprised if there were a dozen long-stemmed American Beauties in a crystal vase next to Emma right now. The setting wouldn't have lent itself to the revelation that one's spouse had been second in line.

"Tomorrow's Christmas Eve; then we fly out the next night straight to the Caribbean. I'd forgotten what being happy feels like, Faith. And I owe it all to you."

"And Michael," Faith added.

"And Michael." Emma agreed.

"I've got to run. There's a large roomful of people waiting for food."

"Will I see you before we leave?"

"Today is crazy, and tomorrow we have a brunch that suddenly came up. I think it was Henri, your caterer again, who, by the way, had had multiple warnings from the Department of Health. You don't even want to know what they found in his kitchen! Then I'm making supper for the family before church, but maybe I can stop on my way over there. I'll call you."

"That would be great. And if not, Merry Christmas, Faith."

"Merry Christmas, Emma."

Faith couldn't decide whether or not to invite Richard for Christmas Eve dinner. As she worked back at her own kitchen after the luncheon, she kept returning to the thought. It made a statement. Bringing a man home to meet her parents for the Good Sibley Stamp of Approval was not something she'd done before. Her parents had known some of her dates when she'd been a teenager, and the biggest thing in the holiday season hadn't been what Santa would bring, but who would take you to the Gold and Silver Ball—a benefit for the Youth Counseling League. She remembered doubling with Emma, who had also been home for the holidays during their freshman year at college—the last year they'd been eligible to attend. They had looked at the tenth graders, the youngest attending, and marveled that they had ever been that young. They'd also marveled at how very sophisticated a few of those young New Yorkers had looked—pretty babies with Mom's makeup and Dad's charge cards.

Maybe she was making too big a deal out of all this. It was a simple family dinner. Hope had invited Phelps, or at least Faith thought she had. That will solve everything, she decided. If Hope's beau would be in attendance, she'd invite Richard. She'd call her sister this afternoon before she left to do tonight's dinner.

"Do you want me to do some more packing?" Josie asked. "There's time."

"No, we're in good shape—and the movers are going to do all the china, as well as the big stuff. Why don't you grab an hour for yourself? Howard will be back at five, and it's just the three of us tonight."

"I hope it's early. I plan to start celebrating early. And you—you need to get some more sleep, not that the alternative is disagreeing with you, but you know what happens when you burn your candle at both ends."

"You get a 'lovely light,' " Faith said, quoting the Edna St. Vincent Millay poem.

"No, you get a whole lot of wax," Josie amended, "and it's a bitch to clean up."

"Go. Go out among the desperate throngs looking for something original, something not a tie or perfume, and spread your words of wisdom."

252

Josie made a face. "It's too cold to walk from store to store. And I'm waiting to do my Christmas shopping the day after, when they have the big sales. But I will get out of your hair. I have to get some sweet potatoes for my pies. I'll make them at home tomorrow after the brunch. Do you think four will be enough?"

"Plenty."

"Then I'll make five. See you in an hour."

Faith sat down at the counter and looked at her doodles on the packing sheet of paper from the day before. She'd drawn thin lines from Emma to everyone else. The result looked like the wheel of an imported sports car. She stared at it some more and then started to crumble it up. She didn't need it anymore. Case closed.

But the case wasn't closed. She still didn't know who had been blackmailing Emma—and she was sure they'd try again. Then there was the big question behind everything else. Who had killed Nathan Fox and Lorraine Fuchs? And who had been at the wheel of the car last night? Could she be sure it was Harvey? Could she be sure of anything?

The phone rang. It was Richard. Case in point.

"Hi, know you're busy, but I wanted to hear your voice."

When someone says something like that, it makes it hard to say anything next. Thou witty, thou wise—thou banal.

"Well, hi there." Brilliant, Faith.

"How late are you working tonight? Could we get together?"

"I have no idea. It's dinner, but sometimes people linger. Certainly not before midnight."

"Then midnight it is."

Whoa, she thought. Last night, tonight? Tomorrow night?

"I really have to get some sleep. I've—"

"Sounds fine to me." His voice was warm and the enthusiasm was neither over- nor underdone.

"Okay, why don't I call you when I'm leaving. The apartment is up on Central Park West."

"See you later."

She hung up, then realized she hadn't invited him to her parents'. Somehow in the course of the conversation, she'd decided to—Phelps or no Phelps.

Sunday morning dawned gray and cold. And brownish green. The only snow they'd have for Christmas was what was in store windows, and the unsightly mounds left by the plows that hadn't melted yet and were serving as dog loos, with occasional garlands of trash. The apartment was warm, but Faith didn't feel like leaving the nest of her bed. Not for a long time. Last night had been a disaster. She roused herself. Coffee. Much coffee. Maybe not a disaster, but certainly a downer. The dinner had gone well and she'd showered her cards like confetti upon the complimentary guests. One man had offered to put money in the business and had given her *his* card. Then she'd gone to meet Richard at the bar at the Top of the Sixes—666 Fifth Avenue, his choice.

"The view used to be better. They're putting up too many buildings in the city."

Faith had agreed. The restaurant had been a favorite of Aunt Chat's when Faith was a child, and they'd celebrated special occasions there. She remembered one time when Chat had let Faith and Hope take turns wearing her new white mink stole—the tangible result of a whopping new account—all through dinner, apparently unperturbed by the catsup they were amply using to cover their fries. The Top of the Sixes was a man-made mountain aerie; they floated not above the clouds, but above the hordes. It had always been hard to come away from the windows to concentrate on the food. As Faith got older, she determined the view *was* the draw. Not necessarily the food.

Last night, some of the old childhood magic had been present. For one thing, it was almost Christmas and the restaurant was filled with reminders—not only the decorations but also the guests. Everyone was a bit more dressed up than usual and the conversation sounded sparkling, even if proximity would have revealed it wasn't. Carols played softly in the background. Faith had changed at work and was wearing a burgundy silk shirt tucked into matching velvet pants—a once-a-year kind of outfit she'd bought on the spur of the moment. She wore the Mikimoto pearl necklace Chat had given her for her twenty-first birthday. As she'd fastened it around her neck, she'd noted the way the beads shone luminously against her throat. She'd pulled her hair back.

Richard was still celebrating. He'd spent most of the day with his agent. "Perrier-Jouët, don't you think?"

Faith had agreed. Not only were the Art Nouveau bottles lovely to look at, but the champagne was damn good, too. She'd settled into herself. Thoughts of Emma Morris Stanstead—thoughts of everything save the moment—had disappeared from her mind.

"You've become very special to me, Faith," Richard murmured. He was sitting next to her, as close as the chair would allow. He took her hand.

"I want to give you something."

"Oh, no, Richard, you shouldn't have," she'd

protested, happily aware that her bag was weighed down with the snow globe she'd bought for him.

"It's nothing." He'd smiled.

And it was. A cookbook. A nice one with glossy photographs. But a book. Impersonal.

"You probably have a million of these, but you have to get ideas from somewhere, and this looked great. It's divided by seasons. You can cook your way through the year."

Oh bliss, Faith thought, and decided to keep the snow globe for herself.

After some more champagne, she had second thoughts. Men were notoriously bad at knowing what to give women as gifts. Her father was a case in point, appealing desperately to his daughters when those times of the year rolled around, and they were more than happy to save their mother from a blender—Dad's idea for one Christmas—or a sewing machine—for Mom's fortieth.

She was just reaching into her bag, Richard nuzzling her neck in a decidedly pleasant way, when she heard him say, "I'm really going to miss you."

Say what? "Miss me? Why?" she said out loud.

"I'm leaving the day after Christmas to finish the book. I've cleared my desk of all but the Stanstead profile, so I'll be gone a month or two, maybe three. I will be back whenever he announces, and we can grab some time then, but for all intents and purposes—and I mean this most regettably—I'll be gone until spring."

"Oh," said Faith. She was not a fan of long-distance romances, especially one that was just getting off the ground, no matter how many stories up they were. She'd never been one to carry a torch—perhaps because there had never been anyone who had caused one to burn brightly enough. Why hadn't Richard told her this before? He must have known last night. Clearing his desk meant forethought. But not a thought for her. She looked into his eyes. Yes, there was a little guilt there, embarrassment. Don't worry, she wanted to tell him. I'm not going to make a scene. I'm not going to try to tie you down.

"Oh," she said, "that's wonderful. The sooner you finish the book, the sooner it will hit the best-seller list."

"I knew you'd understand. Merry Christmas," he'd said, clinking her glass with his.

He'd taken her home in a cab. She had pleaded fatigue and the brunch the next morning to do. As she'd gotten out, he'd handed her her bag. "What do you carry in this thing? Rocks?"

"Yes," she'd said, smiled, and waved good-bye.

"That's it. See you tomorrow. You sure your mother's oven is big enough for the turkey? I'd be happy to do it here and bring it over," Josie offered. The brunch was a great success, especially the Big Apple pancakes [see the recipe on page 282], and they'd cleaned up quickly together.

"I'm sure, although all she ever uses it for is to broil a nice piece of fish or, alternately, a nice boneless chicken breast. That's what they eat—with a little salad or a few vegetables, depending on the time of year."

"This does not sound like the kind of clergy *I* know. Being God's Go-Between is strenuous work, and they need more than a shriveled-up dry piece of chicken to do it. You bring your daddy over to Josie's when I open and I'll give him a real chicken breast—soaked in buttermilk, coated with my special seasoned flour, and deep-fried, with a crust as light as an angel's wing."

"It's obvious you're going home soon. Your accent is getting deeper and deeper and you're starting to talk like someone out of a Zora Neale Hurston short story."

Josie laughed. "Nothing wrong with that. Anyway, you need cheering up." Faith had given her an abbreviated version of the last two dates with Richard. "I think it is positively wicked to dump someone at the holidays. The man has no class whatsoever," Josie added, fuming.

"I don't think I was being dumped. More like put on hold."

"Same thing."

"Same thing," Faith agreed glumly. This was a new experience for her. She had never been the dumpee—and she didn't intend to let it happen again, no matter how many verses the man could sing, or how well. If she hadn't been so preoccupied with Emma's problems, she might have paid more attention to the signs Richard had been giving her. They'd been there.

"I'm leaving, ladies. Merry Christmas to you both." It was Howard. He'd delivered all the surplus food to an agency that fed the homeless. "I'd hate to be on the streets tonight. It is colder than a witch's—toe. And with that, I'm off to start trolling my Yuletide treasure, or maybe it's Yuletide carol. Whichever, I'll be doing it." What little family Howard had lived in California, but he'd often remarked to Faith that you could make your own families—and he had. The same group had been celebrating all the holidays, plus times in between, for years now.

Faith handed him a brightly wrapped present. "Put it under your tree."

"Thank you, love. Yours is in your big pocketbook. I hid it there. Open it whenever you like. Check yours out, too, Miss Josephina."

Faith had gotten him a camel-colored cashmere muffler at Barneys. Howard was not above brand names.

"You'll have to wait for yours until tomorrow," Faith told Josie. "It's not wrapped." Nor were any of the other presents she'd gotten for friends and family. She was so used to doing this chore in the wee hours of Christmas morning, after the Christmas Eve service, that it had come to seem part of the day, a tradition. Wrap presents, fall asleep. Wake up, open them.

"You sure you're okay here? This thing with Richard hasn't bummed you out too much?"

"I'm leaving soon to go across town to my parents. And no, the thing with Richard hasn't gotten to me, and I think it would have by now if it was going to— that's a mouthful, but you know what I mean." Faith was surprised. She really wasn't that upset. Maybe the cookbook had some good cookie recipes. She needed new ones. They often served cookies and fruit. Maybe fruit cookies? A Big Apple cookie [see the recipe on page 284]—a cookie with an attitude?

"I know what you mean—and count yourself lucky. You didn't go spending a fortune on some Christmas present for him. I did that once—beautiful gold-filled pocket watch. I was fool enough to give him his first. All I got was a black lace garter belt, and you know who that was a present for. Picked his pocket next date—last date, too."

When Josie had gone, the kitchen felt unusually empty. Faith had taken down the posters and charts she'd put up on the walls when Have Faith moved in.

She allowed herself a nostalgic moment. The new place was bigger, brighter, yet this had been her first place, and it would always be the most special.

She packed the equipment she needed to cook tonight and tomorrow into a large zippered bag. The only thing she couldn't find was her strainer. She had two of them. They were essential for sauces—metal and shaped like a dunce's cap, not mesh, but solid. They had wooden pestles to push the food against the small holes. Josie must have packed them. Then Faith flashed on the party at the Stansteads'. Hope in the kitchen, fooling around with the equipment; Faith taking the strainer and pestle out of her sister's hands, shoving it out of the way on the counter. The Stansteads' apartment was close to her parents. She could stop by for it, say Merry Christmas—and return all of Emma's keys, too, very discreetly if Michael was home. She went to the phone and called. No answer, which was what she'd half-expected. They'd be at the Morrises' or the Stansteads', dividing their holiday time.

She sat down again, feeling ever so slightly triste. Christmas Eve. It would have been nice to have had somebody. She thought of all the couples she knew— happy and unhappy. Hope was bringing Phelps, which left Faith paired with her grandmother. They'd had an uproarious lunch at a much-denuded Altman's, where Mrs. Lennox had regaled her granddaughters with tantalizing tidbits of past scandals—most of the chief figures long gone—interspersed with department-store remembrances of things past: percale sheets like silk, the divine hats, and the only china department with all her patterns. Definitely Granny was a great dinner partner, yet the holidays were one of those arklike times, when you felt a bit peculiar if you were a female zebra, say, without a matching male striped creature at your side.

If there was still no one home at the Stansteads', she'd stop anyway and get the strainer. The only thing resembling one at her parents' was an ancient colander, and it would never do to strain the shrimp sauce for the fish mousse. She'd saved some of the mousse from the luncheon the day before, but you had to make the sauce up fresh.

No more sighing. No more looking back, she told herself. She had a terrific business and there were a dozen men out there in Gotham who would be more than happy to dance attendance—or more. And there was always that one she hadn't met yet. It wasn't Richard. Even before last night, she'd known that. But he existed. It was simply a question of time.

She stood up and reached next to the counter to turn off the overhead light. The list she'd made on the packing paper stared up at her mockingly. A challenge unmet. The names circled around Emma's. Faith stared at them again. They almost seemed to move. Birds of prey. She picked up the pencil and drew a dark line across Nathan Fox's name and then across Lorraine Fuchs's. The two deaths. The two murders. They were out of the running.

For murder, there has to be a motive—or at least a reason. Nathan could have been killed by a junkie. That would provide a reason. But Lorraine? Faith found herself sitting down again and gazing intently at the sheet. There had been a peephole in the door of Nathan Fox's apartment. He would never have let a stranger in—and he had opened the door to his murderer. It effectively ruled out the robbery theory. Had there been time for a greeting? For the recognition of what he'd admitted into his home? Death. Or did it happen fast, right away? The door opened, the shot—he never knew what hit him?

But the motive.

She looked at the other names. Who benefited? What was the legal term? Cui bono. What did Nathan have? He had his manuscript. What did Lorraine have? The same thing. Arthur Quinn wanted it. But it would probably have made its way to him anyway—he'd have no need to kill for it. Who else? Poppy wouldn't have wanted it published. "You know there's nothing I wouldn't do for my daughter—*nothing.*" Nothing she wouldn't do to get her hands on something she thought would destroy Emma's happiness, threaten her own? Poppy Morris a murderer? Extremely unlikely. Killer instincts didn't necessarily translate into the real thing. And what about Todd Hartley and his respectably bourgeois new life? How far would he go to protect it? And Harvey? Harvey was available to the highest bidder.

People kill for money. Neither Fox nor Lorraine had had any. They also kill for revenge. That might apply to Fox in some way, but Lorraine? Yet, people also kill to protect themselves, Faith thought with a start. To keep from being found out. Had Lorraine known who'd killed Fox?

Means, motive, and opportunity.

She stared at the names, crossed some out and willed the rest to sort themselves out, willed them to speak—send a Ouija board message, send one name flying away from all the others.

And they did.

"Opportunity," she whispered aloud. "Opportunity."

Traffic was heavy, and by the time she got across town, it was getting late. Her father had very noncosmopolitan notions of dining hours. Besides, he had to get to church. She was tempted to keep the cab, but the doorman had his arm out for one, so Faith let it go. It was Christmas Eve, after all.

"Merry Christmas, Bobby," she said to him. "It's okay. I have the key."

"Merry Christmas, miss," he called back, helping the woman loaded down with parcels into the cab.

Ever since she'd left work, Faith had been repeating the same thing over and over to herself: How could I have missed it? She'd been missing a lot lately. She wasn't worried, though. She knew exactly what she was going to do. The elevator was in use, so she took the stairs, running up, filled with the kind of energy she hadn't known for weeks. It was almost over now. Really over this time.

She let herself in. The apartment was dark and empty. No welcoming fire. No hum of conversation. She walked down the hall to the kitchen. There was light streaming from beneath the door. She pushed it open and stopped.

Michael Stanstead, assemblyman from New York City, clad in a long rubberized raincoat like cops wear over their clothes, was pressing his wife's hand on the grip of a gun. The muzzle was in her mouth and she was tied to a kitchen chair with wide strips torn from a bedsheet.

"Sorry, didn't know you were into bondage. I'll just be going now," Faith said, trying to bluff as she backed out the swinging door. Tears were running down Emma's cheeks, but she wasn't saying a word. Faith wouldn't have, either. Not with a Smith & Wesson stuck between her teeth.

Michael whirled around. The gun was now aimed at Faith.

"Get in here. And don't move."

She took a step forward and let the door swing shut behind her. "How did you get in the apartment? Nobody called up!"

Faith sincerely hoped he had distributed his Christmas largesse to the staff already.

"They know me. I have a key. From when I catered your party," Faith stammered.

"Shit!" he screamed over his shoulder at his wife. "You give the fucking key to everyone!"

A slight look of guilt crossed Emma's face. One more thing she'd done wrong. She probably should have kept better track of the keys.

"What are you going to do now, Michael? You can't very well stage two suicides," she whispered.

Three, thought Faith. Three, counting Lorraine. All the names she'd written on the sheet were falling into place now. Falling, leaving only one suspended in the air: Michael Stanstead.

She glanced at the kitchen table. A table like the one where only a little over two weeks ago she'd seen the headlines about Fox's murder. Now she saw a piece of Emma's engraved stationery. She didn't have to read it to know what it said. It was one of those very polite notes saying it was really too much, that this was the end—one of those sincere missives that might have been dictated by the blackmailer himself, the blackmailer—her own husband.

I figured it out, Faith thought in despair, but not soon enough. She'd planned to come in, call until she found out where the Stansteads were, then alert the police. They'd think she was crazy at first, but she knew she could prove it. The money had to be somewhere. And so would the wig he must have worn Friday night while driving the car in his first attempt—quick and easy—to kill his wife.

His wife! Why hadn't Faith gotten on to him right away? It's *always* the husband!

Emma's question seemed to be taking a moment to register with Stanstead. He was standing with the gun trained on Faith's forehead. A strand of hair worked its way down across one eyebrow, but she dared not push it back in place.

Then he exploded. Not moving the gun, he began to swear at Emma.

"You fucking bitch! You haven't been able to do one single thing right since the day I married you!"

Michael Stanstead was definitely insane—and he was on a roll.

"All you had to do was look pretty, smile, and say the right things—not the crazy shit that was always coming out of your mouth. And Jesus! You knew I was in the toilet after Black Monday, and you *still* wouldn't give me any money for the campaign! I'm running for office, in case you haven't noticed! What did you expect me to do!"

Kill me, my father, and two other women totally unrelated to either of us? seemed a wildly inappropriate answer, but apparently not to Michael, thought Faith. She was watching him intently, willing him to at least pace up and down, so she might have a faint chance of getting the gun away from him. But he kept it trained on her without budging. The man must work out—not a bicep was quivering, although it would have been hard to tell through the coat. No bloodstains on his Armani—that would be for sure. Drop the coat in the river and no one would ever be the wiser.

"Wouldn't touch your capital! Wanted to keep it for our children! What children! You couldn't get pregnant if I drilled you from now until *next* Christmas."

Both Faith and Emma winced.

"You and your pathetic little miscarriage! Lucy told me all about it the summer we got engaged. Wanted me to dump you and marry her. She would have been ten times the wife you've been! But no, I wanted you. Wanted the beautiful golden princess.

"My family warned me. Dad told me over and over again what a whore your mother was, but Nathan Fox! He wasn't even a Democrat! A Commie! Your father was a Communist!" Spittle dribbled down Michael's chin. He was literally foaming at the mouth.

"And then that Commie bitch of his tried to blackmail me! Me! Told me he left a book and it might hurt my wife's feelings. You were young. All sorts of crap like that. Said she didn't want any money. But they always want money, women like that."

Michael was raving. Michael was insane. But he was the one with the gun and one of his victims was tied up.

"The whole world was going to know what color nipples my mother-in-law has, for God's sakes! This Lorraine said she was offering to sell it to me instead of a publisher. Had a list of Commie charities she wanted the money to go to. Sure, sure, I said. Right before I put the pillow over her mouth."

Emma gasped. Faith remembered she hadn't told her that Lorraine was even dead. Lorraine, the person who had spent the most time with Emma's father, the person Emma most wanted to meet.

Poor Lorraine, Faith thought. She was trying to do the right thing. Trying to make something good come out of the venomous manuscript Fox had left behind. Had she deleted the sections about herself? Faith hoped so.

"Okay, okay. You come across Emma trying to kill herself. There's a struggle for the gun and it goes off. Or Emma just kills herself and I take you for a ride." Michael Stanstead was thinking out loud. He ran his free hand through his hair in agitation. "Emma comes home, thinks you're a burglar, shoots you by mistake, and kills herself when she realizes what's she's done." None of the possibilities appealed to Faith.

Although Michael had been addressing his wife, he had been keeping his eyes on Faith. Now she realized that while he had been talking, Emma had been quietly inching her chair closer to him across the highly polished wood floor coated with many layers of polyurethane. Faith immediately leaned back against the door, swinging it slightly open.

"Stand up! Don't move or I'll kill you," Stanstead screamed.

Emma scuttled closer.

"It's the same gun, isn't it? The same one you used to kill Fox." Faith wanted to keep his attention focused on her. "Your wife had been despondent over her inability to get pregnant. You've been playing the caring, concerned husband all over town, all the while hinting that there has to be another explanation. Drugs? You've floated that idea? An eating disorder? When the police investigate, they're going to find erratic withdrawals of large sums of money. Her own personal dealer? Then

267

voilà, the same gun, and all the ends are neatly tied up. She killed Fox to prevent him from publishing his book. A book that would have wrecked your political career. She's eaten up with guilt over the patricide and in despair takes her life on Christmas Eve, unable to stand the happiness of others at the holiday. You become the object of sympathy and in a few years, find a more suitable mate."

Just as Faith thought he had reached the point where her words had driven him to pull the trigger, Emma pitched forward and caught him off balance. He fell heavily onto the floor.

But he still held the gun.

Faith leapt forward and groped on the counter for the implement she'd seen out of the corner of her eye. She grabbed the wooden pestle with its sharp point and drove it directly into Michael Stanstead's left eye with all her strength. He screamed in agony, bringing both hands to his face and dropped to his knees. She picked up the gun and raced to the phone, punching in 911.

Emma was on the floor, too—a few feet away from her husband.

"You certainly know your way around a kitchen," she said to her friend, and then she passed out.

The room was dominated by Maxfield Parrish's *Old King Cole* mural, which ran the full length of the wall behind the bar. The sky at the top of the painting was indeed the artist's signature blue, but the king, his fiddlers three, and other attendants were autumnal— browns, scarlets, and golds. Emma sat across from Faith, leaning back against the banquette, slowly sipping a martini.

"Well, I'm not in the Caribbean," Emma said pensively, "but then, neither is Michael."

"No," Faith concurred, savoring her own drink. Some occasions—and places—call for martinis. Both this venerable Big Apple bar at the St. Regis Hotel with its vague suggestion of not just one but many bygone eras in the city's history and the chance to sort things out with Emma qualified.

No, Michael Stanstead was dressed in an orange jumpsuit or some other prison garb, far from any beaches. Even the Stanstead Associates team of lawyers hadn't been able to arrange bail. At the apartment, screaming in pain, Michael had alternated between cursing Faith and insisting he had the right to kill his own wife if she deserved it and that it was nobody's business but his. Hearing his Miranda rights seemed to incense him even further. Possibly a clever attorney might have been able to explain away the latex gloves, the rubber raincoat, his wife bound with bed sheeting so as not to leave marks, but even a neo-Clarence Darrow couldn't have done much with a client who kept insisting on this wild droit du seigneur. "Do you know who I am?" he kept repeating.

Bobby, the doorman, had come up before the police arrived, after Faith's frantic call, and had responded automatically with his boss's name the first couple of times, then given up, wide-eyed. His first act had been to untie Emma, who had come to almost immediately, while Faith kept the gun steadily aimed at Michael.

"Why don't you go to the Caribbean anyway?" Faith asked. It was the day after Christmas, late in the afternoon. Both Emma and she had been spending long periods of time both at police headquarters and with lawyers. And when they weren't there, neither of their families had let them out of their sights. This was the first time the two of them had been alone together.

Michael's father and Jason Morris had had a long meeting Sunday night, which included Adrian Sutherland, and apparently all three men called in a lot of chits. The newspapers were busy covering the overthrow of Ceausescu in Romania and trying to insert a bit of holiday coverage into the grim news of world affairs. Michael's arrest got buried in the Metro section of the *Times*. Faith knew the story would break sometime, but maybe not. Certainly not the whole story. Powerful people were involved. They'd decided there was no way Michael Stanstead would be running for anything except exercise under the eyes of guards in watchtowers.

"People kept asking me how I was in these very heavy, meaningful voices and I was getting all these flowers. I just thought maybe I looked a little tired and the flowers were because of the holidays. Now I know that Michael was spreading it all over the city that I was, you know, sick."

It had been a clever plan, Faith reflected. Michael would rid himself of a wife he didn't want and get his hands on her money, which he wanted very much. Since Sunday, she'd learned it was true Michael had lost a great deal of money in the crash and that he hadn't recovered yet. His parents had always believed what was theirs was theirs. Emma's continued insistence on not touching hers was literally driving him crazy. So, spread a few subtle hints around about his wife's state of mind, add some "Puff the Magic Dragon" stories in the right places as well, and then all he had to do was play the part of the noble, bereaved husband after her tragic suicide. He'd had no idea his wife was *that* seriously depressed. He'd make some tearful speeches about not ignoring warning signs and the need for more mental-health programs. Emma would at last become the perfect political partner—docile and quiet as the grave. With such a perfect plan in place, Faith had wondered why Stanstead had attacked what he thought was his wife with the car. Apparently, he'd meant to scare her, have the doormen see her distraught, but he'd gotten carried away in the actual act. It was part of the crescendo—resulting in her absence at the luncheon the next day, for one thing—that would lead to Christmas Eve and her "suicide." Faith shuddered.

It was interesting that Emma, so compliant, had been stubborn about giving Michael the money.

"A couple of things have been bothering me," Faith said, nibbling on one of the giant Brazil nuts from the assortment the bar provided—fresh, crisp, and not too many peanuts. "Wasn't the whole money thing arranged in your prenup? Michael must have known he couldn't touch it."

"We didn't have a prenup," Emma confessed. "Funny to think about it now, but he wanted one and I didn't. It seemed so unromantic, so businesslike."

No prenup! With this kind of money involved! Then it hit Faith. If they had had one, Michael would have known that on one subject Emma was firm—financially safeguarding her children's future. She'd had the wind knocked out of her own sails and wanted to be sure no one ever did that to her offspring. Would Stanstead have married her if he'd known he could never touch her money? True, she was gorgeous. Every head had turned when they'd walked into the bar, and Faith was used to this happening when she was with

Emma. And yes, Michael must have thought he could mold her, but money was money. He probably wouldn't have married her and then . . . well, then none of this would have happened.

But it had.

"Easy for him to write the notes and plant them. He must have dropped the first one at that party, knowing someone would pick it up and give it to you, thinking you had dropped it. But how did he manage to make the call telling you where and when to bring the money when he was home at the time? Oh, I'm being stupid—"

"Separate line," she and Emma said at once, hooked pinkies for luck, and ordered two more martinis, plus some very expensive food from the bar menu.

"I was really in love with him," Emma said. "It's like there were two Michaels. Mine and the one, you know, the one in the kitchen. This last week, he was so affectionate, so caring—bringing flowers, little gifts. I was thrilled. His schedule has been so packed that these last months we haven't had that much time together, even in bed." She looked a little embarrassed. "Not this week, though. It seemed to be all he wanted, which was fine with me."

Great, thought Faith in revulsion, picturing Michael getting his kicks from the ultimate "good-bye sex."

The drinks came, and Emma wanted to hear about Lorraine Fuchs. Faith told her, and both women felt a deep sadness at the path Lorraine's life had taken—and where it led at the end. The police were now treating her suicide as a homicide. As she'd told Faith, she'd seen Nathan Fox the day before he was killed. He must have called her to come get the manuscript and put it someplace safe. Faith could imagine his saying that he wasn't planning on going anywhere but that he wanted her to keep it—and keep it sealed until his death. The death that was waiting for him on the other side of his door the very next afternoon.

"We know Lucy told Michael about your pregnancy, but how did he find out Nathan Fox was your father? Do you think she knew?"

Emma shook her head. Faith had been interested to note that alcohol had the opposite effect on Emma from that of most people. It made her more lucid.

"I wondered the same thing. The lawyer said Michael had found one of my postcards when we were on vacation a year and a half ago. I'd used it as a bookmark and hadn't mailed it, but it had the address, and I'd written, 'Dear Daddy.' Michael didn't know then who Norman Fuchs was, but he's very smart. He figured it out. I had all of Daddy's books when we got married, and Michael used to tease me about them."

"But how did he know that you'd be at the apartment?"

"He looked in my appointment book and followed me a few times, apparently."

"You mean you wrote, 'Go see Dad' after 'Have Manicure' and before 'Tea at the Plaza'!" This was a bit much even for Emma.

"No, don't be silly. I wrote in code. Don't you do this? Like a little star when you get your period, that kind of thing? I would never forget when I was supposed to see him, but I still wrote a little *d* on Tuesdays at three o'clock."

And after a team of top cryptographers worked for several weeks, this arcane code was cracked.

"What do you think happened to the book?" Faith asked.

"What book?" It was Poppy Morris. She sat down next to her daughter and a waiter instantly appeared. "What they're having, but no olives, a twist. And very dry."

Her hair was pulled back in her trademark chignon. She was wearing a long, full dark skirt and a Valentino shearling-lined jacket with hand-painted suede appliqué designs. Beneath the jacket, Faith could see several ropes of nonfaux pearls and a few gold chains. She looked like a very chic, very rich gypsy queen.

"Oh, that book," she said, answering her own question, then began picking the cashews out of the mixed nuts. "I would love to have read it, before I burned it, that is. See what he had to say about people I knew, about *moi*. And probably Michael did what I would have done. It's not something he would have kept around. Evidence, you know."

Faith was sure Poppy was right. Michael's remark about Poppy's anatomy revealed he must have at least skimmed it before he tossed it on the Yule log. She wondered what else Fox had written about Poppy. There was still the unanswered question of who had driven the getaway car during the bank robbery. Poppy at the wheel with her Vuitton driving gloves? They'd never know.

Poppy was addressing Faith. "Of course, I know what you did in the kitchen, dear, and you do know what I'm so inadequately trying to say." She patted Faith's hand—and Faith did know. "I suppose that's why they call it *batterie de cuisine,*" Poppy added as an afterthought. "Now, Jason and Lucy have gone to Mustique. Emma, I thought we might head off for Gstaad, stop in Paris on the way. You need a trip. It's

274

been horrible, I know, but you've got to put it behind you. That's what I always do. And just think, darling, there won't be any question about grounds for divorce."

Emma looked stricken. Faith could read her mind. One more thing on an increasingly nasty "To Do" list—testify against Michael, find new apartment—too, too upsetting to walk into the kitchen—get divorce.

"I'm sure the lawyers will handle everything, and going away for a while is a terrific idea," Faith advised.

"It's settled, then—and you'll come, too, Faith." Poppy drained her drink and stood up.

"I have to work, sorry," Faith said—and she was. Just for now. Just for a moment.

"He really was the most divine man. I miss him."

There was no question about whom she was speaking.

"I miss him, too," Emma said.

Poppy nodded briskly. Things were getting a bit too mushy. "Now, call me and tell me where you'll be after you leave here. I'm off to Marietta's. You know how to reach me." When they'd met at the St. Regis, Emma had called her mother right away. Poppy was keeping a close eye on her daughter.

Emma kissed her mother good-bye.

They talked some more, but after a while fell into their own individual reveries. It would be the New Year soon. A new decade, and in not too many years, a new century. You can't stop time, no matter how much you do or don't want to, Faith reflected. Richard had been right about one thing: Nathan Fox's murder was tied to his past. A line from Shakespeare's *Tempest*—she'd been Miranda in college—popped into her head: "what's past is prologue." She looked over at Emma. She was shaking the snow globe Faith had given her and watching the flakes swirl about the tiny city inside.

Epilogue

How could I have thought I was so invulnerable? How could I have taken such a thing on? At the end, lives were lost, reputations destroyed, peace of mind shattered forever. But we were safe. Emma and I. Does she see what I see in my dreams? As we've grown older, we've become the kind of friends who don't keep in touch. Looking at each other is too painful. We know too much—know how close we came to never knowing what we have: small arms reaching up for us, large ones reaching down, encircling, engulfing.

How could I have taken such a risk?

But there really wasn't ever any question.

Sometimes life lets us make choices. Sometimes it reaches out and chooses us.

EXCERPTS FROM
HAVE FAITH
IN YOUR KITCHEN
BY Faith Sibley
A WORK IN PROGRESS

PORK LOIN STUFFED
WITH WINTER FRUITS

*4½ to 5 pounds boned pork
loin, center cut*
*1 large apple, peeled, cored,
and cubed*
Juice from ½ lemon
*Approximately 12 pitted
prunes*
3 tablespoons unsalted butter

*3 tablespoons
vegetable oil*
Salt
*Freshly ground black
pepper*
¼ cup dry white wine
¼ cup heavy cream

Ask your butcher to cut a pocket in the center of the pork
loin and tie it at one-inch intervals, or do this yourself at
home.

Preheat the oven to 350°F.

Toss the apple cubes with the lemon juice to prevent dis-
coloration. Then stuff the pork, alternating apple cubes and
prunes.

Put the butter and oil in a large casserole with a lid, a
Dutch oven or Le Creuset–type cookware is good. Place the
casserole on top of the stove over medium heat. When the
butter has melted, add the loin, turning it so that it browns
evenly on all sides. Season with the salt and pepper as you
cook it. Remove the fat with a bulb baster.

Pour in the wine and cook in the center of the oven for approximately an hour and a half. Use a meat thermometer to
check to be sure it's done, but not overdone.

Place the loin on a heated platter and finish the sauce by
first skimming off any fat produced during the cooking, then
bringing the remaining liquid to a boil. Reduce the heat and
add the cream, stirring constantly. Serve the sauce separately
in a gravy boat.

A cranberry chutney or Scandinavian lingonberries go
well with this dish. Serves six to eight.

WALDORF SALAD

1 cup diced crisp celery
1½ cups cored (but not peeled), diced Granny Smith apples
¾ cup coarsely chopped walnuts

¼ cup sour cream
¼ cup mayonnaise
Pinch of salt
Freshly grated nutmeg to taste

Combine all the ingredients and mix well. Refrigerate for at least one hour before serving; then let it warm slightly. Serve as is or on a bed of greens. This recipe tastes best with a slightly tart apple, and Granny Smiths are also pretty with the green celery.

The original recipe was created by Oscar Tschirky, the maître d', not the chef, at New York's famous Waldorf-Astoria Hotel. It called for equal parts of diced celery and apples combined with mayonnaise and served on lettuce. Walnuts were a later addition. Faith has altered it still more, and on occasion she replaces the walnuts with pecans, adds seedless green grapes or golden raisins, and often a slight squeeze of lemon. Serves six.

BIG APPLE PANCAKES

¾ cup milk, plus 2 tablespoons
2 tablespoons unsalted butter,
  melted
1 egg
1 cup all-purpose flour
2 teaspoons baking powder

2 tablespoons sugar
¼ teaspoon salt
¼ teaspoon cinnamon
1 Empire apple, peeled,
  cored, and cut into thin
  slices, halved

Put the milk, butter, and egg into a mixing bowl and beat lightly. Sift the dry ingredients together and add to the liquid ingredients, stirring just enough to mix. Add the apple slices and stir. Cook on a griddle or in a frying pan, making sure that the apple slices are evenly distributed in the batter. Makes sixteen four-inch pancakes.

Serve with warm maple syrup—they don't need much.

FRENCH APPLE CAKE

2 cups sliced, peeled cooking apples	1 tablespoon cassis (optional)
Juice from ½ lemon	4 tablespoons unsalted butter, melted
½ cup sugar, plus ⅓ cup	
¼ teaspoon grated nutmeg or cinnamon	1 teaspoon baking powder
	¼ teaspoon salt
1 cup all-purpose flour, plus 1 tablespoon	¼ cup milk
	1 egg, plus 1 egg yolk

Preheat the oven to 400 °F. Grease a cake pan. Toss the apples with the lemon juice and arrange in a spiral on the bottom of the pan. Cover the pan completely, overlapping the slices if necessary. Sprinkle with ½ cup sugar and the nutmeg. Cover the apples with 1 tablespoon of flour and drizzle with the cassis, if using, then with 3 tablespoons of the melted butter. Set the pan aside while preparing the batter.

Sift the 1 cup flour, ⅓ cup of sugar, the baking powder, and salt together. Beat the milk, egg, egg yolk, and 1 tablespoon of the melted butter together. Add the liquid mixture to the dry ingredients and stir until you have a thick, smooth batter.

Spread the batter on top of the fruit and bake for twenty-five minutes. Do not overcook. The cake should be light brown on top. Cool slightly and invert on a serving plate. Serve warm or at room temperature with a small dollop of whipped cream. This cake is also delicious when made with peaches or pears.

MANHATTAN MORSELS

½ cup unsalted butter
2 1-ounce squares semisweet
   baking chocolate
1 cup all-purpose flour
½ teaspoon baking powder
½ teaspoon baking soda
¼ teaspoon salt

2 eggs
½ cup white sugar
½ cup brown sugar
1 teaspoon vanilla extract
½ cup applesauce
½ cup chopped walnuts

Preheat the oven to 350°F. Grease a 13 x 9 x 2-inch baking pan and set aside.

Melt the butter and chocolate in the top of a double boiler. Cool slightly. Sift the flour, baking powder, baking soda, and salt together. Set aside. Beat the eggs, sugars, and vanilla together. Then add to this the chocolate-butter mixture and the applesauce, mixing well. Stir in the dry ingredients and mix well again. Add the walnuts, stir, and pour into the greased pan.

Bake in the middle of the oven for approximately twenty-five minutes. Cool in the pan on a rack. This recipe makes twenty-four squares.

One of Faith's favorite apple recipes is the apple version of Denouement Apple/Pear Crisp found in the recipe section of *The Body in the Cast*. Make it with New York State apples to give it a Big Apple twist.

As always, all of these recipes may be modified, substituting Egg Beaters, margarine, low-fat milk, and low-fat sour cream. The only exception is the sauce for the pork loin. It doesn't need to be heavy cream, but it does need to be creamy—light cream or half-and-half.

Author's Note

The Big Apple. Jazz musicians coined the city's familiar moniker in the twenties. There were plenty of apples to pick from the tree, but only one Big Apple, only one New York. If you had a gig there, you had it made. The ultimate destination.

Growing up in northern New Jersey, I felt much the same. As teenagers, my friends and I used to say we lived "just outside the city," omitting the fact that we had to cross a state line to get there. At twelve, we were deemed old enough to take the DeCamp bus together to Port Authority—in the daytime. Armed with the small penciled maps my mother would draw, we'd head for Manhattan. One Saturday, it would be museums. My cousin John convinced me to stand in line with him for several hours outside the Metropolitan Museum of Art to catch a sixty-second glimpse of the *Mona Lisa,* on loan from the Louvre. It's the wait I remember best now, the mix of New Yorkers and out-of-towners, the jokes, the stories—holding places while people dashed off for a dog from the Sabrett's "all beef kosher franks" stand. Another Saturday, we'd go from box office to box office on Broadway until we got tickets to a matinee (prices were much lower in the early sixties). We saw everything from Richard Burton in *Hamlet* to Anthony Newley in *Stop the World, I Want to Get Off*. Sometimes we'd just wander, walking miles, entranced by the dramatic changes in the neighborhoods from one block to the next. Bialys and bagels gave way to egg rolls, followed swiftly by cannolis as we moved uptown.

No time of year was more magical than December, and from the time I was a small child, there was always a special trip during the season to look at the Rockefeller Center tree and the department store windows. Other times of the year, my parents took us to the ballet, opera—the old Met with the "cloth of gold" curtain—concerts, and special exhibits at the museums—the Calder mobiles, like nothing anyone had seen before, spiraling in the enormous spiral of the Guggenheim.

Then there were the restaurants—or rather, one restaurant: Horn and Hardart's Automat. My 1964 Frommer's guide advises: "Inquire of any passer-by, and you'll be directed to one that's usually no more than a block-or-two away." Sadly, they have all disappeared, and trying to explain the concept to my fifteen-year-old son—you put nickels in the slot next to the food you wanted, lifted the little glass door, snatched it out, and watched the empty space revolve, instantly producing another dish—is well nigh impossible. Fortunately, there are old movies. Just as difficult is describing the food—the superb crusty macaroni and cheese with tiny bits of tomato, the warm deep-dish apple pie with vanilla sauce, the baked beans in their own little pot. Most New Yorkers of a certain age wax nostalgic about Automat food—the meat loaf! And a whole meal for one dollar.

My husband is the genuine article. A native New Yorker, born and bred in the Bronx. "The Beautiful Bronx" when he was growing up, and we have a book of the same name to prove it. When he meets someone else from the borough, talk immediately turns to the Grand Concourse, the "nabe," and egg creams. Where he lived is now part of the Cross Bronx Expressway, but he can still point out his elementary school as we whiz past. New Yorkers are very sentimental.

And to continue in the manner of Faith's sweeping generalizations, New Yorkers are also very rude, very generous, very funny, very stylish, very quirky, and very fast. Genetically, they have more molecules than most other Americans. The moment I step off the train or plane from Boston, my pace quickens in imitation, my gaze narrows, and my senses sharpen. Forget all those New York designer fragrances. The essence is adrenaline, pure and simple.

This book is a paean to New York City past, present, and future—written about the end of one very distinctive decade as the city is poised for another—and a new century at that. At the close of 1989, the last thing Faith imagines is that in a few years she'll be in exile—living in the bucolic orchards west of Boston. She'll keep her edge, though, will continue to read the *Times* and make periodic journeys back to Bloomies, Balducci's, and Barneys, always keeping in mind what the comedian Harry Hershfield said: "New York: Where everyone mutinies but no one deserts." 1900 or 2000—some things never change. It's a wonderful town.